the 34 in the floor

The Sadie Gray Mystery Series

sadie gray
book one

R.B. Schow

Bailey James

RIVER CITY PUBLISHING

copyright

This book is licensed for your enjoyment only. This book may not be resold or given away to other people. If you are reading this book and did not purchase it, or it was not purchased for your use only, then please purchase a copy for yourself. Thank you for respecting the hard work of the author.

THE 34 IN THE FLOOR

Copyright © 2024 **R.B. Schow, Bailey James**. All rights reserved, including the right to reproduce this book, or portions thereof, in any form. No part of this text may be reproduced, transmitted, downloaded, decompiled, reverse-engineered, cloned, stored in, or introduced into any information storage or retrieval system in any form, or by any means, whether electronic or mechanical without the express written permission of the author. The scanning, uploading, and distribution of this book via the Internet or any other means without the express written permission of the author or publisher is illegal and punishable by law. Please purchase only authorized original or electronic editions and do not participate in or encourage electronic piracy of copyrighted materials.

Author's Note: This is a work of fiction. Names, characters, places, and incidents—and their usage for storytelling purposes—are crafted for the singular purpose of fictional entertainment and no absolute truths shall be derived from the information contained therein. Locales, businesses, events, government institutions, and private institutions are used for atmospheric, entertainment, and fictional purposes only. Furthermore, any resemblance or reference to an actual living person is used solely for atmospheric, entertainment, and fictional purposes.

The publisher does not have any control over, nor does it assume any responsibility for the author or third-party websites or their content.

For more information on these authors and their works, visit: *www.SadieGrayBooks.com*.

one
the driver

THE NOISY '70's wreck of a pickup rumbled through the pre-dawn darkness, a single headlight casting an amber glow over the quiet Reno streets. Something loose and metal rattled in the back of the truck. The noise wasn't alarming; it was oddly soothing.

The clean, middle-class neighborhood slumbered, the homeowners unaware of the killers in their midst. The driver searched street signs and house numbers, looking for the right address and potential witnesses.

Ahead, out of the darkness, a corpse-colored house with an old roof, unkempt lawn, and filthy window screens appeared. It was far nicer than where they lived and in a much better neighborhood. Then again, their targets weren't squatters.

The driver verified the address, cut the V8 engine, and extinguished the lone headlight. The truck coasted to a stop against the curb. For a few long moments, the passenger refused to move a muscle. It wasn't time yet. The driver quietly turned and glanced through the cab's fixed rear window, where the third killer—a perpetually restless and offensive creature—writhed with predatory intent.

The passenger leaned forward, and from a footwell full of fast-food wrappers and shriveled French fries, picked up a large metal ring holding more than a dozen large combination locks and various padlocks. He lay the grotesque bundle on his thigh and stared sideways at the driver. The driver noted the padlocks and imagined the passenger was smiling behind the plastic, full-faced mask. All three wore masks.

When last they used the lock bundle to beat their targets to death, there was so much blood and hair stuck in it that it took an hour of cleaning to pass a visual inspection. It might look clean, but there could also be trace evidence from dozens of kills embedded in the metal grooves. It didn't matter. They were too far from home for it to matter.

The killers in the truck's cab looked at each other—two pairs of eyes behind shiny, dollar-store masks. The driver nodded to the house. Both turned in unison to where their targets were likely asleep.

"Ready?" the driver asked the passenger.

A soft murmur of acknowledgment.

The two in the cab were anxious for action, but the third was a wildcard. The driver knew the killer in the back well enough to know he'd be growling low in his throat like a restless dog with the house now in sight.

"The moron?" the passenger asked.

"He looks ready."

When they first stopped the truck, the idiot, *the psychopath*, had crouched low in the bed of the old Dodge. But then he grabbed the side panel's top railing, pulled himself forward, and hung his ugly head and half his torso over the sidewalk, rocking back and forth like a lunatic.

"God, I hate him," the driver said, receiving an agreeable nod from the passenger.

The psychopath's backlit silhouette was an awful sight. It was a wild explosion of unwashed, untamed hair, a malnourished body writhing and contorting, and nine perfect fingers perpetually moving to the noises in his head. At first glance, he appeared uncomfortable, like a person with a terrible itch to scratch and no way to reach it. As with the killers inside the truck, this ferocious, pint-sized monster wore the shiny, pink mask, which they modified to fit his abnormally large skull and slightly malformed jaw.

Sensing that the two in the front were watching him, the psychopath jerked his head sideways and twisted his skeletal frame toward the cab's dusty window. He and the driver locked eyes, neither blinking nor pulling away, both physical manifestations of humanity's most insidious impulses, the psychopath more so than the driver.

When they were children, the driver dreamed of choking him until he was blue in the face, or beating him to death with a shovel, or maybe even shoving him into traffic just to watch him get hit by a car or run over a few times. How far would the bloody skid marks go before they stopped? There was no way to tell. Despite the psychopath's shortcomings and the driver's murderous desires, they were siblings, and siblings didn't kill each other unless they had to.

"You're sure the dome light is out?" the passenger asked, gripping the door handle, his voice muffled by the mask.

The question broke the driver's homicidal trance. Turning to address the passenger, the driver gave an affirmative nod, the movement silent and spare.

The passenger quietly opened his door, and the psychopath slid out of the truck's bed. The two moved simultaneously toward the house, both as quiet as a whisper. The driver trailed them, carrying a ball of fresh latex gloves.

They crept up the home's footpath to the enclosed front porch. The three occupied the same cramped space: nothing more than a concrete stoop and busted planter boxes on either side of a weather-beaten, wooden door. The dried plants were wilting, the leaves like crispy potato chips. There was one pink flower in bloom, though—the driver plucked it from the box, crumpled it like an old receipt, and tossed it backward where it lay ruined on the concrete.

"I'm ready," the passenger said.

While trying to hand out the latex gloves in such a tight space, the psychopath nudged the driver, who then turned and shoved him off the porch. The youngest of them fell into an ugly, overgrown hedge.

The idiot, the psychopath, the absolute moron, shot to his feet, puffed out his insignificant chest, and balled his hands into fists at his sides. The driver ignored him, focusing instead on the passenger—he had pressed his ear to the wood-paneled door and was listening. But for what? What did he expect to hear?

"Gloves," the psychopath hissed.

The driver turned and threw the last two at him, hitting him in the face. The psychopath put them on, grumbling and cursing under his breath.

The night was bone silent and cold, an empty tomb; the passenger listened with his ear to the front door anyway. The man was like that: patient, cautious, hyper-observant in the stillness that preceded the chaos. He was the best of all of them, the reason they could even do this or exist in society.

The driver blew a soft but impatient snort, leaned in, and harshly whispered, "Knock already *dummy*."

The passenger faced the house and slowly ran the padlocks up and down the door's panels. The scraping, dragging, weighted sounds caused the psychopath to break into a small, almost girlish giggle. He clapped a hand over his mask, smashing it into his mouth to keep quiet. Irritated, the driver spun and held up a fist, a guarantee of punishment if the psychopath were to have another outburst and give them away.

"Go on now—*say it*," the driver turned and told the passenger in what felt like a needful whisper.

The passenger leaned toward the driver and psychopath, his plastic mask creaking lightly with the effort. Using a clean, somewhat theatrical voice, what he would call his best game-show-host voice, he whispered, "Behind the closed doors of this decaying suburban hovel, and unaware of their impending doom, the three residents slumbered, their Barbie-demon dreams nothing like the murderous thoughts of the savage, almost inhuman force now lurking outside their walls."

The psychopath rocked back and forth, rubbing his hands together while stifling another creepy giggle. Behind his mask, his hair was a tousled mess, and his body was reminiscent of a young female who stopped growing just before puberty. It was easy to look at him and consider him harmless to anyone but himself. But the driver knew better. The psychopath was the youngest and smallest but also the most dangerous.

"We are the unfathomable horror," the driver quietly purred. The words skittered like impatient spiders from a spoiled brain to the edge of a milky, rough tongue, where they tumbled out, restless, into the night.

"Unfathomable horror," the psychopath crooned low and anxious.

"It's time to find out what's behind door number one," the passenger whispered, still using his game-show host voice.

"C'mon, dummy," the driver said impatiently. "They ain't gonna kill themselves."

With that said, the passenger gripped the bundle of padlocks, reared back, then flung them forward, hitting the front door as hard as he could.

two
the realtor

MARY TAGGART WAS HEADED to the small hunting cabin in the middle of nowhere, sitting next to a man—a prospective client she had only just met. She opted to drive because she had just leased a beautiful new Toyota Camry, whereas her client showed up in a '68 Mustang he had yet to restore.

Blake Landry was a handsome man and a Marine, a plus in her book. It didn't hurt that he was six feet tall with a great build and deeply tanned skin. The man was no conversationalist, though. Instead of talking during the drive, he sat in an almost brooding silence, his face fixed with the kind of distant gaze you see on men who had seen too much war.

"Blake Landry, USMC," he said when they met earlier that morning. He shook Mary's hand firmly, his intense eyes locked on her like a vise. The action bore a palpable weight in her chest as if pinned down by some invisible force.

She wasn't bothered by his energy, not as she would be if he was ugly or a creep. Blake Landry, USMC, was anything but that. The Marine could've purred the words to her if he wanted; she was smitten at first sight.

How did I get this lucky?

Most days, Mary felt like fate had kicked her in the teeth. But she knew there were other times when you least expected it, that fate would deal you a good hand because you needed it, earned it, and most certainly deserved it.

Blake called her last week looking for a local hunting cabin on acreage—five at least with up to twenty on the high side. Unfortunately, no local listings fit that bill. However, as a young, hungry real estate agent often was, Mary was resourceful, so she scanned the FSBOs, hoping for an owner who would let her sell their property. The search was a bust. Determined to keep the lead alive, she poured through endless foreclosure listings, widening her search as far as Blake would allow, going as far away as Grass Valley. It didn't help, which left her a bit frustrated. While Mary was discouraged by the lack of inventory, which was nothing new in California, she pretended she was working a cold case looking for something, a thread to pull, a solid lead—*anything* to sell because she wasn't in the business of saying no.

And then she came across "the property." The moment she saw it, she held her breath, hopefulness within her grasp. She poured over the property details once, twice, three times. Satisfied and feeling victorious, she reclined in her office chair, breathed a sigh of relief, and let a smile break over her face. She had finally hit pay dirt!

The property wasn't charming at first blush, but the foreclosed and seemingly forgotten cabin sat on ten beautiful acres of wooded land along the edge of Grass Valley.

The quaint California city in the western foothills of the Sierra Nevada Mountain range was home to over fourteen thousand souls and was perfect for hunting, fishing, and hiking. Naturally, Blake was thrilled. The other realtors he'd tried found nothing of interest to offer.

"What kind of game do you hunt?" Mary asked as they navigated one of the many winding roads heading toward the property.

"Deer mostly, but rabbit, too," Blake said, watching the road. "I want it to be somewhere the boys can chill for the weekend. You know, smoke cigars, drink bourbon, play cards."

She often practiced holding a smile longer than expected because "good people bought homes and property from good people." With Blake, however, smiling was easy because he was a feast for the eyes.

"Well, you're going to *love* the land," she beamed. "Maybe you and your friends can take the first weekend and give the cabin a little TLC? The bones look good, so maybe with a little work, it will be something you can be proud of."

"How bad is it, Ms. Taggart? The no-B.S. answer."

Mary cleared her throat and laughed softly at the forthright question. "Not as bad as the pictures would suggest, I'm sure. But it *is* a foreclosure, so I brought bolt cutters and boots." She glanced at him sideways, donning her best smile. Unfortunately, she caught a glimpse of doubt creeping into his eyes.

"So, basically, we'll see soon enough?" he asked. "That's your answer?"

With a stab of pride, she said, "Exactly."

Her laugh was one of her best qualities, but so was her gaze. Mary glanced at him again, hypnotizing him with her big blue eyes and go-with-the-flow personality. He seemed to relax. And, if she wasn't mistaken, he might be giving her "the look."

Mary Taggart liked men and men liked her, but she was also a realist. Age had sneaked up on her over the years, leaving noticeable smile lines around her lips, crow's feet in the corners of her eyes, and the slightly weathered look of a woman who was not in her twenties anymore and darn near out of her thirties. But maybe she still had it, that "it-girl" quality she'd chased so hard in her twenties.

"You said you were married?" Blake asked.

She smiled and nodded.

"What happened?"

"Love runs in cycles, but sometimes it ends," she said plainly. "He's a good man who deserves the kind of love I just couldn't give him anymore."

"What about you? What do you want these days?"

She appreciated the question, but only because she loved to talk about herself. "I want to feel wanted—I miss that."

A long, disappointing silence stretched between them. Then, Blake leaned forward, peering up through the windshield, and said, "This is pretty deep in."

The trees were taller and thicker, the foliage so dense in spots that it blocked out the sun for minutes at a time. And the two-lane road had narrowed. The almost overbearing intensity of the landscape swept through her like vertigo. She eased her foot off the accelerator and stole another glance at Blake, overcome by an unexpected, albeit disturbing, thought.

Is he the kind of man who would kill a woman like me out here?

She devoured the sight of his bulging biceps, broad shoulders, and strong-looking thighs. And that barrel chest! She relaxed inside, her thoughts shifting. Yeah, he could overtake her in a flash. But, would that be so bad?

Perhaps.

When you were miles from civilization, close to being swallowed by endless trees, an encroaching landscape, and not a whole lot else, no one could hear you scream or save you. The woods were so thick now that they blotted out the sky, leaving Mary with a deep shiver in her bones. She should have previewed the property first. At least she would know what she was getting into before leaving herself so vulnerable.

"When you said it was rural, you weren't kidding," Blake muttered. "It's *rural* rural, like *Hills Have Eyes* rural."

"Or *Wrong Turn* rural," she said, mentioning another famous horror movie.

"Are you a little creeped out right now?"

"Well, *yeah*," she said nervously.

The new Camry's suspension soon took a beating on what had become a battered asphalt road. To her chagrin, the bumpy surface, already breaking apart, finally crumbled, giving way to a packed, dirt road. She slowed the car to navigate several gently sloping hillsides and then a dense canopy of trees. Moments later, they emerged from the shadowy darkness into the sunshine of another straightaway and the vast cloudless sky.

"At least it's beautiful," he said.

"And peaceful," she added, feeling anything but peaceful.

That was when she saw the beat-up old truck charging around the bend, headed straight for her. She swerved to the road's shoulder, her front wheel bouncing into a rut. The maneuver bounced her and Blake around and did a number on the Camry's undercarriage and possibly even the front fender.

The pickup swerved, but the narrow road ran along a sloping hillside. When the truck's tires dug into the grassy hillside, the rig bounced back onto the road and clipped the Camry's rear bumper.

"Son of a bitch!" Mary growled under her breath.

She fired the driver a nasty look, but the heathen glanced at her, startled but angry. It was the worst feeling ever. She blinked to clear her eyes, but the Camry had come to a swift and grating halt by the time her vision sharpened.

"Are you okay?" Blake asked, breathless.

Dust boiled over the top of the car—a rolling, light brown cloud. Mary fought to catch her breath, but she was shaking too badly.

In the rearview mirror, she watched the Dodge speed off.

"I need to check the car," she grumbled, removing her seatbelt. "You might have to push us back on the road and change a tire, but it shouldn't be too hard with those biceps."

She wanted to smile, to play it all off as no big deal, but she couldn't stop thinking of the truck's driver, that disgusting-looking *lunatic*.

Mary crawled out of the car and appraised the damage, which was minimal—a scraped undercarriage, some scratches to the rocker panel, and a smooshed corner on the rear bumper. It could have been worse, but her mind was elsewhere, locked on an image of the driver. The foulness of his features stuck to Mary's brain like glue. That horrible face was so *wrong-looking* that it agitated her senses and left her with a stone in her gut. Was he... wearing someone else's face?

She was desperate to shake off the memory, but flashes of the encounter were quick and sharp as a knife. From what Mary could recall, the creep had rotting teeth, flaking skin, and deep-set eyes. His chin was weak, his neck pencil thin, and his hair so unkempt and windswept he could've been an extra from the hillbilly inbreeder horror movies she watched as a kid. Most alarming, however, was the driver's size. He was not much larger than a teenager, yet he looked old—*a redneck Benjamin Button.*

"Well?" Blake asked as he opened his door, pulled himself out, and leaned against the car.

"Did you see his face?" she asked, unnerved.

Blake swallowed hard; his gaze was unwavering. "For a second, yeah," he answered so low Mary had to strain to hear him.

Was he spooked, too?

She forced a smile, shrugged, and tried to regain her composure. Maybe if she sounded chipper and unflappable, she would feel both. "There's nothing that a body shop can't repair, and I have insurance coverage for these situations."

"What about you, Mary?" Blake asked with concern, slightly suspicious. "You look shaken. Are you okay to drive?"

She laughed and waved him off. "Looks like we're fine here. And yes, I'm okay to drive. It will take worse than *that* to rattle this California girl."

When they finally arrived at the property, Mary realized the cabin was in poorer shape than she thought. What in God's name was she doing out there?

Play it cool...

She and Blake climbed out of the car and trudged through some overgrown foliage and up a rough driveway to the large, wooden porch. Once there, she took a breath and looked out from where she stood. The whole ordeal was fast becoming one of those awful experiences your brain blocks out so as not to worsen the trauma. Talk about a professional blunder!

"Wow," Blake said, holding his nose.

Mary smelled it, too. "Probably raccoons or a dead squirrel," she replied, her stomach rolling at the meaty, dank scent.

A heavy padlock hung from the door, one with flaky brown residue in the grooves and a few stray hairs caught in it. *Gross.* She knew the drill, though. Without a word, she returned to the Camry's trunk, popped the lid, and grabbed the heavy-duty bolt cutters. When she returned to the locked door a moment later, Blake reached for the bolt cutters and said, "I can get that."

"It's no problem," she said, dodging his grasp.

It took her a minute and some unwomanly grunting, but she finally cut the lock, removed it, and tossed it aside. It landed in the brush, the disgusting thing gone.

She turned to Blake with a satisfied smile. She needed a victory. But when she tried to open the door, she found the damn thing was stuck! She leaned sideways, dropped her shoulder, and rammed herself into the door.

The seal popped, the door flew open, and all resistance disappeared. Mary stumbled into the front room, nearly toppling sideways into a filthy house with a stench so atrocious that the scent hit her like a right hook from a young Mike Tyson. It was a one-two shot that had her wondering who died. She was a professional, though, so she regained her balance, fixed her hair, and turned around with an Oscar-winning smile.

"The lighting in here is simply divine!" she beamed. Then she took a deep breath and gagged. Blake covered his mouth to stifle a gag of his own.

If she wanted to salvage the awful moment, she would have to hurry to the nearest window and open it as quickly as possible. "We could do with some fresh air right about now, don't you think?"

"Yeah, I think," he grumbled.

She shoved a few nasty cobwebs aside and popped the seal on the old window; it was as sticky as the front door against its frame, so she muscled it up the wooden tracks and breathed deeply. When she turned to Blake, she smiled like it was no big deal.

The Marine, however, was busy toeing the old wood floor, which had darker spots of muck and grime on a few exposed planks. Mary noted fresh boot prints in the dust but didn't think much of them—until she did. Had someone been there recently? Her body bucked under an involuntary shiver, one that had her thinking about the true crime shows she watched and how people like her died in places like this.

Forcing the awful imagery out of her mind, she cleared her throat and said, "What would a hunter's cabin be if it didn't smell like dead meat?"

Blake half-sniffed the air and made a beeline to the open window. "Something died in here."

"These are *man* smells," Mary said theatrically.

Blake wasn't impressed by Mary's ability to ignore the obvious, so she found herself fidgeting. It was time to drop the beauty pageant act and address the issue point-blank.

"Things die under houses all the time," she said. "Especially in the woods. As I said earlier, it's probably a rat, possum, or something nasty. If you've ever had a rodent die in your wall, you'd think a human died there, too."

"That's what it smells like now," Blake said, hanging his head out the open window.

A light sweat broke out all over Mary's body; if she didn't get this train back on the tracks, all her efforts would be for naught.

"Now that the air's circulating," she said, "you can bring your face back in. The breeze inside is almost magical in the way it cleans the air."

He did as she asked but wasn't happy about it. "Yeah, if you say so."

"Let's do a quick walkthrough," she said. "Consider the cabin a perk. Mostly we're here for the ten gorgeous acres."

Mary walked Blake through the modest-sized living room with little, if anything, positive to say. She spotted a few dust-covered photos of ugly kids posing for the camera; they stood as stiff as statues and refused to smile. Were they kids or hostages? The sight of one boy's facial deformities nearly buckled her knees.

They breezed through an afterthought of a kitchen and stopped at the back door where the wooden casing bore the hash marks of a young family chronicling the kids' heights, including the scratched-in dates for each measurement.

The single bathroom had an ancient toilet bolted to a rotting linoleum floor and a porcelain sink streaked with rust marks from years of a leaky faucet. The cabin's foul smell persisted despite the abundance of outdoor air, which Mary found humiliating.

She lifted the toilet lid to check for water; what she saw hit her like a slap. She stifled an unintentional gasp, but her eyelids flew open so fast she nearly lost her glue-on lashes. She quickly lowered the lid, hoping Blake hadn't seen the petrified turd stuck to the dry side of a waterless bowl.

"It seems they fired the maid a hundred-and-fifty-thousand years ago," Mary joked, still fighting to make light of a miserable situation.

"Obviously."

While standing in the doorway of one of the two bedrooms, she and Blake stared at a rickety, queen-sized bed on an old rug covering most of the rustic hardwood floors. Someone without standards might crash there if they were drunk enough, stoned enough, or close enough to a self-induced coma to be okay with it.

"I've seen the insides of corpses that were cleaner than this house," Blake grumbled as he turned and headed back down the hallway.

"At least the bedroom is cozy," she called out, her face so pale and bloodless that even *she* couldn't believe it.

"I can see myself eating a bullet here," he said from the kitchen.

Mary caught up to him in the living room only to watch him take a few steps onto the medium-sized area rug and break through the floor. The rug sank under his foot, causing him to twist his ankle, step wrong, and torque his knee.

Mary stopped short, her mouth opening in shock.

Blake cursed under his breath and grabbed his knee. "Un-freaking-believable!" he growled, as if injured.

Did he tear something?

Oh, dear, sweet Jesus, she wanted to die *right there and then*—stop her heart, toss her lifeless body onto a conveyor belt, and feed her into the incinerator! What do you even say to something like that? Please, don't sue me?

"That answers my question about the foundation," he spat.

"Yeah, it's not concrete."

"Apparently."

"On the bright side," she heard her dumb mouth say, "it's nothing we can't fix with a few new boards." For a moment, she wondered if she was a real human being. Because who says things like that?

"I wouldn't have been upset if you asked about my ankle," he said.

"What would you have said?"

"That it's fine."

When Blake finally managed to hobble to a nearby chair, Mary grabbed hold of the rug's edge and pulled it back, holding her breath against a billowing cloud of dust. The smell that wafted from the hole in the collapsed floor had her covering her nose and staggering backward.

"That's a trap door here," Mary breathed, pointing to the framed opening in the exposed flooring. It was close to where the floorboard broke under Blake's weight.

Either Blake hadn't smelled what Mary smelled, or he had smelled too much death overseas and was immune to the effects. Nevertheless, he limped to the trap door, kneeled before it, and lifted the lid. The smell was so bad and immediate he shot to his feet and slapped a hand over his nose and mouth.

"The hell?" he barked through a cupped hand.

Eyes that might have once looked at Mary with interest now glared at her as if this was her fault. Technically, it wasn't her fault, but did she blame him?

"Could be something died down there," Mary muttered, cupping her mouth and nose. As a realtor, she felt the wind leave her sails. *Hello Defeat, I'm Mary. It's not lovely to meet you.* There was no saving the sale now.

"Something died, for sure," Blake said, staring at the black hole as if offended. "Or maybe *someone*."

"Probably a rat or a squirrel," she said, gagging as the rotten meat smell sneaked past her defenses, "or it could be an age-related illness, too. You know stagnant air and animal guts don't make for great bedfellows."

"Are you cracking a joke?" he asked.

Mary stared at him with uncontrollably moist eyes, unable to reply due to her stomach's sudden sloshing and roiling. She told herself to be a professional and regain her composure. Was it that easy, though? She swallowed the huge lump in her throat and said, "If this place was for hunters, if hunters had used it…?"

Blake approached the trap door cautiously, activated his cell phone's flashlight feature, and leaned over the hole. When he shined the bright light into the darkness, everything changed. With one look, Blake's eyes bulged with a great fright as if he had seen a ghost or something worse.

He stood and backed up quickly as if moving away from a threat. Then he turned and hobbled through the front door. Mary followed him.

Outside, on the front porch, Blake grabbed the railing and vomited out into the dirt, pine needles, and scrub brush. Mary wasn't sure what to do. She only knew that the smell was worsening, leaving her feeling sick, too.

"What did you see?" she breathed, her face breaking into a cold sweat. "Deer guts, or something, maybe a… a—?" She couldn't say it. Dear God, she didn't even *want* to say it.

Blake wiped his mouth, blew his nose, and looked at her with throw-up tears and revulsion etched deep into his features. "We need to go to the sheriff because... because..."

"Is it a... did you see a...?"

Blake slowly shook his head, pausing momentarily to look up through the deep canopy of trees into the blue sky beyond. When his traumatized eyes returned to meet her gaze, Mary saw that Sexy Blake, with his dark and dreamy eyes, was gone. The disturbed man occupying his body plopped down on his butt, inhaling all the clean mountain air he could take.

"Blake?" she asked.

He spat out into the dirt and blew a snot rocket from his nose, unwilling to look at her. Finally, he said, "It's not a body, Mary."

He shook his head as if rejecting his memories while trying to put his mind back together. Did the glimpse into the floor trigger his PTSD? She knew it was a real thing with returning soldiers and wondered what had caused such a severe reaction.

"If you didn't see a body," she asked breathlessly, "then what *did* you see?"

He refused to answer for a long time, acting as if he hadn't heard her. Finally, he glanced up and said, "Oh, my God, Mary. It's so much worse than you can imagine."

three
chief cormac miller

GRASS VALLEY POLICE chief Cormac Miller received word of the dumpsite late in the afternoon as he was checking his watch and wondering when to call it a day. His blood pressure was normal one minute; it doubled the next. Detectives Ruiz and Peters were on the scene, along with the patrolman who was first on the scene. He reclined in his chair as a light sweat broke across the back of his neck. If he stared hard enough at the phone, would it ring? Would it be Ruiz telling him it was nothing, a deer carcass or maybe a collection of dead bunnies?

Life for the Grass Valley Police Department, and him as its chief, was about to spin wildly out of control. He didn't need this crap—not now.

Before the mayhem started, he opened an available line on his office phone and dialed his wife to say he wouldn't be home on time but to keep his dinner warm. When she asked what happened, he said, "Something awful."

"Dead children?" she asked as if terrified of the answer.

He closed his eyes and rubbed his temples. "Worse, I think. Way worse."

He almost absentmindedly stared at the office phone when the other lines lit up like a Christmas tree. His cell phone buzzed on the desk before him, rattling across the polished wood surface.

It's starting. He wiped his face with a moist hand and said, "Honey, I'll call you when I can."

"Love you," his wife said.

"Same-same, darling."

He hung up the phone, grabbed his cell phone, and checked the number. His lead detective, Detective Pablo Ruiz, was calling, hopefully with a report.

"Talk to me," Miller said.

"Oh my God, Chief," Ruiz exclaimed, breathless and rattled. "It's bad."

"How bad?"

"Worse than what we first heard." He paused to catch his breath. "Guys... *oh, man*... the guys out here are puking everywhere. Not just because of the smell, but... because—"

It suddenly sounded like Detective Ruiz had turned the phone away so Miller didn't have to hear him retching.

"Are you throwing up, Detective Ruiz?" Miller asked. The police chief didn't get an immediate response. Instead, he got more gurgling, horking, and coughing sounds. Miller shook his head, fearing for himself, the department, and the city in the days and weeks ahead.

He stared at his office phone, ignored the blinking lights on multiple lines, and wondered which one to take or if he should ignore them all. The last thing he wanted was to speak to the media, and he refused to talk to anyone who was dying to know what was happening. Miller didn't know enough about the situation to have that conversation.

Miller's Executive Assistant, Barbara Mentz, knocked on the door but didn't wait to be summoned before she walked in. Miller glanced up at the otherwise composed woman and found himself staring at a bloodless face and startled eyes.

"What have you got?" he asked.

"The county coroner is on the way," Barbara replied. "I told her you're headed to the scene now."

"Dr. Eliana West, or one of her minions?" he asked.

"Dr. West."

He waited for her to speak, but she said nothing.

"That's it?" he asked.

She shook her head, not yet finished. "I have the *Sacramento Bee* holding on line one, but I can't stall them for long. *The Union* is still holding, saying that we are obliged to verify news of this nature with them before going to anyone else. I think they're referring to the *Sacramento Bee*."

"How do these people find out so quickly?"

"Lesser people love to gossip."

He snorted an agreeable laugh, then said, "Well, I happen to agree with *The Union*," Miller said, standing and grabbing his coat off the back of his chair. "Make sure they know that but don't say anything, okay? Not until I figure out what's what."

Barbara licked her lips and swallowed before saying, "How many bodies have they found so far, Chief?"

"I don't know yet."

"A lot?"

"Detective Ruiz was supposed to let me know, but he's busy puking his guts out along with everyone else, so it looks like we're both in the dark." Miller breezed past her, saying, "I need to leave now if I want to beat forensics to the scene."

She turned and tried to keep up with him, but he was on the move.

"What can I do to help, Chief?"

Over his shoulder, he said, "Check with the Nevada County Sheriff and see if we can get his forensics team to lend us a hand processing the bodies."

"When he asks for a count?" Barbara asked.

"Just tell them there's a lot."

"Yes, Sir."

Miller headed outside, got into his new F-150, and fired it up. Before dropping it into gear, he breathed and reminded himself that being on the scene would look good for the press when this thing went national. Besides, he was the police chief and needed to do everything right, or else everyone at the GVPD now and for years to come would suffer.

"No pressure there," he grumbled.

Moments later, he left the parking lot to meet the others. When he arrived on the scene, however, he saw a circus of other officers, Nevada County deputies, a forest green Ford Explorer he knew belonged to the coroner's office, and long lines of crime scene tape strung between various wooden saw horses to form a makeshift barrier.

A slew of people fired off questions at the lone patrolman assigned to watch the crowd, which had gathered behind the crime scene tape. Miller turned and saw a car from *The Union* arrive, a lone woman with sloped shoulders and big, worried eyes. There was no designated crime section at *The Union* despite the uptick in crime since budget cuts, so whatever this woman was about to walk into, he prayed for her sake that she was mentally prepared.

The woman saw him, and they locked eyes, holding each other's gaze for a prolonged moment. When she moved to get out of the car and approach him, Miller quickly turned, ducked under the yellow crime scene tape, and headed up the broken dirt driveway toward the cabin. If she called out his name, he didn't hear her.

Detective Ruiz met him on the porch, where the unmistakable odor of dead bodies assaulted him. No amount of fresh mountain air could mask that gut-clenching smell.

"Is Dr. West here?" Miller asked Detective Ruiz.

"In here," she called from inside the cabin.

"Where's Peters?" Miller asked.

"Puking out back."

Miller nodded, stilled himself against what was coming, then nudged past Ruiz and stepped into the house. Kneeling, Dr. West was peering into the hole in the floor. He stopped before walking too closely. It had been years since Miller had visited the scene of a homicide. The last thing he wanted was to contaminate it with puke and draw the ire of a woman he liked and respected.

"How many?" he turned and asked Ruiz.

He heard Dr. West gag before catching herself, which was saying something considering her affinity for the dead and decade-long position as the county coroner.

Ruiz's eyes were running, and he wiped his nose. "Flashlights in the floor's opening... they show... it's like someone built this cabin over the top of a massive hole. We can't tell if someone designed this as a dumpsite or if it evolved into one over time."

"Dammit, Ruiz," Miller said, his anxiousness getting the better of him, "how many bodies?"

Ruiz straightened his back and squared his shoulders. "In the teens. Maybe more from what we can see. Do you remember watching any of those documentaries on John Wayne Gacy? How he had all those bodies buried under his house?"

"He's that guy from Chicago who dressed up as Pogo the Clown and killed teenage boys, right?" Miller asked, jogging his memory.

"Yeah," Ruiz nodded.

"Late '70s?"

"Yeah."

The details of the case were coming back to Miller, but he wasn't someone drawn to true crime or the serial killers of decades past. He noticed something in the air—a fat black fly. A few more flies appeared, the winged garbage cans creating a low, underlying buzzing sound. He gulped hard and clenched his jaw. He plugged his nose, his eyes starting to water.

Ruiz pulled a small tube of Vick's VapoRub from his jacket pocket and handed it to Miller. "Put a dab under your nose."

Miller thanked him, smeared the ointment under his nostrils then handed it back.

"Gacy was one of the most prolific serial killers of his time," Ruiz said, ignoring Miller's reaction to the scene and the Vic's. "He was considered a charming predator and a man of the people, but he was also a contractor who liked to offer good-looking young men jobs. He'd pick them up, take them back to his house, and murder them, burying their bodies in the dirt under his small suburban house."

"Twenty-six victims, right?" he asked, swatting a rather portly fly that wouldn't leave him alone. The thing was trying to land on his face. Miller wanted to tell the stupid fly he wasn't dead; he just needed a day off.

Ruiz acknowledged him with a nod, his nose and eyes running. "Under the house, yes. But I think they found thirty-three total, maybe more. I can't be sure since it's been so long."

"That's a lot of bodies," Miller said, coughing and fighting to keep his stomach down. His eyes started to water as he broke into a light sweat. "Why are you bringing him up?"

"Because there might be more bodies here."

That sinking feeling Miller had since his patrolman's frantic call doubled and doubled again until all he knew was the God-sized pit in his gut.

He watched Dr. West lift her head out of the hole; whatever she saw there rattled her. She was and had always been a level-headed woman, so her pained expression scraped Miller's nerves. When it was clear she was not inviting him into the crime scene, he stepped outside to wait for her.

Dr. Eliana West, a forty-something forensics expert with a plain body, pleasing features, and a tight platinum-blonde ponytail, walked out of the cabin a moment later, her face ashen—something Miller still couldn't believe he was seeing. She headed toward him, all business. More than anything, Miller wanted to escape that cabin and its appalling stench.

"This is huge, Chief Miller," she said. "Never seen anything like it."

"Quit beating around the bush, Eliana—how many?"

"We have a man in his late thirties to early forties, a woman of similar age, and a young girl—maybe twelve or thirteen—stacked on top of a huge pile of bodies. The pile spreads out pretty wide at the base, and from what I could see, there were bones at the bottom of the pile, which tells me this dumpsite has been in use for a while."

"Years?" Miller gasped.

Dr. West nodded and said, "At least."

Ruiz looked squeamish again.

Miller leveled his detective with a contemptuous glare and said, "Pull yourself together, son."

"With all due respect, Chief," Ruiz said, "you head in there, get a good look, and then come tell me how you feel."

Miller didn't like others challenging him publicly, but maybe Detective Ruiz was right. He donned a pair of latex gloves, slipped booties over his shoes, and looked at Eliana, the question clear on his face. She nodded, letting him know he could enter the scene.

Before going inside, he said, "Any hint of airborne contaminates, or are we just smelling the dead?"

Dr. Miller said, "Just the dead, from what I can tell, but my crime scene techs will verify that shortly. Judging by the first bodies, the likely causes of death are blunt force trauma and exsanguination. I'll do a tox screen back at the office, but there are a lot of bodies, which means it's a crap shoot, Chief Miller. If molds or toxins are present, we'll know when we test the air. Until then, you're welcome to stay outside."

"Everyone's puking," Miller said.

"That's because it's disgusting and smells worse than normal, Chief Miller," Dr. West replied. "Wear a mask if you want, or don't. Or smear more Vick's under your nose."

"That's your professional opinion?" he flippantly asked. "Wear a mask? Smear more Vick's under your nose?"

Dr. West flashed him a sharp look he tried to ignore. Instead, he walked into the house and into a smell so meaty and damp and utterly foul that it was all he could do to keep his knees from buckling. He turned and desperately looked outside, ready to escape had his lead detective not challenged him, which he did.

Those who weren't busy being sick were watching to see if he would join them in the barf brigade.

Deep down, and from personal experience, Miller knew the second he turned his back, the guys would start betting on whether or not he'd lose his lunch.

Miller approached the trapdoor on the floor and opened it. A wave of dizziness flashed through him, accompanied by the sensation of heat and nausea you get before passing out. He kneeled and gripped the wood casing with one hand. He then grabbed the Maglite flashlight left on the floor with his free hand. With great determination and much trepidation, Miller pressed the flashlight's ON button, igniting a thousand lumens of light. But he couldn't direct that light into the hole before him. He closed his eyes against the rolling sensation in his stomach.

Just do it, you pansy.

He mopped the sweat off his brow, wiped it on his pants, and opened his eyes. Then he braced himself against the urge to cough, which would surely be the start of his puking.

He flashed the light inside the hole and saw the tower of bodies stacked face-up. A few stared at him through the darkness with foggy eyes, hair the consistency of straw, and faces with flaky, graying skin tightly stretched over their skulls. He wavered, instinctively turning away, but he couldn't avert his eyes for long. The child on top of the pile—her body was fresh, but someone had snapped her neck in half. Sadness found him with brutal force. He didn't recognize the child; she was so small and vulnerable. Tears boiled in his eyes at the thought of this little girl suffering this measure of violence before she could even make her mark in the world.

Miller was hit with a swoop of vertigo, setting his cheeks on fire and aggravating his stomach further. If asked, he would say the sensation was akin to a baby seal stretching inside his belly after a long nap. He loathed that feeling but had never puked on the job.

"And I won't start now," he muttered, the edges of his eyes

burning. A string of clear snot drizzled from his nose. He caught it with his glove and wiped it on his pants. If he contaminated the scene, Dr. West would never trust him again.

He shifted the powerful beam of light, tracing the edges of the body tower. The bottom of the vast, cavernous hole was shovel-scraped dirt with some exposed rocks. Holding the wall in place were bricks and rocks, some odd pavers, and even an old log—all held by chicken wire and four-by-four posts.

The only way to get to the bodies would be to tear out the floors and widen the opening. Crime scene techs would do that after they photographed everything, collected whatever trace evidence and fiber they could find, and dusted for prints. Looking around, he wondered about the shoe prints, if there were any in the dirt below, or if they missed them in the front yard and had already contaminated that section of the crime scene.

He shifted his weight backward and plopped onto his butt on the floor. He turned and stared out the open front door at Dr. West, Detectives Ruiz and Peters (who finally appeared), and a few others watching him. What he thought about saying next bothered him immensely. It would rub some guys the wrong way, but no single department could handle a crime scene of this scope and savagery. To Ruiz, Miller said, "Call the Sheriff and let him know what's going on, that we need an assist."

"One of the deputies here already called," Peters said, still looking green. "He's on his way."

Miller looked at Dr. West and raised a brow at the look on her face. He said, "You were thinking it, too, Eliana. I know you were, and it's the right move. We'll need help on this one."

She nodded without comment.

Miller flashed the Maglite's beam on the young girl under the floor again, her face within reach. He absorbed all the little details, committing to memory her brown hair, old bed clothes, and the unnatural turn in her neck. The realtor and her client hadn't stumbled onto an old dumpsite—the killer was active, and he had just struck.

He peered around the girl and saw a mother with her throat raggedly sliced open and a man beneath her with a face so battered and bloody it was hard to tell what he ever looked like.

"My first impression is that this could be a family," Miller turned and said to Dr. West, who had walked back into the scene. "Was that your impression, too?"

She nodded thoughtfully and said, "Perhaps."

"The three bodies on top are all dressed in bedclothes," Miller observed.

"This qualifies for a serial if that puts your mind at ease," Dr. West said. "Don't feel bad about outsourcing. You have to get your arms around this one way or another."

"I know," Miller conceded. Dr. West wanted to bring in the FBI—he knew that now. "We need to see if we can ID these three ASAP. We need to see if these folks are local, out-of-towners, or undocumented."

"As soon as we print them, we'll run them through AFIS and see what we get," Detective Ruiz said, referring to the Automated Fingerprint Identification System, as he walked inside with his nose plugged.

Dr. West quietly said, "If they're not in our system, we could use the FBI for IAFIS, in case any are international or already in the fed's criminal database."

"I'll make the call, Eliana," Miller said, accentuating every word while trying not to sound too irritated. He considered himself a realist but still hated giving anything to the Feds. They were a prissy bunch he never did like very much.

He breezed past her and Ruiz, retrieved his cell phone, and made the call. The reception wasn't great, but he had enough bars to call his assistant and say, "Reach out to the FBI's Sacramento field office in Roseville and tell them we have a double-digit dumpsite with fresh bodies. We're pooling county resources, but with budget cuts, limited personnel, and an active serial killer, we'll need help in all aspects of the investigation."

"Wow, double digits?"

He didn't have time to listen to Barbara marvel over the case. Time was of the essence.

"Do it quickly now, Barbara, and be sure to let them know this little city is about to become an all-out circus as soon as the media catches wind."

Barbara paused first, then said, "I hate to say it, Chief, but they already have." She sounded nervous about the development and felt obligated to warn him.

"Who leaked it?" he leaned into the phone and growled.

"I'm not sure, but it certainly wasn't me. How many guys are on the scene right now?"

Miller glanced around and saw at least two dozen people. "Twenty, maybe? I don't know for sure. But it's too late to worry about the leaker now. I'm going to talk to the two witnesses who found the bodies, then see what the sheriff has to say when he gets here. You know we aren't the best of buddies, right?"

"I'll ask kindly and thank him graciously should we speak again," she said, understanding the political climate between the two.

"In the meantime, call all available personnel and get them in," Miller said. "I'll authorize the overtime, but I need you to monitor the budget. The second we look like we're dipping into the red, I'll reverse the overtime allowance, and we'll deal with the shortfall then. If we mess this up, and it negatively affects our ability to protect and serve the people of this city, the loudest ones will start asking about your salary and then mine."

"What about those who don't want to come in?" Barbara asked.

"Tell them they can volunteer to come in, or I can hit them with threats, public humiliation, and less-than-subtle berating."

She snorted out a laugh, then stopped herself and apologized.

"You get the point," he said.

"Yes, Sir. Absolutely."

"This is big, Barbara. Bigger than we've seen in decades." She remained silent, knowing there was no time for interruptions.

Miller squeezed his eyes shut and felt the tension spreading like molten heat through his temples and down the length of his spine.

Down the hill, Miller saw the witnesses who discovered the bodies. Detective Peters, a man who looked like a wiener in a suit, was interviewing them. He quietly wished Peters would grow some hair and facial hair already. With his skin-heavy look, and a name like that, he practically invited the dick jokes.

"Sir?" Barbara said, startling him.

He almost forgot he was still on the phone with her. "I'm just thinking this crime spree is going to make the serial killers of the '80s look like amateurs."

She sighed softly; the impact wasn't lost on her. "It's that bad?"

"I almost puked."

"Wow."

"You said the sheriff is on the way, right?"

"Yes."

"Okay, then. We'll see what we can figure out together, but you know what the sheriff's office deals with now that the cartel has partnered with local growers."

"They're dealing with their homicide investigations," Barbara said.

"Terrance Graham, the FBI's Special Agent in Charge at the Sac Field office, is a class-A, blue-ribbon, knuckle dragger, so don't ask for him. Ask for the Assistant Special Agent in Charge, ASAC Blackwood. He's good people. As for us, we need to ID these bodies, get this case solved, and arrest those responsible, and then we're going to crawl back under the radar. Bad press isn't good press for small-town law enforcement agencies."

"No press or good press is the best press," Barbara said.

"Exactly."

"I'll make the call," she said.

"Between you and me, if this case goes sideways, I want the weight of it falling on the Feds' shoulders, not ours. GVPD just got out of former Chief Davenport's spotlight—God rest his soul—and we don't need a rehash of the old days, which were bad."

"You weren't here then, Chief," she said.

"Neither were you, but Davenport and the department screwed up then, which is why Earl Gray is in NorCal on a twenty-five-year stretch, and Davenport drank himself to death. I came here to put a good face on this department, and I'll be damned if we screw the pooch because I was too proud or thought we could do more than I know for certain *we cannot do*."

"I know you don't need my opinion, Chief," she said. "But it feels like the right call."

Miller nodded. "You're the best."

four
sadie gray

WHEN TWENTY-EIGHT-YEAR-OLD SADIE GRAY left Sacramento to enroll at the FBI's training academy in Quantico, Virginia, she eventually asked her instructors what she would need to do to get an East Coast assignment. They told her that the FBI's Human Resource Division made final assignments. Not only did they consider the staffing needs of various field offices all over the U.S., but they also weighed the merit and performance of the graduates.

Sadie was looking for a better answer.

Her instructor saw this and said, "They'll consider requests from graduates seeking assignments at specific field offices, but nothing is guaranteed."

Sadie prayed they would assign her to any state but California. While she had no problem with the state or its capital city where she lived, her complex family history had her aching for a dramatic change of scenery.

After pushing herself to her limits and graduating second in her class at Quantico, she again asked her instructors to put in a good word for her with HR. They promised to do so. After graduation, Sadie returned to California with a renewed sense of optimism. Rather than saying she didn't want an assignment in California, she reiterated her desire to be assigned to the East

Coast. She even offered options by stating she was okay with the South or anywhere in flyover country—*just not California.*

After landing in Sacramento, she took an Uber straight to her tiny rental home and began packing, more ready than ever to make a move, even if it was a cross-country move. Knowing she was leaving the state and not likely to return, she visited her estranged father in Vacaville's NorCal State Prison—a man she hadn't seen in more than ten years due to a decades-long prison sentence. She didn't expect much from the visit, and she couldn't have imagined the turn she took toward happiness in seeing him. But when she left, she received a call from her new SAC, a polite man named Terrance Graham, who blindsided her with her assignment: the Sacramento field office, located on the outskirts of Roseville.

That night, she started drinking at sundown and didn't stop until the 2 a.m. last call. She was drunk and eventually disorderly, and she both puked and soiled herself on the way home, where for the next two days she lay moaning on the couch with a headache, a stomach on spin cycle, and a debilitating bout of depression.

There were fifty-six different FBI field offices or satellite offices in the country; she would have gladly accepted an assignment at fifty of them. So, why here? Was she being punished for not finishing first? She toyed with the idea of requesting a reassignment, but how do you take a job you *badly* want, and before you even start, say, "Gee, thanks and all, but I want to go someplace better." That was how you made a poor first impression and quite possibly set the tone for your future at the Bureau.

Sadie told herself countless times that most graduates got their first choice. But, in all fairness to the Bureau, her instructors said that if that proved otherwise with her, it was because the mission came first, and she was lucky even to have a job. Did her instructors know something she didn't?

After seeing her father in prison for the first time in a decade and enduring the tidal wave of emotions that followed, she came to accept that she was not leaving the state. In hindsight, guzzling copious amounts of alcohol might not have been the best reaction. She likely got a bit of alcohol poisoning in the process and a few new wrinkles for sure, but after two days of recovering, it was time to put on her big-girl panties and face reality.

Rather than lament her luck, she told herself she'd rent in a safer community using the money she had saved for her move. On the upside, she could now afford better living arrangements. With her anticipated salary, she might even consider a nice loft in midtown if one became available. Of course, if she took that route, she wouldn't be able to buy new furniture or likely anything else for a while. But at least she wouldn't have to listen to rats crawling through the walls or her next-door neighbors, who were always getting into fights and rocking the walls with makeup sex. That alone would make the move worthwhile.

The first week at the Bureau was so overwhelming that it nearly melted her brain. She forced a smile through most of it and told herself Quantico was a grind, but the rubber had met the road, and the jolt was nearly enough to snap her neck. She considered quitting in her darkest moments that week, not just because of the new job. She found a quick move-in deal for a mid-town loft, but the logistics of moving and simultaneously starting work proved challenging, and it wreaked havoc on her mind, body, and soul. As a result, she had difficulty focusing during that first week. Fortunately, she didn't have to move her possessions alone. Her friend at the property management group, Aria Butler, set her up with a loft—something she called "a rare opportunity"—also referred a few guys who would help her move because "Sadie Gray is super-hot." Sadie dismissed her friend's statement with an embarrassed laugh, but that was what she said. It seemed to do the trick.

"You're not getting free work because of your good looks," Aria said, which caused Sadie to frown. She wasn't exactly rolling in the greenbacks. "I promised the guys you would cook them dinner and buy beer afterward."

Okay, that's not so bad.

"I can make that happen," Sadie said immediately. "But it's going to be budget everything—food, beer, snacks, that off-brand stuff from the dollar store, and some cheap cuts of meat, like gristle and fat with a small veining of meat running through it."

Aria found that funny and tragic. "I forewarned them," she said with sympathetic eyes. "They're all fine with it."

Sadie failed to cook an award-winning meal for the boys, but she told them she tried. It helped that she splurged for decent beer. As for her looks, Sadie hadn't fared well that day. With her beat-up tennis shoes, baggy jeans, and black *KISS* tee-shirt faded to a charcoal gray (not to mention no makeup and messy hair pulled into a loose ponytail), she wasn't getting any dates out of it. But that was never her aim.

Later, Aria said the guys liked her, and she said she liked them, but when they left after dinner that night, Sadie knew they weren't coming back. She could live with that. On the upside, by the end of the week, she had set up all her utilities and put a solid week on the job behind her.

Even though she was exhausted, it felt like a win in the end.

But then came Friday night, and the force of nature that pushed her through the week ebbed, leaving her bored senseless. Sadie had yet to make any real friends at work or in her new building, and her other friends were with their boyfriends, so she spent the evening alone, pacing the floors of her bare, beautiful loft while trying not to cry. Looking at the absence of life in her home, feeling pathetically alone, she wondered, *Is this the actual value of my life?* To her name, Sadie owned an old queen-sized bed, a hand-me-down couch she bought at a second-hand store three years ago, and the same flat-panel TV she'd purchased on her eighteenth birthday, along with toiletries, dishes, and cookware she stole from her foster parents the day she left home. Everything else was worthless to her in her new life, so she threw them out before moving to the loft.

Just recently, she told herself that was all she needed to live. Now, she wasn't so sure. How she felt wasn't the same as living a fulfilling life. She looked around her new home. The loft had great bones, but without warmth, was it anything more than a nicer place to squat? That was when she turned to her Everlast punching bag where it lay in the corner, the long chain coiled on the floor beside it. She halfheartedly kicked it a few times before bed, then promised to find someone to hang it tomorrow.

A thought occurred to her the following morning, and so she acted on it. Sadie walked barefoot to her bathroom, pulled her hair into a high ponytail, and appraised herself in the mirror. "I can do better than this, right?" she muttered, rocking her head back and forth like she was unsure of her appearance.

Now is as good a time as any.

She forced herself to walk next door and knock on her neighbor's door. She had seen the man who lived there a couple of times, mostly in passing, but since she just moved in, she hadn't found that practiced ease of interacting with others. The man seemed friendly and looked strong enough, and she didn't hate that he was cute in a manly way.

He answered the door in jeans but nothing else except a smile and paint splatter on his hands. From deeper inside the space, Sadie heard the lofty sounds of folk music playing—a tune with the power to grab your soul and have its way with your emotions. It wasn't music you'd hear at Starbucks, but you might listen to it in an upscale coffee shop or at a music festival.

"Are you casing my loft?" he asked with a smirk.

"For a robbery?"

"Yeah."

Okay, she thought when she saw the canvases, *painter.* With a smile meant to disarm him, she subconsciously bit her lower lip, tilted her head, and said, "I uh... I need some man strength. Can you hang things from the ceiling?"

He stared at her with an amused look.

She glanced past him at several large pieces of artwork displayed from long chains he had hung from the open rafters. She couldn't help herself. But she also knew that she had come to the right place.

"I can pay you," she offered with both hands behind her back, one hand clutching her wrist. She hoped she didn't sound desperate, but she *was* desperate. She needed to punch and kick things to feel better, not that she would admit that to a stranger.

"You seriously want to pay me?"

"Yes, but not too much." Her face broke into an embarrassed smile. "I just moved in, and I'm starting a new career, so..."

"I'm a starving artist who's used to starving," he grinned. "Does that help?"

"You tell me," Sadie replied.

He stuck out a hand, which she took immediately. It was strong and felt good in her hand, a feeling of warmth she didn't experience often. They shook hands, but there was nothing formal about their meeting—he had a good grip, and she enjoyed the feel of his skin pressed to hers. Neither blinked, and both couldn't stop smiling.

And this is how most romantic comedies start, she thought. She began to bite her lower lip again but caught herself. Did she want romance? *No way!* She relaxed her hand into a dead-fish grip and slid it from his grasp. She felt like a disappointed lover sneaking out of bed in the morning, careful not to wake the man beside her.

"So, that's a yes, then?"

He nodded. "Give me a few minutes to clean up and grab a ladder from the super if you're good with that."

"Of course I am," she said with delighted eyes and a smile she couldn't put away to save her life. "Thank you, by the way! Oh, and I'm next door." She pointed to her door, but he smiled like he already knew.

When he showed up twenty minutes later, dressed and

carrying a ladder, Sadie opened the large rolling door and invited him inside.

"Wow, you're living like a Spartan," he commented as he looked around. "You might be poorer than me, something I didn't think possible."

"I said I just moved in, ding-dong," she laughed despite suddenly feeling self-conscious.

"Are you a starving artist, too?" he asked.

"Maybe?"

"What do you do?"

"A job requiring an NDA."

"What do you mean?" he asked.

"It's a non-disclosure agreement," she explained. "Sorry, but contract law *is* the law, and I'm a law-abiding citizen." She performed a cute curtsy. He seemed to appreciate it enough to stop asking about her personal life.

"I didn't get your name," he said.

"Hey, Lady," she replied.

He chuckled lightly. "Nice to meet you, Hey Lady. I'm Yo."

"Hey, Yo," she said, mimicking a surfer chick.

They laughed, and then he pinned her down with smoldering eyes and said, "Hey, Lady." Sadie knew he was being cute, so she joined him in laughter. Yeah, she liked him already. But then he said, "So, I'm assuming you want me to hang the heavy bag?"

"I do."

"You a fighter?"

"NDA."

He started to speak but stopped himself. "That's right, no questions."

"Personal inquiries give me polyps," she replied.

"I get hives."

She appreciated a good sense of humor over almost every other quality, and the ease with which she and this man interacted was surprising and charming. She put *Kygo's* latest album on her iPhone, hooked it up to a small Bluetooth speaker, and offered him a beer—which he declined.

"I appreciate you doing this," she said. "I'm going to keep an 'emergency egg' in my fridge should you ever need one."

He grabbed the bag, and then said, "That's kind of you, but my girlfriend is the baker in my household."

The statement stopped her so quickly that she felt a flush of disappointment hit her face. *God, how embarrassing!* But she wasn't as embarrassed by her response as she was by the fact that he turned in time to witness it. Seeing this, he broke into a mischievous chuckle but said nothing.

Sadie narrowed her eyes and tried not to make excuses for herself. But then she got it, and now she felt worse. "You don't have a girlfriend, do you?" she asked.

He lifted the bag, and before he climbed the ladder, he shook his head.

"You slick turd," she grinned.

He barked out a laugh as he climbed the ladder. Sadie handed him the heavy-duty metal bag mount with the swivel attachment, two three-inch screws with washers, and an old drill she had charged earlier.

"You're going to mount that in the exposed beam, but it doesn't need to be perfect since it's got the swivel."

"Who hung this bag at your last place?" he asked.

"I did, but I sprained my wrist and ankle, dislocated a finger, and cried and drank a lot. The good news is that when it was up, all I wanted to do was hit it because I was pissed off that it was so freaking hard to hang."

He screwed in the mount and looked down in time to hand her the cordless drill and take the heavy-duty coil spring.

"Attach that to the swivel bar," she said. "We'll hook the carabiner to it and then the chains. When that's finished, we'll hang the bag."

"You dislocated a finger doing this?" he asked as he attached the hook and chains.

"There was alcohol involved."

He found her stories humorous enough to keep smiling, which she appreciated.

When he was ready, Sadie lifted the heavy bag and watched him hang it at the desired height. He was about to clasp the stainless-steel carabiner hook to the D-ring when she handed him a custom sling—a rounded length of heavy fabric—and told him to slide the sling through the D-ring first, then hook the carabiner in the sling.

"Without the sling, the metal-on-metal movement will eventually wear through the D-rings," she explained. "When that happens, I might as well buy a new bag. But when it wears through the sling, I'll buy a six-dollar replacement, not a two-hundred-dollar heavy bag."

"Someone's not new at this," he said, balancing the bag on the third step against the ladder. He pressed his body against it and the ladder hard enough to take the small sling when she handed it to him. A moment later, he hooked the sling, let the bag hang against the ladder, and moved it away, ensuring it remained at her desired height. When he finished, he folded the ladder and said, "Unless there's anything else I can do for you, I'm all done."

"There is one thing," she said, causing him to raise a brow. "Bait me again like that, and I'll eat your emergency egg."

"Bait you again?"

"The girlfriend comment," she said.

He held up his hands in mock surrender, backed up, and leveled her with a look of boyish charm she found utterly intoxicating. Straightening his back and rising to his full height, he said, "I just wanted to know if we felt the same thing."

She crossed her arms and fixed him with a look. "And what's that?"

"The desire to take a quilting class together, duh."

Okay, she liked his sense of humor. "I'm not the dating kind of girl, and I have a black belt in playing hard to get, so..."

"I'm not the dating kind of girl either," he teased.

"I'm a virgin, saving myself for marriage."

"As am I," he winked.

"No egg for you, sucker," she said as she opened the loft's only door and motioned for him to leave already.

He strolled to the door, refusing her one last look, but then turned and said, "Hey, Lady."

Her heart squeezed. "Yeah, bro?" she said as if they were homies.

"I'm glad you let me hang your bag for you."

She gave him her best "Oh, really?" face, then said, "I'm going to think of your pretty face whenever I kick it."

"You're not paying me, are you?"

"If you need the money, then yes," she said. "But do you need it?"

"Not really."

So, with a smirk, she closed the door and thought hot guys were too much work for a girl trying to get on her feet and put her life together. *But they sure are fun to look at.*

Later that day, when Sadie went to check her mail, the superintendent asked if she was the one who needed the ladder. She indicated that she was and that her neighbor—the painter—was kind enough to help her hang some things.

"He's a painter but also a day trader," he said casually.

The superintendent was a nice, older man with a thick Hispanic accent and pudgy arms and legs she found adorable—if only she were into short, older men. While he was cute like a teddy bear and disarming, he also had a kind of over-the-hill, run-down cherub look. He smelled like Old Spice and hints of body odor. In other words, he was all right in her book.

"You said day trader, right?" she asked.

He nodded.

"So, he's not a starving artist?"

"I think he starves himself to look like that, but he's not going hungry because he's poor if that's what you're asking."

"Does he sell his artwork?"

The super shook his head and smiled sadly. "No, but he should. I've seen it, and he's got talent. But he said it would increase in value when he died, and then, hopefully, he'd be a millionaire."

"Sounds like him," she laughed. She wasn't sure what to make of her new neighbor. The man was an enigma so far, one who might have gotten under her skin the slightest bit, and in a good way. "What's his name, if you don't mind me asking?"

The super waved her off. "It doesn't matter."

"Really, why?"

"He's not the dating kind."

"Gay?"

He shook his head. "No, just uninterested in the drama. At least that's what I heard him telling Jane, the renter before you. She was cute, too."

"Hmmm."

"How good are you with mysteries?"

"Mysteries are my job," she said, beaming.

"Well, when you figure him out, be a sport and share."

She thanked him, returned home, and hit and kicked the heavy bag to ensure it was sturdy. Then, she plopped down on her couch and turned on the television. Nothing was interesting, so she shut it off and grabbed a nearby book. An hour later, she set the book aside, grabbed her cell phone, and scrolled through several Facebook groups searching for a local pet adoption agency. After an hour, she locked eyes on the cutest Boston Terrier she'd ever seen.

"What's your name, cutie pie?" she asked aloud, her hand over her heart.

She scrolled through the dog's photos and saw that his owner had named him Droolius Caesar, or Caesar for short. A quick email to the adoption agency let her know the dog was a forever pet for serious pet owners only. Sadie messaged the woman from the ad, indicating her intention to adopt; the woman messaged back to ask if she was married with kids. Sadie let her know she was single and gainfully employed. When the nosy woman asked about her job, Sadie messaged her the truth.

I'm with the FBI.

Oh. Pause... Then: *Here locally?*

Yes, I'm running a task force investigating domestic pet adoption fraud.

Am I under investigation???

I want to adopt Droolius Caesar. Can I schedule a doggy date today or tomorrow?

Today, if you're close.

I am.

She messaged Sadie the address and the dog's pertinent details, then promised to supply her with everything she needed to hold her over for a few days.

Within an hour, Sadie pulled up in front of the woman's home, politely introduced herself, and walked inside when invited. She saw Droolius Caesar and lowered herself before him. The pup came right to her, and she let him lick her face, melting her heart all over the place.

Maryanne, who adopted Caesar out to Sadie after requiring her to fill out a questionnaire and do a ton of paperwork, said, "I know love at first sight, and this is it."

She was right—it was.

Saturday was halfway over when she returned home, showed Caesar around, and poured him a big bowl of food. She soon found out why he was named Droolius Caesar. What seemed like an entire gallon of saliva appeared along his lips, flooding his mouth so fast that Sadie could hardly scoot a bowl in front of him before he soaked the floor.

"My God, Caesar," she gasped as he wolfed down his food. "A duck could float in that gigantic drool pond you left on my floor."

Ten and a half seconds later, the pup's bowl was clean, and he looked up at her with those big, beautiful, *begging* eyes.

"First off, *no*," she said clearly. "We eat slowly to better digest our food, stay fit and trim, and always be in fighting shape. So, this one time, if you promise to slow down and *not* devour your food in less than ten seconds, I'll refill your bowl. Bark once for 'yes,' twice for 'no.'"

Sadie stared at him a long time before Caesar barked once.

"Okay then, you know the drill. Not ten seconds this time—shoot for twenty."

She grabbed the bag of kibble, and the drool gathered in Caesar's mouth like a magic trick—the warm, slimy joy of a hungry dog waiting anxiously for seconds. The instant Sadie poured the kibble, Caesar shoved his snout into the bowl and ate so fast that she was flabbergasted. The little fella was finished in under six seconds, licking his lips and looking up at Sadie as if satisfied.

"*Rude*," she said, dragging out the word. At least the little guy stopped drooling. Now, if only she had a mop large enough to absorb the ocean of slobber left behind...

She made herself a burger from grass-fed, grass-finished meat that was so expensive and tasty that she couldn't afford to buy hamburger buns or mustard; she was fresh out of both. After cooking the meat, she slapped it between buns made of crispy lettuce leaves. With a shake of pepper, a splat of ketchup, and a few bread-and-butter pickles from *Trader Joe's*, she was in business.

Sadie stacked everything on a paper plate, grabbed a napkin off the counter, and sat on the couch, which doubled as the kitchen table. Caesar jumped on the couch and plopped beside her. He ignored her and focused on the burger, his nostrils opening and closing as if powered by pistons.

"No freaking way," she said, pushing his face away. His head was on a spring, though, and he whined like he was in the worst pain ever, making him the consummate beggar. She looked at him sternly and shook her head. "You ate. Now *I* eat. Sit down and watch TV with me, or go to your bed and sulk. It's your choice. Either way, you're not getting any more food."

Little Droolius Caesar lowered his head, jumped off the

couch, and walked over to his bed, where he curled up and closed his eyes. Satisfied, Sadie turned on the television to the local news, then grabbed her burger with both hands and took a big first bite while watching the talking heads run the gamut on various local issues.

And then the headline, MURDER IN THE FOOTHILLS, appeared, dominating the entire screen with attention-grabbing, eye-catching colors. The second Sadie saw that the location was Grass Valley, California, she frowned and muted the television.

Grass Valley was her hometown, located maybe an hour away. She wished it were a hundred hours away, a thousand. Suddenly grumpy, she took another bite of her burger, chewed it noisily, and hoped the segment would end before the PTSD kicked in. But then the studio switched from the news anchor to the on-the-scene reporter, bringing the location into perfect view.

She lay the sloppy half-burger on the paper plate, wiped her hands on her good pants, and immediately shut off the television. For a moment, she sat in complete silence, remembering the past and the horror that unfolded there as a child. These memories were not limited to her abduction, though—she also held the horrible memories of her sister, mother, and father, and what happened to all of them in that miserable, beautiful city.

When she started to cry—because she couldn't help herself—Droolius Caesar climbed out of his bed, trotted back over, and jumped up on the couch. To her delight, the pup didn't go after her food. Instead, he made whimpering noises and licked the side of her face.

The doggy kisses were what she needed, but having seen a nightmarish crime scene set against the backdrop of her hometown rattled her heart and threatened to undo everything she had done to put those awful times behind her.

After seeing the city, everything changed. While she buried the specifics of those dark days in the recesses of her mind, the resulting emotions existed in a different part of her. She could tuck them away, but there was no way to control them. She knew that now. Would the horrors of those days ever go quietly into the night?

Probably not.

Sadie sniffled hard, wiped her eyes, and rubbed Droolius' ears. He curled against her thigh and glanced up to be sure she was okay. She had managed to steady herself, but being a special agent with the FBI while having a father in prison for murder... sometimes she wondered if it was too much to take.

At that moment, she wondered if—based on her past—she was perfect for the FBI or plum crazy for joining. She would know soon enough. Then again, she was supposed to get her partner assignment on Monday, which she learned from her ASAC, a man named Angus Blackwood. When she asked who he was thinking, Blackwood said, "I don't know, maybe Special Agent Tulle or someone else. I'm evaluating personalities right now." She didn't give anything away by her expression, but she ran into Special Agent Tulle, *Brad,* and he rubbed her the wrong way, if anything, by just his appearance.

"You can do this," she told herself.

Finally, Sadie picked up her burger, took another bite, and swallowed, telling Droolius Caesar he was a good doggy and that she was happy he came home with her. As if to prove her right, Droolius licked her hand once, then curled up beside her and let her finish her burger in peace.

five
sadie gray

THE FBI TAUGHT her to fight using sound techniques and good body dynamics; four years in foster care taught her to fight dirty—if needed. Now, if she didn't work and re-work her newfound techniques with the heart of a girl who refused to be bullied by others, Sadie knew they might fail her when she needed them most. That was the reason for the heavy bag.

As a federal agent, it was possible for her to one day find herself in a fight with a full-sized man, a lunatic fighting for his life. Her one hundred and twenty-five pounds wouldn't cut it unless she possessed an indomitable will backed by constant training in proven techniques.

In addition to working these techniques on her heavy bag in the privacy of her loft, she focused on the timing and placement of her shots, working through multiple fighting scenarios in her mind. She drilled the bag like it was a man, a killer, an inhuman nightmare who stood between her and the preservation of life—hers and others.

After every shot, she asked herself the same question: *yes* or *no?* Yes, she stopped the fight, or no, she didn't. Sadie fought hard to stop the proverbial fight, but that was rarely the case, so she chastised herself, knowing her ability to stop it with even her best shots was still a hard no. She was too small, didn't have a man's bone density, and any use of body mechanics still bore the force of a woman weighing a buck twenty-five. For these reasons, she trained and fought harder, pushed herself longer, and dug in with more determination, especially when squeezing out the last of her energy.

Then there was the matter of her father and that thing that happened as a child—the thing that sent her otherwise normal-ish life into a tailspin. She fought hard to put the memories of that terrifying time out of her mind, and though that worked for a while and the details of her abduction were fuzzy at best, the feelings could sometimes hit her out of the middle of nowhere with enough force to leave her shaking. Thinking about the man who took her and her sister and what happened to their family afterward gave her an extra push near the end of her workout. Most times, she felt anger, but other times, fear consumed her. And then there were times when she trained hardest to push out the soul-swallowing vulnerability she'd suffered at the hands of that freaking madman.

Over the years, Sadie fought to leave her past behind. The fact that she could now finish her workout without collapsing and gasping for breath, or worse—quitting, was impressive even to her for as hard as she trained.

A few days ago, in prison, her father was beaten to within an inch of his life, then stabbed in the back four times with a prison shank. When the prison informed her, and she spoke with him about the attack, he told her he didn't die because there was no quit in him and he was too powerful to kill. He told her that with a raspy voice and a chuckle from the prison infirmary. He also said life was not fair and you had to fight for every breath in the hellish world in which you lived.

"They got me four times, but I ended up winning the fight because I wasn't afraid to drive my thumb into the man's eyeball and try pushing it into his brain," he said. "No one came out of that fight unscathed. But only one came out victorious, and I decided long ago I would always be that man. You need to make that same decision for yourself, Sadie."

This mindset saved his life: soft targets, willpower, and forceful determination. With her music playing, she hit the heavy bag from multiple angles, working it like it stole her money and was trying to kill her.

Droolius Caesar watched her from his bed, curious or entertained. She smiled and told him he was a good doggy.

Her music changed from a pulse-pounding, head-banging riot of noise to a slow-starter that would ramp up to a blistering crescendo.

She checked her watch: twenty-two minutes left in her workout, twenty-two live-or-die minutes. Considering her father's advice, Sadie intensified her efforts, training with the vigor required to beat a man twice her size. She wanted to earn that "yes"—the "yes" meant she stopped the fight and cleaned her attacker's clock.

The song ended a few minutes later, her core seized, and sweat dripped off her hands, arms, face, and everywhere else. She looked at her knuckles and saw some were skinned and bleeding. It didn't matter. It was a Sunday and she felt good. As if to highlight her determination, her black workout pants, white top, and sports bra were soaked. She pushed damp, matted hair off her forehead, drew a shaky breath, and tried to steady her heart rate. Caesar was now asleep, which was okay with her. So, she went back to work on the bag.

Her body continued to sweat, the perspiration running down her face and throat, all along the base of her neck in her hairline, darkening her nearly black hair and leaving it wet. Sweat also ran between her smallish breasts, and a swamp formed in her armpits, the moisture spreading down her torso and lower back and gathering in the crack of her butt. At a gym, she would feel gross enough to worry about the judgments of others; at home, such inconveniences only mattered as they related to pride and effort.

She drilled the heavy bag with fist after fist, envisioning her prey, those criminals she would capture, the smug sons of bitches whose faces she would rearrange with more violence than allowed as a fed. Then she stepped back and threw various kicks—the hard, focused kicks she reserved only for days off.

Sadie was in the final stretches of her workout when she stopped mid-stride, froze momentarily, and made a beeline to the kitchen. She bent over the waste basket and threw up, pawing sweat from her eyes between the convulsions. A quick look at the clock told her she had nine minutes left. Sadie blew her nose, spat in the can, then stood and returned to the heavy bag. Lifting her hands with sweat still dripping from every pore, she reminded herself that if she was in her father's position—getting beaten, stabbed, and nearly killed—she couldn't let anything slow her down the way a little vomiting was trying to slow her down. So, she went after it again, stopping only seconds later due to heavy pounding on her front door. Caesar woke up and started barking. If her sudden spell of nausea had irritated her before, then this new disruption was beyond infuriating. She only had a few minutes left!

"Droolius Caesar!" she said.

He looked at her.

Curse words ached to fall softly from her lips, words she felt in her heart but refused to say out loud lest she come to rely upon them for every form of expression. While dropping f-bombs and GDing had been the ways of people from her past, Sadie swore to rise above that kind of low-brow countenance. If anything, she wanted to one day prove she was worth recommending to the Behavioral Analysis Unit in Quantico—her long-term goal. She wanted to be a profiler and hunt down serial killers, serial rapists, and kidnappers.

She shut off the music and stalked to the door, thinking that whoever had cut her workout short by a few minutes would know her fury from the look in her eyes. Part of her wanted to finish her workout on them, whoever they were.

"Unacceptable," she grumbled as she unlatched the door and unfastened the lock. She grabbed the handle on the sliding door, pulled it open along the tracks, and stared into Special Agent Brad Tulle's Ken-doll face.

"Hi."

"*You*," she all but spat. She meant to say "hi," but the interruption and her emotions about it got the best of her.

Brad was dressed in standard bureau attire: a three-piece suit and tie, stylish dress shoes, and a gentleman's haircut. His face was young-looking, and he seemed to possess an air of self-importance, which was immediately off-putting, not that he would care.

"And here I thought I'd catch you in your pajamas," he said, his eyes wandering over the curves of her body.

She frowned and crossed her arms over her breasts. "What do you want, Brad?" she asked in a tone that didn't fall on him as much as it smacked him in the face.

He smiled as if he had never seen her before, as if this was the first time, and he wanted to take the sight of her in completely. His eyes now moved over her in slower, more purposeful glances, which was an odd feeling to experience and a bit uncomfortable.

"Don't do that," she said. "Harassment laws extend beyond the workplace."

Brad had never been to her loft before, which didn't affect his demeanor. However, he should have been more sensitive to the fact that he was intruding on her privacy—and on her day off, no less.

Droolius was suddenly beside her, growling at Brad. "It's okay, Caesar, he was just leaving." The dog sat at her side, just to be sure.

Brad cleared his throat and said, "Then, next time, don't answer your door looking like... *that*." He motioned at the length of her body with his hand, allowing himself a third generous look. At this point, she wondered if this were the start of a hazing she'd have to endure like a rite of passage.

"Let me guess, you have a thing for gym bunnies and yoga girls?" she quipped.

"First off, which man doesn't? And second, it's not that."

"Then what is it?" she asked. "Because I'm getting a pervy vibe that I don't like right now."

"No, you just look... *smelly,*" he said, not the least bit ashamed. "I'm super embarrassed for you right now."

Sadie shut the heavy rolling door, watching his face disappear behind the metal. She turned and stalked back to her bedroom amid renewed pounding and Caesar's barking.

To prove a point, she donned a winter jacket and the pants she wore when she was one-hundred-and-fifty-five pounds—pants that reminded her to never accept anything less than your very best, lest you end up out of shape and feeling miserable again. The pants covered her skin-tight bottoms and gave off that formless, homely look she despised so much. She then cinched the belt to hold things up and quickly fashioned her hair into a loose ponytail. After that, she pulled her FBI ball cap onto her head and smiled a hostile smile.

Brad was still pounding—the weasel. Her scared pup now looked at her nervously. "It's okay, boy," she said.

Sadie grabbed the door's handle, rolled the sliding door back open, and found Brad standing there, red-faced and less than amused.

"Better?" she asked, modeling her new outfit for him.

"You just went from a solid seven to a two," he said, trying to calm down.

"And you went from a three to a one, you feckless pig," she snapped. Droolius barked in agreement. "Now, what do you want on my day off? And why would you come here when you or anyone else could have used the phone instead?"

"ASAC Blackwood wants to talk to you," he explained. "I said he should call you, but then he told me you weren't answering your phone."

"Because it's my day off, I've muted my ringer, and I'm not working a case yet. That will change when I get my partner assignment and a case."

"Which is why he thought it best to stop by unannounced," Brad said.

She frowned and shook her head, knowing she was rude and that you shouldn't judge a book by its cover. With her hands on her hips, she said, "Tell him I'll see him tomorrow when I'm back in the office."

Brad looked immediately uncomfortable with her answer. "He said you might say that, thinking you work this job like any other. Well, you don't. The FBI employs us, and when we're on, *we're on.*"

"We're not on until tomorrow."

"Wrong," he said.

She bit her tongue to keep the rudeness at bay.

Brad, however, seemed to consider his next words carefully, but only for a moment. His expression darkened and suddenly became more serious. "Most times, it won't be like this, but when it is—as it is now—get in the boat and row."

"Get in the boat and row?" she asked, cocking her head sideways.

"In case you haven't figured it out yet, and now I'm sure you haven't, this is... *special.* ASAC Blackwood is not a sadist. He takes care of his agents, and he will only adjust protocol when it's important, which it is. When he tells you why he wants to talk to you, trust me, you'll understand. He also said he'll make up for it after this case."

"He's got a case for me?" she asked, instantly perking up.

Brad nodded, smoothed his right eyebrow with his thumb, then folded his lips inside his mouth to keep from saying more. She loved and hated the sight of him, yet she was also annoyingly curious about his thoughts.

Finally, Brad nodded—this was no longer "fun Brad," "judgy Brad," or "almost-sexy Brad" in front of her. He became Special

Agent Brad Tulle, going into business mode on the turn of a dime.

"I should have dialed down the snark," she admitted.

He waved off the comment and said, "This is ASAC Blackwood asking, not me. We could get off on the right foot, but maybe we're left feet people."

Her eyes cleared, and she looked at Brad with a bit too much intensity. "Whatever, that's fine. Tell him I'll be there in an hour."

At that point, Brad should have left. Instead, he remained in the hallway, staring at her as if he had nowhere else to go. Then, he said, "You have dreams of being in the BAU, right? You want to hunt serial killers?"

With one hand gripping the sliding door's handle, Sadie looked for an excuse to pull the door shut in Brad's face, but his expression and the question stopped her.

"Yes," she conceded.

Brad eyed her, turning his head in the appraisal, then shifted from one foot to the other, less confident and cocky than before. He glanced down at Droolius Caesar, who had been behaving so far, then back to her. Was he holding something back?

"Did you even see the news?" he finally asked.

She shook her head. *Is there a serial killer on the loose?*

"Better make it thirty minutes, not an hour," Brad said, choosing to be coy. "I can drive you there if you want since you don't have your bu-car. It'll be faster."

"My what?"

"It's fed-speak for your car from the motor pool," he said. "That's what we call them—bu-cars. We're all assigned one, but someone just totaled one, and the other isn't back from the body shop. Some guy t-boned Special Agent Callaway."

"Too much information, Special Agent Tulle," she said. "I have to shower first and grab a protein shake, so I'll shoot for half an hour, but it'll likely be an hour."

The morose expression on his face broke, and "fun Brad" was

working on making a comeback. "A shower, huh? Can I stay and watch?"

Sadie thought she knew where this was going and didn't want it. "Watching me drink a protein shake is so boring," she said, speaking in a leaden tone she hoped would squash his efforts to establish dominance. He began talking, but she cut him off instead. "However, if you're suggesting I let you stay and watch me shower, I won't bother reporting you to ASAC Blackwood because I'm not an HR-type of girl, but I will make sure that tomorrow morning you're shitting out blood and most of your teeth."

Droolius barked once again, as if to emphasize Sadie's point.

Brad seemed to think he could alleviate the tension with bright eyes and a well-timed smirk; she didn't hate his look, but she had come to understand he was testing their limits, the same as you'd push a sports car into a slide to find the car's threshold for breaking traction. As much as she despised the hazing, it was a ritual that ordinary people expected, endured, and overcame. She would take it if she had to, but no one said she had to smile doing it.

"They say you're good at your job," Sadie said. "You want your spot at the BAU, don't you?"

"Most of us do," he said.

"I also hear you've been to the BAU several times, that they're looking at you as an agent of interest, right?"

"That's correct," he replied with pride.

"So read me, then," she said, stone cold. "Read me while I'm looking right at you."

He grinned, raised his hands in surrender, then stepped back and said, "I have a thing for protein shakes and perspiration, I swear. Besides, I have a girlfriend who is cleaner and more my type than you. No offense, but I don't go for sevens or twos."

"None taken," she mumbled. "Props to the charity case you call a girlfriend for landing such a winner." She gave him an underwhelming slow clap she hoped stung.

Brad took the blow gracefully, his eyes locked on hers, unblinking. She razzed him, made her point, and waited for him to leave. So, why wasn't he leaving?

She folded her arms and said, "How can you do that? Just go from jerk to deadly serious, then back to jerk again?"

"What can I say? It's probably the combination of good looks and charm," he replied, his serious demeanor giving way to a light-hearted, airy personality. "See you back at the office, stinky."

And with that, he left.

She blew out a frustrated breath, rolled her door shut, then latched it and stood there, wondering what bug crawled up his ass and died.

"Freaking clown," she finally grumbled as she turned and headed to the bathroom for a quick shower. She heard the ticking of Droolius' nails on the floor as he followed her to the bathroom. She stopped for a second and fought the urge to turn on the news, but whatever story broke would only draw her interest enough to slow her down.

"Go sit in your bed," she told Droolius Caesar.

The dog knew the word "bed" and readily complied, exhausted from protecting Sadie at the front door.

"Good doggie," she said in a baby voice.

Brad was correct when he asked if she wanted to hunt serial killers, rapists, and kidnappers—the worst of the worst when it came to predators of every sort. She wanted this because she never wanted to become her father. He was a good man, but he put himself into a position he should never have been in, forcing himself to make a life-changing choice. Sadie didn't hate him for the things he did or stood for; instead, she loved him for the sacrifices he made for her to be less dysfunctional than she was now. In the end, because he was a man who loved the fight, he was now forced to pay a price that was too steep for his reactions.

She got into the shower and focused on efficiency over enjoyment, thinking that if she could hunt down and stop monsters like the one who stopped her father—the one who preyed upon

Sadie and her sister, Natalie, when they were kids—she wanted in on that and then some. That made her wonder about Brad's reference to a serial killer. Was she going to get her crack at taking one down fresh out of the gate? She laughed and told herself not to dream that dream. Because she wouldn't get that shot—that would be stupid.

Wouldn't it?

six
sadie gray

SADIE DRESSED QUICKLY, downed a pre-made protein shake, and drove straight to Roseville, to the FBI's Sacramento field office. She walked inside, saying hello to those in security, then walked back to ASAC Blackwood's office. A small group of agents and personnel had gathered in his office... waiting for her. *Oh, God.* Was she holding up everyone else?

Embarrassed, she lowered her head and apologized for not being there sooner. Blackwood nodded but said nothing about it. Was he mad? Disappointed? She shouldn't have been such a jerk to Brad, but she had dealt with the Brads of the world most of her adult life, and kindness or respect for his ilk wasn't in her repertoire.

Speaking of the Devil, she eyed Brad where he stood. He gave her a wink, which she hated right away. He was so full of himself, standing at attention like a superhero with the ego to match. But it wasn't just the two of them and ASAC Blackwood. Several other agents or support staff she didn't know were in attendance, people who regarded her with nothing more than a cursory glance.

Blackwood turned everyone's attention to a large flat-screen television mounted on the wall in his oversized, ornate office. Sadie turned around, stepped closer to Blackwood's desk, and saw that he had put on the local news but muted the sound. Blackwood unmuted it, and they watched a scene of horror, one eerily reminiscent of some of the most gruesome serial killings the country had ever seen. The '70s and '80s were the heyday for serial killers, especially those who were prolific. There was no internet, forensics had severe limitations, and people trusted the newspapers and national media enough to take them at face value. Thinking of the fear those men and women had inspired back then, she prayed for a different outcome. She shook off the ick she felt and, instead, watched the TV, where she was quickly sucked into the crime scene's gravitational pull.

While local camera crews, on-the-scene reporters, small-time bloggers, and dozens of spectators and potential witnesses remained behind the crime scene tape, the towering pines, a long dirt driveway, and a creepy cabin set the stage for something horrible.

Crime scene techs moved in and out of the run-down structure like lines of worker ants, and several officers from GVPD and a few deputies from the Nevada County Sheriff's Office seemed to be talking, maybe even coordinating their investigative efforts. Two men from the coroner's unit suddenly emerged from the front door with a body bag strapped to a gurney.

So, what's the body count?

The camera panned from the cabin back to the reporter. Behind the female reporter, witnesses lined the street—people from all walks of life congregating between the police cruisers and sheriff deputy's patrol cars near the meat wagon. The police left the flashing lights on their patrol units active; the sheriff's deputies used their vehicles for traffic control. A second coroner's van arrived at the scene, waiting for one of the LEOs to lift the crime scene tape so the driver could pull closer to the cabin.

"Did they reach double digits yet?" Brad asked. Behind the second meat wagon was a third, a vehicle on loan from a funeral home, by the looks of it.

Blackwood said, "It's still early, but it's starting to look that way."

Hot and cold sensations flooded Sadie's face and neck. Her breathing quickened as the anxiety took hold. The world around the television faded from her vision, leaving her a bit woozy and locked into something akin to tunnel vision. The scene held her hostage in so many ways; she tried to swallow, but her throat had constricted.

As much as she tried, Sadie wanted to avert her eyes but couldn't. Before long, the visceral effects of a very physical reaction began to diminish, leaving her with an eerie feeling she couldn't shake. Could she leave the office and use the bathroom? Splash some cold water on her face and pull herself together? *No, that'll look weak.* A terrible, aching sadness did nothing to lessen the pit growing in her stomach. Worse, a sudden clap of desperation grabbed her, taking her by surprise. She forced herself to blink, to break the stare and look away, but she could not get away from the intense pull of the scene or its many implications.

Even though it was not yet noon, the sun had climbed high into the late morning sky, but you wouldn't know it by looking at the crime scene. The dense trees and intensely thick foliage, reminiscent of a familiar, low-mountain feel, blocked out much of the sunlight while casting the ramshackle cabin and everything else in shadows that made the scene look cold, unsettling, and just plain wrong.

Then she saw the words on the lower portion of the screen, which cut through her like a blade: Grass Valley, CA.

Sadie swayed under a groundswell of dizziness, then closed her eyes only to bump into an intruding memory. The flash of a pitch-black basement snapped into her mind, sharp and cruel, and then, as quickly as it had come, it was gone. She drew a breath, trying to shake off the memory, but it hit her like a gut punch. Desperate to control herself, she pulled a chair around and practically fell into it, gripping the handles until the feeling passed.

"Are you okay, Special Agent Gray?" ASAC Blackwood quietly asked.

Turning to him with a terror-stricken gaze, she nodded. Blackwood narrowed his eyes and stared back at her, not so sure that he should believe her.

"All good, Sir," she finally said.

He motioned for her to return her attention to the television, then increased the volume as the picture-in-picture coverage shifted from Grass Valley back to the studio. In the background, another gurney and accompanying body appeared. The reporter looked stricken from the start, but her face seemed to regain some of its original color.

"Thank you for your detailed coverage, Sharon," the news anchor told the reporter. "It has to be surreal to be standing somewhere so beautiful while reporting on a horror of this magnitude. Honestly, I can't find the words."

"I'm here so our viewers don't have to be, Stew," Sharon said. "I'll keep you and our viewers posted on the newest developments. Until then, back to you and Erin in the studio."

The lead anchor, Stew, was handsome, with slick black hair, a prominent jawline, and a plastic-surgery nose. He wore an expensive suit and tie with a tie pin and cuff links. If she could see his shoes, Sadie would bet they cost a fortune. The man was clearly in his prime and gunning for a larger network, seemingly prepared to have his face memorialized in the archives of history should coverage of these murders captivate his audience.

Just before the small box in the upper right-hand corner disappeared, Sadie and the group, along with thousands, if not tens of thousands of other viewers, watched Sharon vacillate on unsteady legs while white-knuckling the mic. Anyone watching knew what was coming next, but to see it on live television was surreal. The woman fought to hold her composure as crime scene techs wheeled out more bodies on gurneys, each affecting her more than the last. The second Sharon thought she was off camera she abruptly turned and sank to her knees.

"Holy cow, she's puking on live TV," Special Agent Tulle muttered.

"Wow," someone else in the room said.

Shocked, the news anchor cleared his throat and said, "I apologize for that, folks. While we do our best to maintain an air of professionalism, Sharon's unexpected reaction is a testament to the depravity of this scene. Our prayers go out to her and those forced to make sense of something so heartbreaking that even this dogged newsman can't make sense of it." He cleared his throat, breathed for effect, and waited for the B-roll to run before continuing. "For those tuning in now, local law enforcement arrived at the scene of this rustic hunting cabin deep in the woods of Nevada County, where they encountered a shocking scene of unspeakable evil, one so appalling that words to accurately convey what we've seen today simply don't exist. Folks, you're seeing a serial killer's body dump. From what we've learned from those on the scene, this maniac is active and prolific, and it would seem he's used the cabin for months or even years."

Stew's co-anchor, Erin, transitioned seamlessly to the stats, then touched her earpiece as if hearing from sources on the scene. She said, "We're receiving updated numbers now. Local authorities report removing a total of seventeen bodies so far: men, women, and children. With the county coroner's unit and crime scene techs on location, as well as police and various sheriff departments, everyone involved is searching for the identities of both the victims and the monster responsible for this. While no clear patterns beyond the obvious have emerged, it is early in the investigation." She turned to Stew with a solemn look.

Stew asked, "Has anyone talked about possible motives here, Erin?" Erin shook her head as if sad she didn't have an answer.

"Everyone's a detective, and no one's a detective," Brad muttered.

"Be quiet," Blackwood said.

On TV, Erin continued: "As if to complicate matters, the poor condition of the older bodies will likely worsen, ultimately slowing the coroner's work of identifying the bodies and determining a cause of death."

"Genius," another person said.

"Shhh," Blackwood snapped again.

Erin then turned to Stew and said, "Sources within Grass Valley PD and Nevada County Sheriff's Office tell us they're preparing to remove a larger section of the cabin's main floor to gain access to the remainder of the site. They say it will be tricky because beneath the home, well... I suppose it's best just to say it."

Stew responded with bated breath and a theatrical look of shock, unable to take his eyes off Erin.

She took a stabilizing breath and said, "There is a cavernous hole, still filled with too many bodies to count, which means we can expect the crime scene techs to be working long into the night and possibly tomorrow."

"My God," Sadie heard herself say.

Others in Blackwood's office nodded to her sentiment, but they misunderstood her and would never know what she meant by the statement.

Sadie realized she was being assigned to the case because she grew up in Grass Valley, not for any other reason. That was why ASAC Blackwood summoned her on her day off, why he sent Brad to retrieve her personally. She turned and flashed Blackwood a desperate look.

"Now you get it," he said with a knowing smile.

"But why?" she whispered.

"You know why."

Sadie swallowed a lump in her throat as panic took hold. Her skin turned clammy, and her lower lip lightly trembled. Blackwood read her weakness like a book and responded in kind.

"Special Agent Tulle, shut off the television. Everyone else, including you, Brad, leave my office," ASAC Blackwood boldly announced. The response to the ASAC's order was immediate. Sadie stood, but he stopped her. "You stay, Special Agent Gray."

"Yes, Sir," Sadie said, sitting back down. Her skin was cool, so bloodless it should be gray.

The office quickly cleared, leaving Sadie with Blackwood. He motioned for her to turn her chair and pull up to his desk, which she did. Somehow, Sadie mustered the courage to look him in the eye rather than stare at her feet. While she was not one to fidget, she suddenly developed a case of restless leg syndrome. Discreetly, she touched her thigh and squeezed the muscles to stop the frantic movement.

"You look like you're about to shit out circus monkeys," Blackwood said.

"Already did that, Sir," she said. "I've got an elephant on deck."

"Hope you have a suture kit on you," he laughed, appreciative of her dark humor.

She laughed along with him, surprising herself. A bit of warmth brought color back to her cheeks; her neck, however, burned with such intensity it could be hives, even though she knew it wasn't. Was she about to sweat through her blouse? Lord knew her armpits were soaked at that point.

"There she is," ASAC Blackwood said with a smile. "I'm sure you know why you're here."

"It's obvious, Sir."

"My agents are spread thin, and though we're not struggling for resources, I can't pull other agents off of active cases to work on this one."

"You don't have to explain your actions to me, Sir," Sadie said. "I understand I'm new, and you're the ASAC. The chain of command dictates I do whatever is asked of me from my SAC, ASAC, or SSAs when the time comes."

"That's a great textbook answer, but not necessary. Special Agent Tulle is competent and well-suited to mentor you on this case."

"The case on the news?"

He nodded.

She swallowed hard and almost closed her mouth, but she couldn't. Not with her body in near revolt. "But... you know what happened to me in Grass Valley," she said in a voice that sounded small and pathetic even to her.

"That's why I wanted to talk to you, Special Agent Gray. You'll see and experience things in this job that will rattle you, test your faith in life and moral decency, and likely stain the very fabric of your mind."

"I understand, Sir," she said as a warm flush returned to her neck. "We don't sell Girl Scout cookies or run swim classes for the elderly. We're the Federal Bureau of Investigation, and we assist law enforcement in hunting down the worst of the worst."

"You were second in your class at Quantico," he said.

"Second place is the first loser, Sir. That said, the minute I'm in the field, I'll shed the first-case jitters and strive to be the best agent possible."

"Are you trying to convince me of your competence, Special Agent Gray, or are you trying to convince yourself? Because you sound like a wind-up toy right now, spitting out all the right answers."

"The latter, Sir," she said, embarrassed. "I'm sorry for my formal responses. I just never expected to return to... *that place* again."

"Surprise," he said with an animated expression that either calmed or infuriated her. Was Blackwood trying to soften the moment or put some proverbial hair on her chest? She would never know. But working around guys meant you couldn't and shouldn't complain, and the answer to most questions was "stop asking questions" or "toughen up."

She nodded at the muted television and said, "You know the kind of press this will get, right? It will be a zoo out there and will likely consume the entire city."

"Once it hit the wire, that was the guarantee."

She nodded. "You need a veteran agent to navigate a case of this magnitude."

"Don't tell me what I need or don't need when you've only been a Special Agent for a week, young lady. Besides, you'll be assisting local law enforcement. Brad is in line for the BAU, has trained with them in Quantico numerous times, and could provide a rudimentary profile for them, should they ask."

She fought the urge to lower her head in shame. "I'm sorry, Sir. I didn't mean to presume."

He waved off the comment with the flick of a wrist. "You're going to try to inch, crawl, or run your way out of this case, and it won't work, so you might as well dig in and embrace it. You have fears about going back to Grass Valley, I know. Sacramento wasn't your first choice of assignments—I know that, too. I know *exactly* what happened to you when you were fourteen, which is why I chose you for this case. You have a rare opportunity to walk back into Hell and face the fears that have come to define you, in some part, today. You can try to avoid this or get on that horse and ride."

"I see the opportunity, Sir," she said, the blood once again draining from her face. Had she not been so scared, she would have said he was right—because he was.

"I will warn you, if you wash out on your first case or torpedo it entirely, I'll hang every piece of bad press around your neck and use it to terminate your employment. The number one rule at the Bureau, albeit unspoken, is don't make the Bureau look bad. But if you screw that pooch, you will create an opportunity for me to demand budgetary increases to bolster better staffing. In other words, like you, I will make lemonade out of these lemons."

"Are you telling me you think I'll fail?" Sadie asked.

Blackwood narrowed his cold, gray eyes and leaned forward, startling her but also prompting her to pull back. "This is the real world, Special Agent Gray. I don't care about your feelings; try-hards have no place in this office or the Bureau, and we don't cry about *anything*, no matter how difficult or unfair it might be. I expect results from you, plain and simple. Now, wipe that sullen look off your face, straighten your back, and act like the agent you intend to be here."

She drew a deep, stabilizing breath and did as he said.

He relaxed his eyes, reclined in his chair once more, and smiled as if the "come to Jesus" part of the meeting had adjourned. "I fought for you to be here because you've already made a name for yourself in Quantico, and I want you to make a bigger name for yourself here in California. Now that I've hit you with the stick, let's give the carrot a shot. Brad tells me you want to go after serial killers. Is that right?"

"It is, Sir."

"Well, this is shaping up to be the mother of all serial killer cases. They're going to pull twenty or thirty bodies out of that cabin, and the public will demand answers to questions you haven't even thought to ask. They'll want the monster who did this stopped, caught, and made to pay for every crime."

"I understand the magnitude of it, Sir."

He rolled his eyes and said, "Drop the 'sir' stuff for now, Special Agent Gray." She nodded. "You can resume when we see each other next."

"Okay."

"Each body belongs to someone, and those 'someones' will want answers, justice, and closure. That's your job. Work with the locals to find the killer, catch them, and give the justice system every opportunity to convict. Do this right, and your name will be etched in history forever. Botch this, and it will also be etched in history—the kind you can read about from whatever fast-food restaurant you end up working at after I fire you for incompetence or worse, negligence."

"Moving speech, Sir," she said.

"Are you being smart with me, Special Agent Gray?"

Her eyes flashed, and she said, "No, not at all. It's what I needed to hear—that's what I should have said."

He relaxed and eyeballed her, unblinking in a show of dominance, as if looking through her eyes to better root around in her soul. Sadie held her ground with her chin up and steady eyes that refused to look away.

"Go meet with Brad; he'll spool you up," Blackwood said. "Grass Valley's police chief, Cormac Miller, asked for the weekend to get his arms around this, so I gave it to him. But first thing tomorrow morning, have your bags packed and be ready to go because you and Special Agent Tulle will leave for Grass Valley at seven. I want you two in the trenches with Miller and his teams at eight o'clock on the button."

"For how long?" she heard herself ask.

Blackwood shot her a look that wasn't kind. "Until you catch the son of a bitch who did this."

"I just got a dog," she said under her breath.

"Well, then give it back!"

She shot to her feet, looked him dead in the eyes, and said, "No worries, ASAC Blackwood, I'll get it handled."

"Pucker up, Special Agent Gray," he all but growled. "Whatever you think will happen in this case probably won't happen. It'll likely be a hundred times worse. But you can handle it. I know you can because you're Sadie Freaking Gray."

"Trial by fire, right?" she grinned.

He forced a smile and nodded dismissively. "That's the spirit." Before Sadie left his office, Blackwood looked at her and said, "Oh, and Special Agent Gray?"

"Yes?"

"Stop acting so... *new*."

seven
chief cormac miller

WITH EVERY BAGGED corpse rolled out on a gurney, the nightmare deepened. When in God's name was it going to stop? Miller had hoped that they'd hit the bottom of the body pyramid before having to dismantle parts of the cabin's structure, but the bodies kept coming long through the night. Finally, he went home for a midnight dinner and a few hours of shuteye but was only gone two hours when Detective Ruiz called.

"Yeah," Miller grumbled into the phone. He felt as if someone had hit every notch in his spine with a hammer. His wife turned toward him in bed, unaware he had come home.

"They're taking out more of the floor," Ruiz said.

Miller ran a hand down his face, pushed himself up in bed, and yawned so deeply that Ruiz asked if he was still there.

"Yeah, I'm here," Miller said.

"You want to meet me at the scene?"

"Sure, but I need to hit the head and get some coffee," Miller said. "Do you want me to pick some up for you?" Miller kicked the blankets down his legs, put his feet on the floor, and felt his wife's warm palm press into his back.

"They've got coffee on the scene," Ruiz said. "It's from Lumberjacks, and it's the good stuff."

"Which angel made that miracle happen?"

"A guy named Hudson Whitlock."

"And he is...?"

"Forensic Pathologist on loan from Sac County's Coroner's Office. He's here to assist Dr. West and her coroner's unit."

"Level One or Two?" Miller asked.

"Level Two, but he brought a colleague who's a Level One."

Miller stood on surprisingly weary legs, shuffled to the bathroom, and waited to end the call before taking a leak. "Who's doing was that?"

"Dr. West, of course," Ruiz replied. "I spoke with her a few minutes ago, and she has calls to both El Dorado and Placer County asking for assistance. Placer promised a forensic anthropologist and El Dorado has two Level One Forensic Pathologists to assist her. They'll work with Whitlock and answer directly to Dr. West and her deputy coroner. She asked for assistance in whatever way possible and that all lines of communication between us are open."

Instead of waiting for the call to end, Miller lifted the lid and unleashed a hearty stream.

"You pissing, Chief?"

"Does it sound like it?" he asked. Rather than wait for an answer, he asked another question that required a response. "What did Dr. West promise?"

Detective Ruiz let out a low chuckle. "She's morbid, this one."

"Yeah?"

Miller flushed, washed his hands, and went for his uniform.

"She said this will be bigger than Gacy, and anyone who wants in on it will be part of a huge piece of history."

He stopped what he was doing. "Is it going to be bigger than Gacy?"

Detective Ruiz said, "Gacy had twenty-seven bodies buried at his house, although I think maybe they found two more. He threw five more into the river. Law enforcement found four."

"What are we at now?"

"Twenty-five."

"Sweet Jesus, we don't need this," Miller grumbled. "Let me get ready. We'll talk more when I arrive."

"Sounds good, Chief. I'll see you in a few."

"Thanks, Ruiz."

Miller drove his truck through the pitch-black night with the windows rolled down and his elbow hanging out the side. The chilly pre-dawn air filled his lungs enough to keep him awake but did nothing for his bad mood. Where the bitter cold would eventually fail to wake him entirely, the coffee would do so in return. Miller likened it to a relay race or wake-up protocol for the diehards.

Miller arrived at the scene and looked around; his jaw dropped. Waves of dread coursed through him. For a long moment, he stared at the ghastly scene. It was something out of a nightmare. Floodlights illuminated pathways from the house to the meat wagons and the cabin while darkness held the night. The amber glow in the windows was so creepy-looking that he wanted to go back home, but he couldn't. The public would crucify him.

A knock on his passenger-side window startled him. He turned and saw Ruiz motioning for him to unlock the door. Miller leaned over and pushed the door open when he saw his lead detective had both hands full.

"Thanks, Chief," Ruiz said. He handed Miller a hot coffee, climbed into the front seat, and closed the door. Neither said a thing. They merely sipped their hot coffee and took it all in.

"You remember Chief Davenport?" Miller finally asked.

"Of course."

"All those girls who were taken and killed, did you know their murderer made snuff films to sell on the dark web?"

"That was what, ten or twelve years back?" Ruiz asked. Miller nodded, which bothered Ruiz into a silent spell. But then he spoke. "I knew he had photos of the girls, but I didn't know about the snuff films."

Miller sat there quietly drinking his coffee, thinking life sure loved contrast. "Grass Valley itself is gorgeous but sees its fair share of crime."

"You were talking about Earl Gray, right?" Ruiz asked. Miller nodded. "Heard he's in NorCal State Prison with that nut job Atlas Hargrove and a bunch of other killers."

"Yeah."

"Think he'll make it?"

Miller shrugged and said, "I hope so. Earl is good people."

"He *was* good people."

Miller turned to him and said, "No, he *is* good people."

"What's your point, Chief?"

"When Sadie Gray and her younger sister Natalie were kidnapped, it was because Davenport didn't do enough to find the missing girls or the monster who took them. It took several murders, a lot of sidestepping, and Earl freaking Gray going 5150 to do what the department should have done years before that point. I know Davenport drank himself to death, and we shouldn't speak ill of the dead, but that man was lazy and inadequate. Furthermore, his department was, too."

"Present company excluded," Ruiz said.

"Naturally."

"What did you do, boss?"

Miller finished the bottom of his coffee, turned to Ruiz, and held his eye. "I called in the Feds."

Ruiz seemed to stop breathing altogether. He stared at Miller like he wanted to tear holes in his soul. Finally, when the detective composed himself, he said, "You see us marshaling our resources, don't you? Dr. West has her team, we have ours, and the sheriff is willing to lend whatever resources he can spare. His crime scene techs are still working!"

Miller wasn't having it. "It's too big, Ruiz."

"Bullshit."

"It's too big," he said again, his tone lower and more somber.

"You freaking quit before we got started."

"I didn't quit anything," Miller turned and barked. "I saw

what Davenport did to this town, how it eroded the community's trust, and how good people died because of his policies. This city doesn't need another stain like that."

Ruiz wasn't offended by his outburst. He said, "We can do this with our resources. We have three reserve officers and two active volunteers."

Miller interrupted him and said, "Do you think that will cut it? Five people? Because it won't, Ruiz. We'll show the city and its naysayers we're fully functional and can handle the worst predators. But we'll also show them we're smart enough to call for backup before the train comes off the tracks."

Ruiz looked like he wanted to press the issue but paused before speaking. He opened his mouth to make his point but closed it without a word, which Miller appreciated—his blood pressure was rising for another reason.

With bulging defiant eyes, Miller said, "We let this demon through our front door, and he dumped his bodies in our backyard by the dozen. There is no use acting in the defiance of our critics, not when we have other options. Because the way it looks now, we're a county that let its people die, and die they did—en masse, Ruiz. They died en masse."

"We can shape it another way."

"The media shapes the story; we solve the crimes," Miller said. "And the best we can do right now is bring in the Feds and combine our resources to reach a quick and thorough conclusion. The faster we can find this guy, this serial killer, the faster we can return to our daily lives. The longer this drags on, the more of these media vultures we'll get, which will exhaust and agitate us all. It won't take long before the public will call for our heads."

"Let them try doing a better job than us," Ruiz groused.

"You're still young," Miller said with a bite. "What do you know about politics?"

"Enough to be your lead detective."

"It's the right call," Miller said, getting out of the truck. Before closing his door, he looked across the seat at his detective, a man he greatly respected. "We can't afford another Davenport debacle, and you know it."

"I do."

"Are you proud of your work?"

"Of course," Ruiz said, getting out of the truck.

"Then don't let what happens here spiral out of control. That's what happens in cases like these: anger, fatigue, desperation—all these emotions eventually take hold. And when they do, our chances of missing something or making the wrong assumption will skyrocket."

"That won't happen, boss."

The two of them watched the crime scene techs roll another body from the cabin on another metal-framed gurney. When they met, Miller asked, "What's the count now?"

"Twenty-nine, sir," the lead tech said.

"Condition?" Ruiz asked.

"Nearly had to suck this one up with a wet vac," the tech said.

Miller shook his head, wondering whose feathers he ruffled to have this crap show up in his backyard. His eyes cleared, and he stared at the tech. The man was exaggerating about the wet vac, but was it that bad? "What does Dr. West say?"

Both techs had stopped for the chief despite working for the county coroner under the sheriff's office. The lead tech, a man everyone called Dirty Boy, said, "Dr. West is calling a Forensic Odontologist she knows in the Bay Area."

"The teeth are intact?" Miller asked. "The ones you're taking now?"

"Some, yeah," the secondary tech said, a man everyone called "Hulk" despite his average size and stature. Rumor had it he could tear apart a dead body limb for limb, bone for bone, with his bare hands. That said, he had a kind face. Hulk continued. "But some of the others... their faces are like meatloaf, man—their skulls obliterated by blunt force trauma."

"Same object?" Miller asked. "Like a hammer or something?"

"No, different," Ruiz said.

The foul stench of the body, the crime scene techs, and even the early-morning air smelled like the inside of a corpse. Miller needed to know everything, but, at that point, he didn't want to know one more thing—*not one*.

"How many more down there?" Ruiz asked.

Hulk said, "Half a dozen more at best. We took out the floors to get better access. I have to warn you, though, it's an open pit in there, and it looks like the entrance to Hell."

Miller hated what was happening, what it would come to represent, and how one stupid-ass hunting cabin would destroy everything he did to restore some faith in the Grass Valley PD after Police Chief Davenport, the murdered girls, and Earl Gray's violent rampage.

A car pulled up on the road, and a woman got out. She stood in the darkness, a lone figure, looking like she could be lost. From what Miller could see, a second woman got out; she was younger and thinner-looking. Both stood at the edge of the light, mere silhouettes against yellow crime scene tape and the backdrop of a black abyss.

"What's up with those two?" Miller asked.

Ruiz shrugged. "You want me to check 'em out?"

"No, I'll go. Check-in with Eliana for me, okay? We need IDs on the vics as quickly as possible."

"You can just call her Dr. West," Ruiz said. "Everyone else does."

"First, don't tell me what to do. Second, Eliana rolls off the tongue just right. I had a thing for Mae West as a kid—although you're not old enough to know of her."

"I know of her, but Dr. West looks nothing like Mae West. She's so much prettier."

"I'm too tired for this, Ruiz."

Miller walked down the rocky dirt driveway to a stretch of asphalt road where two women stood, waiting for him or someone like him.

"Can I help you two?" he asked.

"You the sheriff?" the older, uglier one asked. Something was wrong with her face.

"I'm the police chief with Grass Valley P.D."

She shoved out a hand and said, "Riley Sharpe with Sharpe True Crime Podcast."

Miller looked at her hand but didn't shake it. The only thing worse than the media was self-proclaimed independent journalists who wanted the fame, didn't make the cut, and ended up there, in the middle of the night, talking about a podcast no one had even heard of before.

"What's your viewership, Ms. Sharpe?" Miller asked, glancing at the other woman, who stood in the shadow cast by the podcaster.

Her eyes bore a lazy, tired look—like his before the chilly air and coffee. "Our viewership is substantial."

He chuckled and said, "Cute."

Sharpe shrugged and smiled, only half her mouth smiling with ease. He caught himself before overreacting. Truthfully, he wasn't remotely interested in her show.

"I see you're still hauling bodies out of there," she said.

"You using this for the show?"

"I don't need nuthin' from you, Chief," Riley said with a subtle edge to her voice. "I just want to see with my own eyes if this is all worth the hype."

"It isn't," Miller said, deadpan.

"Bullcrap, it ain't," the blonde girl in the shadows said.

Her tone stopped Miller cold. "Maybe you could enlighten me, Ms....?"

The mysterious woman didn't move into what little light the scene could provide. Instead, she said, "You've been hauling bodies for three days. You gotta be shoveling 'em outta the ground by now, right?"

"This is my research assistant," Riley said. "Forgive her passion—she's the one who finds and vets my stories, which means she's the reason we're here."

Miller stared at the two for a long time before deciding. "Come back with the rest of the media at eight o'clock. There will be a press conference."

"Why not speak now?" the girl asked. "You got a final body count? Or maybe knowledge of the killer?"

Miller stepped forward to get a better look at her; he saw only untamed hair and intense eyes. She looked like she should be a local, one of those backwoods types.

"Where are you ladies from?"

"I have my studio in Colfax," Riley said. "Coupl'a addresses over from the Colfax Market. You know where The Wrecking Crew Bakery and Café is, right? Next to Pastime Club on North Main Street?"

Miller nodded.

Riley Sharpe pulled a card from her pocket and handed it to him. "We've been renting there for a few years. This'll be the twenty-fifth show, which could be something special."

When he looked down at her card, Miller pressed his lips together and shook his head. He already had too many business cards, so he refused hers. "There's nothing special about something like this."

"To the right person there is," she said, sliding the rejected card back into her pocket. "Plus, if we do this show right, we could be out of that dump we're in now and living the high life in Auburn."

"Wouldn't that be amazing," he said with gobs of sarcasm.

"Could you perhaps spread the word about us at the press conference?" Riley asked, ignoring Miller's cutting remarks. "We'll be moving quickly and releasing multi-part shows. People like high production value in their movies, but something like this?" She smiled like a Cheshire cat. "Crime scenes with a lower production value remind people of the dark days before forensics, laptop cops, and podcasters like me."

"Forgive my forthright nature at this hour, ladies, but I don't give a rat's ass about your show. I just want to process this scene and ID these bodies so we can notify the families and try to solve this case."

"How long do you think you'll be at it?" Riley asked.

"I could ask you the same question."

The nameless blonde in the shadows smiled, hinting at an awkward row of teeth. "We'll be at it until you catch the person responsible for this. So, start doing your job, and let us handle our job, which is to entertain and inform the public."

Miller withdrew his flashlight and hit the blonde in the face with the near-blinding beam, startled to find a young woman with a bit too much wear and tear for her apparent years. She blocked the light with her hand.

"The fuck's wrong with you?" Riley hissed, shoving Miller's flashlight aside.

"Touch me or my tools again, and I'll haul you in for assault," Miller snapped. He raised his light again, aiming the beam at the blonde, whose hand now became a middle finger. He looked at the two of them for a long time, then clicked off the light. "Do whatever you want as long as you don't step foot on my crime scene. That means you're welcome to report it however you see fit because this is still a free country."

"Can we expect your cooperation if we need clarification on a few things?" Riley asked.

"If you can talk to me and I can hear you, I'll give you what I can, but you won't be able to talk to me, and I won't be able to hear you." With that, he turned and tromped back up the driveway, thinking serial killings draw out all the crazies.

When he met Ruiz at the cabin's front door—which someone had removed earlier—he saw his lead detective standing just inside the house. The man was staring into the ground. Miller took a step in, which was as far as he could go without falling to his death.

Before him, a monstrous hole was dug meticulously into the ground, one at least twenty feet in diameter and maybe that or more to the bottom. Several extension ladders lined the sides of the pits, and men and women wearing gloves, booties, and respiratory masks were at work below, nearing the end of the arduous process of separating the smashed stacks of bodies.

"It's like taking apart old pancakes," Ruiz said. Miller's face reflected his distaste for the comment, but Ruiz was fixated on the scene below, almost mesmerized. "Dirty Boy said it looked like the entrance to Hell. What do *you* think?"

Ruiz turned and stared at Miller.

Large stones, bricks of every color, and quarried pavers reinforced the walls—all held in place by layers of chicken wire, which was pulled tight and stapled to four-by-four support beams. Roots had pushed through in areas, and the layers of sediment were transparent; below, smaller rocks and dirt cave-ins gave the dirt floor a scary, storied look. Whoever dug this hole likely did so before they built the cabin. That or they replicated the old cabin with a new build over a freshly dug hole. Of course, to do that, they would have had to remove the structure, its footings, and all former traces of it. It would have to have been a long time ago, judging by the apparent condition of the first victims.

A slick-looking layer of moisture added a glossy sheen to the damp walls and old bedrock layers, something Miller found disgusting. Was that moisture from the soil? Or were those the evaporated juices of the dead clinging to the earthy walls?

"When Dirty Boy called this the entrance to Hell, he was generous," Miller finally said in response to Detective Ruiz's question.

With that statement, as if Dirty Boy himself had heard Miller's exact words, the crime scene tech looked up from below, saw them, and gave them the thumbs up.

"Something's wrong with these guys' heads if they like doing this crap," Miller grumbled.

"Everyone has a hobby and a job," Ruiz said.

"Jeffrey Dahmer liked to mutilate his victims and eat their brains for dinner, Ruiz. Not every hobby is a good hobby."

"At least you're used to the smell by now," Ruiz said.

"I'm not," he admitted. "I just have a strong stomach, which I fortified with hostility for whoever did this. What I can't stomach is sitting on our thumbs waiting on forensics or the Feds, who are coming this morning."

"Are you handing them the case, then?"

"I'm not handing over anything. I'm merely requesting assistance because we may need their databases and forensics lab. That said, play nice and do your best to impress them because we don't want them telling their SAC we're a bunch of incompetent rednecks who can't find our asses with both hands."

"That goes without saying, Sir."

"Does it, though?"

"Of course."

eight
sadie gray

THE WEIGHT of the day hit Sadie with speed and force: her dressing-down by ASAC Blackwood, the scope of the case in Grass Valley, and a quick briefing of the murders by Brad—a man she did not like who was now her partner. There was also the dog, which she bought impulsively. What a dumb thing to do! What would she do with Droolius Caesar now? Give him back? Hire a dog sitter and pay them with money she didn't have?

Caesar hopped out of his bed the second she got home and ran straight to her. She kneeled and love-bombed the little fella, knowing she should not have adopted him. Leaving him alone so much wouldn't be fair to him in the long run.

"I'm afraid I already suck as a doggy mom," she said, scratching him behind the ears. He turned his head into her affection, then rolled over and exposed his belly for a proper scratching.

Sadie felt terrible thinking about offloading the pup, but someone had to take care of him now that she was leaving town for her first case. She could try her neighbor, then the superintendent; if neither option worked, she needed to return the dog to the breeder.

God, what a failure...

Sadie drew a weak, defeated breath, shook her head at her bad decisions, and realized that if she was going to be a proficient agent, she couldn't live such a carefree life.

She looked down at Caesar. "Well, wish me luck."

The pup stared at her as she stood, then he stood with her, taking a few tentative steps toward her before stopping. Her heart was already aching. When Caesar saw her leaving again, he began to whine low in the back of his throat, the noise growing louder by the second. She wanted to cry. *What have I done?*

"I'll be right back," she promised.

She walked next door, steadied herself, and knocked on her neighbor's door. He pulled it open a moment later and smiled as he quickly gave her the once-over.

"Yo," she said with a sly smile.

"Hey, Lady," he grinned.

She was dressed in a fitted yet flexible business suit, with her hair pulled back and her makeup done sparingly but on point. She looked good but felt great.

"You're walking your eyes up and down me like a perv at a frat party," she teased. "I almost don't like it."

"Guilty as charged," he laughed.

"Sad to see me?"

"Yeah, broken-hearted," he replied, a natural flirt. "I wasn't sure what you did for a living, but I didn't expect you to look like this."

"Like what?" she asked with a soft head tilt.

He held her eyes like a playboy and couldn't stop the smile on his face, meaning she had him right where she wanted him.

"All I'm saying is I'm not hating how you look right now," he replied.

"Truthfully, I'm not hating it either," she said, glancing down at her suit and shoes. "I had to sell a kidney to buy this suit, though."

"Do you need another?" he asked.

"Kidney or suit?"

"Kidney."

"Why?" she asked with a sly smile. "Are you offering?"

He shrugged, playing coy.

She kind of liked the game and was good at it. "Who said it was *my* kidney I sold?"

He seemed to appreciate their interaction, but then a realization dawned on him, draining some of his playful energy. "Let me guess: You're going out of town on a fancy business trip and need me for my dog-sitting expertise?"

"You heard him barking while I was gone?"

He smiled as if it were a sad truth. And, just like that, all the fun, flirty, sexy vibing between them melted like a pat of butter on a hot summer sidewalk.

"Are my intentions so obvious?" she asked.

He nodded. "When you return, I want to share a meal with you, one you cook for us at your place."

"Why do men always want a home-cooked meal?" she asked. "It used to be sex or a date, or… something else—a night on the town, maybe a Broadway play. But now, it's just… cook me some dinner."

"I want to see how well you cook," he said.

"Why?"

"I'm trying to decide if I want us to be friends or a one-night stand."

"Friends," she said.

"Then you'd better be a good cook."

"So, that's the deal, then?"

He nodded, some energy returning.

"I could be gone a few days, maybe a week," she warned.

"That's fine," he replied. "Old dogs love young dogs. I have a thousand things I want to teach him about life. But, if you're gone longer than a week, make it two meals."

"What's your real name?" she finally asked.

"One thing at a time," he replied, still so mysterious. "When do you want me to pick him up?"

"Tomorrow at seven a.m. would be perfect."

nine
sadie gray

SADIE WAS ready to go when the knock at the loft door sent Droolius into a barking fit. "Protector engaged," she said as she walked to the door.

She rolled the door open to her neighbor's lovely face.

"Yo."

"Hey, lady."

"You're a seven-a.m. dream," she said, looking him over.

He did a mock curtsy for her, which she found hilarious. Then he glanced past her, where Droolius Caesar was poised to either attack or empty his bladder on the floor. She prayed for something in between, preferably something she didn't have to clean up.

She turned and called his name, giving him a firm hand clap. He didn't come at first, but when she clapped again, the dog trotted over. To his credit, and maybe this was because her neighbor was harmless-looking and attractive, Caesar went right to him with his tail wagging a bazillion miles per hour. The two were fast friends.

Yo looked up and smiled, giving her the kind of smile you'd give when you want her to know you're capable and have everything under control. "Is that really his name?" he asked with a grin.

"Of course, it is. It's fitting, too."

He snorted out a laugh and scratched the pup's ears. "What did you get me into here?"

"You own a mop, right?" she asked.

"Yeah."

"Keep it handy."

Sadie had his food, bowls, chew toy, pee pads, and fluffy bed available. The three went to his place next door, and Yo invited her inside. The space reminded her of a beautiful art studio, but with a bed and nice furniture. What captured her attention most were the large paintings hanging on the brick walls. Not only were they gorgeous, but his artwork elicited an unexpected surge of emotions for which she was unprepared.

Breathlessly, she said, "Wow, you are talented."

"I can't wait to be dead and sell them for millions," he replied with a wink.

She glimpsed a separate side of the loft, one with a large desk and multiple monitors—one that appeared to be tracking the stock market and two more displaying what looked like corporate earnings reports and maybe a start-up prospectus.

"Not just a painter," she said.

"And you're not a broke kickboxer."

She rubbed her hands together and smirked. "Ah, the mystery thickens."

"So it would seem," he grinned.

She checked the time and thanked him, then left a hundred dollars in twenties for food and other incidentals and a number to call in an emergency. As an afterthought, should she die on the case or worse, Sadie also left him the breeder's number. She was saying goodbye when Special Agent Brad Tulle strolled into the building, entering through the front door behind one of the residents.

"All set?" he asked when he saw her, Aviator sunglasses still on. She hated to admit it, but the man could wear a suit and tie, and he was pretty freaking hot.

If only he weren't such a douchebag...

Yo stuck his head into the hallway, saw Brad, and gave him the chin-lift nod of acknowledgment.

"Oh, do you two need a moment?" Brad asked.

"No," Sadie said.

Yo chuckled to himself.

The pup popped his head out, too, and Brad said, "Oh, this is the little showstopper. Look at you, bud. Pretty fly for a furry guy."

"So stupid," Sadie muttered.

Brad stuck his hand out; Yo took it and said, "And you are?"

"Brad Tulle," he replied. "She and I work together."

Special Agent Tulle turned to Sadie with a pointed look, saying he didn't care to know anything about Yo, like his name or anything else, which would have been polite. "Sorry to rush you, but if we don't leave, we're going to be sucking fumes in rush hour traffic, which won't bode well with people we're trying not to upset."

"I know the drill," she said. She looked at Yo, smiled generously, and said, "You're a lifesaver, I swear."

"See you when you get back," Yo replied. Instead of saying goodbye to Brad, he nodded sparsely. Brad returned the gesture.

The two went to her loft, where Sadie grabbed two pieces of luggage she had purchased at a second-hand store yesterday afternoon. Then she followed Brad to his bu-car, which happened to be a black Chevy Impala.

He looked back at her luggage, did a double take, and then said, "That's the saddest overnight bag I've ever seen, but at least no one will accuse us of being pampered."

"Or polite," she mumbled.

"Oh, I can be polite. Was that your boyfriend back there?"

"Neighbor."

"Prospective boyfriend?"

"Neighbor," she reiterated. "I don't even know his name."

"What do you call him?"

"Yo."

"Does he know you?" he pressed.

She shook her head.

"What does he call you, then?"

"Hey, Lady."

He chuckled. "Yeah, you're creating a boy toy."

She loaded her bags into the Impala's trunk, climbed into the front passenger seat, and said, "Mind your own business, *Brad*."

Impervious, he started the car and said, "Do you know how easy it is to get under your skin, Agent Gray? For the love of God, you'd better thicken that hide and quickly."

She hit him with a sideways glance, warm eyes becoming hot. He ignored her as he pulled into traffic, heading for the freeway.

"Let's try this again, but with thicker skin this time," Brad said a few minutes later. "Was that your boyfriend?"

"One of many."

"You sound like a slut."

Jerk.

"I am," she said.

"How many diseases are you carrying around?"

Okay... I can play this game.

"All the STDs and you, you jackass. How often do you jerk off to your perfectly mediocre face?"

He barked out a laugh and said, "Every time I can." When traffic opened up, he turned to her, smug and grinning. "See, that wasn't so hard."

She leaned back in her seat and said, "I guess not."

He signaled and moved into the fast lane, accelerating to eighty-five miles per hour. Despite going twenty miles per hour over the speed limit, they kept up with the flow of traffic.

"Why is it so important for you to toughen me up right now?" Sadie asked.

Brad seemed to really think about the question. Then, after some contemplation, he cleared his throat and said, "Human nature used to be predictable, but I think society has changed us."

"How so?"

"With all the division out there, people are more triggered than ever, and they're going from zero to psychopath in a few seconds flat. They play the victim game, get their feelings hurt over nothing, and act like the rules should change to suit their weaknesses."

"This is painfully true," she conceded.

"Sorry for being so harsh, but that's a game losers play. Not us. We're the FBI. What we do and see, we have to deaden those parts of us—the outrage, the sensitivity, the need to cry over our woes so people will come to our rescue, all to feel important in our small and largely insignificant lives."

"Yeah, that's harsh, but I've been guilty of those things."

"Me, too," he admitted.

"So...?"

"When you're carrying your credentials and your weapon, you don't get the luxury of having feelings—even with me or how I act. We operate not on emotion but on instinct derived from training and hard-earned wisdom, which you'll hopefully begin to develop on this case and the many others to come."

She sat back and smiled, understanding what he was trying to do. "Life lessons by Brad Tulle," she teased. "Can I call you Daddy?"

His face lit with amusement, but he refused to comment, which let her know he had thicker skin than she had.

"Some guys in positions of power get off on teaching cute, young girls, new things," she said, continuing to poke at him.

He glanced at her sideways. "I'm one of them." Then he made a screwy face, which caught her off guard. She snorted a laugh and started to understand. He said, "You see now?"

"Yeah," she said, humbled. "Message received."

"I'm not even attracted to you, for the record," he said flippantly, as if it were nothing. "I just wanted to give you a tiny nudge to see where you're at."

"Now you know," she said.

"Yeah, you're a fast learner, but that pride will get the better of you," he warned. "Why did Blackwood choose you for this case? There were five guys on their freaking knees begging to partner with me."

"How should I know?" she asked, wondering if Blackwood lied to her about being unable to spare others because of their active caseloads.

"Were you asleep when he spoke to you?" he asked.

"Yeah, I was asleep," she said sarcastically.

"This is the mother of all cases, Agent Gray. Thirty-four dead as of today. All found in a cabin in the woods, in a massive pit dug under the floor."

The number shocked her, but she tried not to show it. "Maybe SAC Graham told Blackwood to put me on this," she suggested.

Special Agent in Charge Terrance Graham had personally called her to let her know about her assignment at the Sacramento Field Office, but she had yet to meet him in person. He had left a nice message, though, so she was anxious to one day make his acquaintance.

Brad shrugged and said, "Maybe."

"Why does it matter?"

He looked at her as if she had asked a stupid question. "Partner assignments and cases matter, Sadie."

"Okay," she said.

The two lapsed into silence.

Around Auburn, Brad said, "Some podcaster—Riley Sharpe True Crime, I think it's called—coined this dumpsite, 'The 34 in the Floor.' The media outlets grabbed the name and, mark my words, by noon this story will be all the nation is talking about."

"Okay..."

He did a double take like he couldn't believe her lack of excitement. But it wasn't that. She was heading right into a nightmare that stemmed from her past; her psychosis was flaring, and all she could do was try not to throw up or jump out of the car and walk home.

"Why did he choose you?" he asked again.

"I don't know," she replied.

"Bullshit."

"It's not," she snapped, her voice climbing a notch. She knew, though.

"If we're going to be partners on this and other cases, you can't act like a crappy wife, keeping things from me and saying things like, 'It's fine,' and 'I don't know.' You *do* know, it's *not* fine, and I know that Blackwood read you the riot act when he kicked us out of his office yesterday."

"So?" she asked, refusing to meet his eyes.

"You were sweating bullets in the ASAC's office before he gave us the boot. I know who you were in Quantico and what you achieved there, but the legend of Sadie Gray doesn't square with this version of you. You look like a scared kid in grown-up clothes pretending not to be shaking in your boots. But you are."

She pursed her lips and breathed an irritated sigh.

"You're not fit for this," Brad finally said.

"I'm fine."

"There it is!" he snapped.

She held her tongue and shook her head. Was she the stupid one here? "Why the trial-by-fire crap, huh? Maybe you can tell me that."

"Just spit it out, Agent Gray."

She finally said, "When I was fourteen, my little sister and I were kidnapped and almost killed in Grass Valley. My dad... he... kind of... he used to be a soldier—behind enemy lines, off the reservation, wet work, those sorts of things. He was pretty much a mercenary for the US Government."

"Holy cow, that's you?" he said, surprised. "You're Earl Gray's kid?"

She turned and didn't say anything.

"I wondered what happened to you and the others after all that," Brad whispered, clearly aware of Grass Valley's dark history.

"My life collapsed, that's what happened," she said. "A few loudmouth assholes in Grass Valley turned the community on us. They said that me, my sister, and my alcoholic mother were a stark reminder of the evil that took hold of our city for years."

"All the kidnappings and killings before that, right?" Brad asked. She nodded. "Wow, Blackwood is a genius."

"Why do you say that?" she asked with a tone.

"I'm not new to this job, but this case could be tough, even for me. And that's without me babysitting you."

She whipped her head around and said, "Hey!"

"If you survive this without making a fool of yourself or having a meltdown, you'll have paid your first dues in the middle of a freaking nightmare, because that's what this is and will become. But if you crack or botch this case, Blackwood will blame you."

"Blackwood said as much," she sat back and admitted. "He said he'd hang this around my neck, cite it as one of the dangers of underfunding, and use it to raise awareness of the perils of decreasing federal funding for agencies like ours."

Brad laughed low and to himself, shaking his head. He said, "He must respect you to tell you that."

"He doesn't even know me, Brad. Not any more than you or the others, anyway."

"He respects that you were second in your class in Quantico."

"If that's true," Sadie said, "he sure has a funny way of showing it."

"Guys bust each other's balls all the time; it's how we amp ourselves up for tough cases, Sadie. We talk smack, bet on the agents failing, and tell each other they suck if they can't close out the case with a win. If you want a nice, polite, politically correct job for young women without experience in actual law enforcement, this isn't it. We're not some little coffee group where we talk about butterflies and baking cakes or fluffy shiny shit like that."

"I know where I am and how women fit in here," Sadie said. "I'm not the kind of girl who takes my hurt feelings to HR if that's what you're worried about."

Brad refused to comment, and so they quietly headed through the city of Auburn on Highway 49 toward Grass Valley.

"Make no mistake," Brad finally said, breaking the silence, "what we're headed into will be nothing short of the ninth circle of Hell."

"If you're trying to scare me," she said, "you're wasting your breath."

"I'm not trying to scare you, Special Agent Gray. I'm trying to prepare you for what's coming. It'll likely shock me, and I've seen some *things*. You're the FNG, and you're a girl. Not even thirty. What we're about to see will wreck your brain several times over."

She turned and said, "Shut up, Brad. *Seriously.*"

He raised his hands in surrender but didn't say another word, not until they reached the crime scene. That was when the craziness began.

"Oh, damn," she heard herself say.

"Yeah."

ten
sadie gray

THEY ARRIVED at a media circus set up in front of a crime scene—a looming cabin in the woods with a dark vibe that screamed "redneck nightmare." Cameras and cameramen were positioned on the side of the road facing a makeshift podium that was, at that point, unmanned.

Sadie noted a dozen blue and light-brown uniforms from police and sheriff departments, a few plain-clothes detectives, and a man who might be the police chief. She and Brad would have to thread their way through a gaggle of concerned citizens and media personalities to get to their people. She took a deep breath, fighting her nerves.

First on her mind when she glanced at the onlookers was whether or not GVPD or the sheriff's office photographed the looky-loos. If they had, would they already have identifications, addresses, and lists of priors? While that was a job for law enforcement and not necessarily part of her job description, she knew Brad had some training in profiling—not the BAU level, but training from the same facility. Could that help? Brad didn't say if they were there to create a profile or not, but with such a diverse crowd of spectators gathered so far into the backwoods of this small mountain city, a few of these folks surely had priors.

The man she thought might be the police chief saw them, broke away from the men he spoke with, and headed their way.

"Special Agent Tulle?" he asked, approaching Brad's rolled-down window.

Brad extended his hand and said, "You must be Chief Miller." They shook hands. "Pleased to meet you. What's going on?"

Miller bent and looked at Sadie, who did not smile or remove her sunglasses, then back to Brad. "First real press conference," he said, kneeling to see them both. "I was hoping you might say a quick word, maybe reassure these folks that the full measure of federal resources is at work, and that we'll catch this guy."

"That's no problem," Brad said.

Looks like we've got a camera whore, Sadie thought, her pessimism in full swing. Was that a bad thing, though? She considered it further. Brad was a good-looking agent with a face the FBI would want to put front and center.

"This is Special Agent Gray," Brad said, interrupting her thoughts.

Miller narrowed his eyes and extended a hand. She took it, gave it a polite squeeze, and then let go.

"Cormac Miller, GV Police Chief," he said. "Pleased to meet you, Special Agent Gray."

She nodded, and Miller looked back at Brad.

Miller then looked at Brad with concern in his eyes and said, "Are you sure you want to bring a young woman to this kind of a scene?"

Sadie was about to tell this guy to shove it when Brad coolly replied, "We grew up in a world where women were delicate flowers with manners, proper etiquette, and the need for special treatment. While parts of the world remain locked in that archaic dogma, the FBI believes our women are tougher than most because we train them that way. Special Agent Gray is just as competent, smart, and ambitious as us men, maybe even more so."

"I didn't mean it like that," Miller said, backpedaling. His eyes were bloodshot, the bags underneath them packed for vacation. "All I'm saying is that it's a kindness to her by not having her here."

"Stop busting my balls, Chief," Sadie said from her seat. "I've seen this and worse, so just let us know where you'll brief us after the circus wraps."

Brad drew a deep breath, pulled his lips in to keep from laughing, and looked away. Miller, however, stared at her like she just crapped in his coffee and told him to start drinking.

"Straight to the point with this one, I see," Miller said, looking up at Brad as if he were a life raft. But was he?

"Well?" Sadie pressed.

"As I was saying," Brad replied.

"I'm going to start the press conference in a moment," Miller finally said. "If you'll say a few words, that would be great. After that, we'll field questions from the media—half a dozen at most, but no more. Detective Ruiz will then walk you up the driveway to the scene, which is... not pretty. Ruiz's partner, Detective Peters, is around here somewhere, so you'll meet him, too. After that, we'll figure out how you can assist us."

"We'll all be assisting each other," Sadie clarified.

Miller stared at her for a long moment, then blinked hard, and said, "You're like a morning hard-on, young lady. Anyone ever tell you that?"

"Just the creative types, Chief. And it's Special Agent Gray, not 'young lady.'"

"Of course," Miller said. Then, with a sheepish look, he glanced between Sadie and Brad and said, "I appreciate you joining forces with us and the sheriff's department. If you'll follow me..."

Brad nodded and exited the car. Sadie took his cue, and the three made their way to the podium. Miller walked with his head down at first but lifted it a moment later. The man's physiology changed on a dime, going from someone put in his place by a woman to the police chief—ready to brief the city, state, and nation on one of the most horrific crimes of the past forty years.

"Thank y'all for coming here this morning," he announced from the podium. "I'm Chief Cormac Miller of the Grass Valley Police Department, and I am overseeing this investigation. I will lay out the facts as best as possible, and then I'll introduce the other agencies involved in the investigation. After that, we'll take a few questions before returning to the trenches.

"Several days ago, we received a disturbing call from a concerned citizen. Officers arrived on the scene right away and, after an initial observation, determined there were deceased individuals inside the home. GVPD Detectives, along with myself, the coroner, and crime scene technicians from GVPD and Nevada County Sheriff's Office were brought in. What we found over the last few days was nothing this small, otherwise peaceful community has ever seen before."

Miller took a deep breath, looked around, and saw the sheriff heading his way. Sadie watched him visibly relax: all three agencies were now present.

Emboldened, he continued. "Our crime scene has been dubbed 'The 34 in the Floor' by some of the more inventive 'true crime' types out there, and though that is technically accurate, none of us here want to minimize the individual value of any of those thirty-four lives, each of which now falls to us to provide answers for.

"We are a small city of around fourteen thousand souls, and this is a monumental dumpsite. Rather than lean on pride, work ethic, and sheer tenacity to solve these murders ourselves, we immediately contacted other agencies to help us get answers quickly, find who did this, and prosecute them to the fullest extent of the law. Our immediate goal is to safeguard our community and our nation from this... *evil*. That said, the Nevada County Sheriff's Office and the FBI are the other agencies cooperating in this investigation. Placer County, El Dorado County, and Sacramento County also stand ready to assist us should we need additional resources. With the help of our expanded task force, the full resources of these agencies, and the hard-working personnel in this community we love, we will hunt this monster down, arrest him, and make him pay for his crimes."

Miller should have turned the podium over to the sheriff or Special Agent Tulle. Instead, he said, "I'd like to introduce you to Special Agent Gray with the FBI. She'd like to say a few words on the bureau's behalf."

Sadie's stomach dropped, and she almost smiled at her distaste for Miller. He hadn't just taken her jabs on the chin because she was a fed and he was police; he intended to get in a jab of his own. And, boy, did he ever.

Roll with it...

Sadie stepped to the podium, thought she might vomit, then told herself not to smile because she wasn't giving a speech. And... *time is ticking... everyone's staring... SPEAK!*

She cleared her throat and said, "Forgive me for my prolonged silence. I was taking a moment to look at all the faces here—not those of the media, but of the concerned citizens. I can't imagine the horror you must feel having someone leave this kind of a stain on your community. The disruption from an emotional standpoint has to be enormous. I say that not to appease you but to assure you that with this measure of concern for your homes, families, and the larger population, the FBI has devoted all our available resources to solving these crimes."

A hand shot up from one of the citizens, and though she thought about telling him to save his questions for the end, how would it look to put him off when she just said how important they were to the FBI?

"Yes?" she asked.

"You're not Sadie Gray, are you?" the man asked.

Oh, no.

She swallowed hard and said, "That's correct."

The man laughed like he couldn't believe it, drawing all eyes on him. "Didn't we run your ass outta town about ten years ago?"

A collective gasp silenced the crowd.

This miserable turd. Smiling away her agitation, Sadie calmly said, "A few of the lesser folks did, yes."

"Her daddy's a fuckin' killer," the man announced to the others, which couldn't have played well on live TV.

Sadie turned to Chief Miller, who was now looking at her with different eyes, and then Brad, who was fuming. In hindsight, she probably should have let Brad take the podium. It was too late now.

"I won't hold that against those of you who took that tack," Sadie said, trying to wrangle herself out of the situation. How she composed herself under this kind of pressure would dictate her ability to function as an agent in the days and weeks ahead.

"It wasn't no tack, Sadie," he said too loudly. "It was a 'repudiation.'" He said this, using air quotes for the word repudiation.

"Be that as it may," she said, "I am here not as a former resident of Grass Valley but as a representative with the Federal Bureau of Investigation. I assure you I bear this city no grudge because it is not about me, you, or anyone else alive. Our efforts are about the thirty-four people who lost their lives to a madman."

"You may not bear us a grudge, but a few of us bear one for you, Miss *eff-bee-eye.*"

The offhanded comment got a few laughs.

Sadie rolled her eyes, sighing at his comment, and said, "If you've finished making this about you, Sir..."

He shook his head in disgust and said, "Just thought the good, law-abiding people of this community ought to know what's slithering around here, calling itself... whatever."

"Perhaps you could take some time to figure out the proper use of metaphors," she said. "In the meantime, I'm going to turn the podium over to the sheriff."

She turned and nodded to the sheriff, who glared at her with disdain. Was she just ostracized? Did she end her career before it started? Her cheeks blazed as she stared into the cold, cruel gaze of a man who looked like he wanted to throw her out of the county.

He moved around her without a word, took the podium, and addressed the media and the crowd. "This is a monumental task, ladies and gentlemen. Identifying dozens of bodies in this state of decay will take every measure of our resources and a tremendous human effort. But we are up for the task, we are confident in our various agencies—including the FBI—and I have a message for the man or woman responsible for these bodies."

He paused, breathed, and glanced at the cameras for effect. At that moment, a breathless hush fell over the crowds, and everyone waited in bold anticipation for the sheriff's message. Like the crowds before her, Sadie found herself wanting the sheriff to say the words that would put everyone at ease.

The sheriff said, "To the human filth who did this: We are the best in our fields, we have significant resources, and now we have a savage desire to find you, rip you from your cowardly den, and break your freaking neck—metaphorically speaking, of course. You picked the wrong county to dump these bodies. As a result, there is no place you can hide, no distance you can run, and nothing that will save you from us. We're coming for you, and you will rue the day you touched one hair on these people's heads."

There was an almost stunned silence, and then the moron who called out Sadie erupted into a redneck hoot and holler while fast-clapping his hands. "Now *that's* why we elected this guy!"

The crowd broke into applause, and the sheriff stepped away from the podium, gesturing to the chief.

Chief Miller said, "I'll take a few questions now."

The reporters asked a dozen questions at once; Miller pointed to only one woman, a reporter from *The Union*.

She asked, "Do you have any suspects yet?"

Miller said, "In any other case, within a few days, we'd likely have someone in custody with all the evidence we need for the DA to prosecute them in a court of law. But with a body count of this magnitude, we must identify the victims, examine their lives, and search for motives, patterns, and past threats. Once we understand what we call the 'victimology' of each person, our detectives and FBI agents will help us chase down every lead, turn over every stone, and create a profile by which we will find this person."

"That sounds like it will take a while," one of the citizens said.

"We have three agencies with two more in the wings, including Sac County forensics and any other resources we need. It remains critical to have your trust, faith, and cooperation if we ask for it. I would also urge the media to be careful about speculating on aspects of the case without first having intimate knowledge of them. Please leave the heavy lifting to the professionals—we eat, sleep, and breathe cases like these, and we *will* find, arrest, and ultimately convict those responsible."

"Are any of the bodies our citizens?" someone asked.

"We don't know yet," Miller answered honestly.

"Have *any* identifications been made yet?" a reporter from the local Fox affiliate asked.

"Yes, three so far," Miller said. "We will contact the next of kin before releasing the names to the press. In such situations, we'll let the families decide how public they want to be. Losing a loved one impacts everyone differently, as you know. Some want their privacy while some are outspoken."

"What can you tell us about the motivation of the killings?" an NBC affiliate asked.

The chief swallowed, paused, and said, "This is the true nature of the horror that we in law enforcement deal with and have come to accept. And while the burden feels impossible to carry at times, it is a burden we signed up for but hoped never to carry."

Sadie didn't like how cryptic he sounded.

The NBC affiliate started to speak, but Miller cut her off. "I was going to allow six questions because I thought it would take that many to reach this question. Now that we're here, this will be my final statement today, and then our agencies will return to the tasks at hand. From what we can tell of the victims we've identified thus far, they appear to be families."

The collective gasp was something Sadie felt as much as she heard. *Families?*

"That's right," Miller said over the murmurs. "Whoever killed the thirty-four people we pulled from the cabin didn't just take lives; he took families off of this earth and will be held to account for that. That's all for now."

Miller turned and faced his teams despite the chorus of questions from the media and pool of citizens behind him.

"Sadie, perhaps you and Special Agent Tulle can walk the crime scene," Miller said. "Detectives Ruiz and Peters will brief you, and then we can reconvene at the station."

"It's Special Agent Gray, Chief Miller," Sadie said.

"The hell it is, young lady."

Miller turned and stormed off, leaving Sadie with the others. The sheriff hit her with a dead-eyed gaze, then turned and left her with Detective Ruiz and Brad, who looked at her with a similar gaze she could only describe as icy. She scoffed at the treatment.

Brad was the case agent and likely experienced at media relations, but Miller practically shoved her to the podium and forced her to speak. That wasn't her fault. But it happened. Making matters worse, Brad was gunning for a spot at the BAU, so holding the first press conference about the FBI's involvement in such a huge case could have helped him shine. Instead, she got up there and flubbed the whole thing.

If she wasn't so angry at Chief Miller for ambushing her or that prick in the crowd double ambushing her, she would have felt bad. But she didn't. Nope, she didn't feel bad at all. She went from logic to emotion and she was *furious*.

"Well," Detective Ruiz told her, "that went off like a fart in church. On the bright side, I know what your dad did when you were a kid, and I'm a big fan."

A bit of the steam left her eyes. "Yeah, well, you might be the only one."

"I assure you, I'm not," Ruiz chuckled, reassuringly touching her shoulder. "Follow me, and I'll tell you what we have so far, saving us time at the station."

"Roger that, Detective," Brad said in a chipper voice that sounded as fake as a three-dollar bill.

eleven
the driver

THE DRIVER LEFT the two idiots at that hovel they called a house, headed to the private coin-fed car wash, and hosed the blood and hair out of the truck bed. While some of it was the psychopath's hair—the moron's hair—there was plenty of evidence that belonged to the last family they killed. It wasn't a mercy killing, not for the parents. But for the girl, yes. She was an innocent, saved by the moron from a life of pain. While killing the children was necessary and humane in some cases, the moron was the only one willing to do *that* task. One day, he would be dead or gone, begging the question: would they have to stop? Or could they carry on?

The driver washed the Dodge pickup, returned the hose to its wall mount, then grabbed a container of bleach from the cab and poured it inside the beat-to-hell truck bed. The disinfectant was not great on the eyes or skin, so the driver didn't wait long before hosing everything down again, hitting it with fresh suds, and giving it a more-than-thorough rinse. The driver then fetched a stack of towels from the truck, dried the vehicle from bumper to bumper, and tossed the towels in the garbage. Now, the job was complete.

Serial killers found so many ways to get caught these days. It was the sloppy, stupid, and unavoidable mistakes they made when they chose the wrong target, the wrong location, and even the wrong dumpsite. And then they got caught. There was also the decision to work together rather than fly solo. No matter the details or the many choices along the way, every serial killer had a reason to exist, a motivation to kill, and a specific driving force.

I am the driver.

A thirty-minute trip down the hill into Rocklin took the driver to the gun shop where the family had purchased their only handgun—a .38 Special. They often dry-fired it in the house and at each other, but they never used it to kill someone. Not yet. The driver, however, was not there to buy ammo or another throwaway pistol. Instead, this was a special occasion that filled the driver with joy.

It had taken a while to save for the rifle—an LWRC International—but having the AR-15 was worth it. And it was beautiful. *My God,* the driver thought when the salesman brought the weapon out, *has there ever been a more beautiful rifle?* California's mandatory ten-day hold following the purchase of any firearm was up, and today was the big day.

When the salesman first inquired about the nature of such a purchase, the driver merely smiled and said, "Tactical home defense." Because everyone needs a fifteen-hundred-dollar AR-15 to protect their home from invaders, especially if those invaders are the police. In the case of this morning's press conference, they needed a defense against the sheriff's department, the police, and the Feds.

While the driver and the two idiots did not watch the actual news conference, they caught soundbites of it on the morning news cycles, especially the threat leveled at them by the sheriff, that sanctimonious prick. After the two clowns in the Camry discovered the dumpsite, the story had gone viral, as expected. Surprisingly, news of their kills terrified the public enough to make the driver smile. There was something about sowing the seeds of panic in an entire country that brought about a low-

swirling ecstasy. The last three days' worth of news and imagery set the world on fire with fear, gossip, and plenty of conjecture.

The talking heads made comparisons to serial murders in the past and speculated as to the killer's identity or motive, tossing their conspiracy theories around like a baseball. Grass Valley and nearby cities warned families, pleading for them to lock their doors and windows and call the local authorities if they saw anything suspicious.

Three days, thirty-four bodies, one cleaned-out dumpsite: *Is that suspicious enough for you?*

The driver opened the rifle's cardboard box, removed it, and turned it from side to side. The ten-round mag sat in the box all by itself. The driver looked up, pointed to the wall of ammo, and said, "I'll take a hundred rounds of the Federal Premium. Also, two extra mags, if you have them."

"Course, I do," the salesman smiled. He grabbed five twenty-round boxes of 5.56 ammo and headed onto the sales floor, where he pulled two extra mags off the rack. He returned with a smile, placing them next to the ammo boxes.

"I can't believe you pay a grand and a half for a rifle, and they give you one ten-round mag," the driver muttered.

"Yeah, most people make that gripe," the salesman agreed. "You smell good, by the way."

His face was closer than the driver wanted. "No shit, I smell good," the driver purred. "I'm going to work after this."

The salesman stopped, looked her over suspiciously, and cocked a brow.

"Oh, don't worry," she assured him. "I'll take the rifle home to lock it in the safe before work. Besides, I love my job—it's the best job ever."

"I wasn't implying anything."

The driver met the salesman at the register and paid the balance for the rifle in cash. Next, they rang up the magazines and ammo. Per California state law, the transactions were separate. The driver paid in cash and asked for receipts.

"Of course," the man said, catching her eyes. He printed both receipts and handed them to her.

The driver's fingers grazed the top of the salesman's fingertips. Instead of apologizing or acting like nothing happened, she curled her fingers just enough to graze the man's skin with the tips of her nails. He wasn't bad-looking, and it had been a while since she'd had sex with anyone she wasn't related to. Could she let him rail her?

Probably.

"What did you say you did for a living again?" the salesman asked.

She knew he was sweet on her—a lot of guys were. She had that look about her, the one that said it wouldn't take much to coax a blowjob out of her.

She smiled, tilted her head seductively, and, as sweet as candy, said, "None'a yer fuckin' business."

The salesman blushed and laughed to cover his embarrassment, but then he said, "It's just that, well, you've got a voice for radio."

"But not the face for TV?" she asked, standing tall, with her lower lip pushed out just enough to come across as pouty-cute.

Slowly, cautiously, he shook his head and said, "No, ma'am. Definitely not."

"And here I thought you liked me."

"Sorry for the confusion."

She grabbed her rifle, the bag of ammo, and the extra mags and walked out to the truck, thinking if she weren't so freaking sweet, she would track that man down and pump a few rounds into his skull to see if having shit for brains was a real thing.

"Nice rifle," one of the gun shop's employees said as he walked past her, presumably returning to the building.

"Thanks," she smiled.

One day, she and the idiots would make that fatal mistake—if they hadn't already—and the cops and Feds would come to their house and try to take them by force. If that day ever came, she had her new rifle and would be ready. Just then, her phone rang. She checked the caller ID and saw her brother was calling from work. She picked up.

"What?"

"Got another."

"Things are kinda hot right now."

"We have a life to save," he said, his tone sounding like a warning.

"I understand our commitment, but in case you forgot, the cops and Feds pulled up our bodies."

"I'm not blind or forgetful." Leaning into the phone and lowering his voice, he said, "The girl I found is getting raped, beaten, maybe even starved. The caseworker marked it for critical intervention."

She closed her eyes and sighed. "Where?"

"Sacramento."

"House or apartment?"

"It's a house in Rio Linda, a five-acre horse property."

"Neighbors?" she asked.

He breathed on the phone for a moment, getting himself wound up. Her brother hated being told no because he saw the inside of the situation. She managed it from the outside. And both managed their younger brother because he was the one with the broken brain.

In a voice eerily reminiscent of a game show host, her older, much larger brother said, "And in this corner, weighing in at eighty-two pounds soaking wet, we have the victimized youth with all her beat-up, battered holes—"

"Stop it," she said.

He didn't listen to her or respect her wishes. "She's a resident of Rio Linda, California, part rural and nice, part shithole and not so nice—a place where a rapist's wildest dreams can come true."

"I said stop it," she growled, this time with urgency.

He continued, "And in the opposite corner, weighing in at a heady two-hundred-and-five fat, hairy pounds, is the crusher of dreams. He's a part-time mason and a full-time pervert complete with a willingly blind wife, a pack of barking mutts to cover the sounds of screaming, and a donkey that's forty to fifty years old and ornery."

"You bastard," she hissed low. She thought of shooting her brother between the eyes with her new rifle just to make him stop talking.

"Soften your heart, little one," he whispered into the phone. "Be at peace with yourself, our past, the pain we endured over the years. We are the reckoning, the answer to a life of unrestrained cruelty."

Sitting in the truck, she pulled her blonde hair over her face as if hiding from the world and said, "Tell me about Momma. Say to me the things I said to you."

He met her request with silence for a while, but then he spoke, using his normal voice. "You watched her get hit with a hammer until her skull cracked open like an egg."

She felt a spark of energy take shape in her hideous, black heart.

"She never loved you because you were an ugly child, same as all of us. And when David was born, when that venomous mongrel passed through that disaster of a vagina, there was one too many unpleasant things in your momma's world."

"Daddy hated him, too."

"He loved and hated us all," her brother said.

"When you read about this new child, what did you see?" she asked, her eyes flooded with tears.

"I saw us in her, but worse. Before there were three of us, there were four created to take the old man's abuse. We could handle that; four made it manageable. But then Momma was gone, and Daddy and Teddy, too. We were down to three, all of us pulled apart and made to face new monsters *alone*."

"I was scared every day," she heard herself whisper.

"How many times were you raped?"

"Can't remember—lots."

"By Daddy?"

"Too many to count," she whispered.

"And your step-fathers? Not separately, but combined."

"I already told you half the time I went somewhere's else," she said with a sniffle. "I'm a walking cliché, Jake. The kind of girl they make backwoods horror stories about."

"We are a backwoods horror story, except we're making things right," he said with a soothing voice her mother sometimes used. "Unless you're gonna sit there crying like a big fat pussy. Because what—the cops are sniffing around? So what? You're better'n them, you know? *You know...*"

"Every serial killer runs the risk of getting caught because they don't know what they don't know."

"What don't you know?" he pressed.

The question and subsequent contemplation caused a fissure in her skull and a white-hot bolt of pain. She sat up fast, the drapes of her hair parting, the world again coming into full view. With wet and swelling eyes, she saw a man standing in front of the truck, staring at her.

"What're you lookin' at, Joe Bob?" she roared, slapping the steering wheel with her palm. "Get yer ass to steppin'!"

The man frowned, shook his head, and moved on without incident.

She finally said, "When Momma was hit with a hammer, and when we saw her eyes roll into her head and her body collapse like a Raggedy Ann doll, I felt that killin' thrill charge right through me. She was dead, Jake. Finally, the miserable wretch was dead, and I was as happy for her as if it was me—as if *I* was the one who got to be dead."

"I remember," he whispered. "And do you remember what you said as she lay there with her brains peeking out of her head, seeing the world for the first time?"

"I told Daddy I wanted to be next," she said.

"But then he was dead."

"I'll kill this family with you," she finally said, "but it's the last for a little while, at least until we can make sure we're in the clear."

"If you want, you can use the locks tonight."

He never offered her the locks.

"Really?"

"That little girl needs us," Jake said softly. "She needs us just as much as we need her."

"We need her," she purred. Then, "Okay."

twelve
sadie gray

SADIE and the others traversed the rocky driveway, avoiding jagged rocks and small puddles, all while trying to disturb as little of the crime scene as possible.

"We made imprints of a fresh set of tire tracks, but we also have a possible description of a truck and potential driver," Detective Ruiz said.

"How'd you do that?" Sadie asked.

"You're asking how we made imprints of the tire tracks?" Ruiz asked.

"Yes," she said.

"We took a cast of the tread and are running it through SICAR, a comprehensive, constantly updated database of shoe prints and tire tracks."

Brad seemed embarrassed that she asked the question, but they weren't detectives, and Sadie didn't have a background in law enforcement. She was merely trying to get an idea of who they were after and what resources were already used.

"Crime scene techs and local contractors cleared the scene enough to pull out the floors, so you'll have to look at photographs to see what it looked like first."

"Who owns the house?" Sadie asked.

"Dead guy—long dead," Ruiz replied. "The property went

into foreclosure years back and for all intents and purposes, was left abandoned. Squatters could have used it, but we think it was purely a dumpsite. If the killer somehow knew this place or stumbled upon it, he likely saw the opportunity, and... well, you can see the rest for yourself. Just watch your step."

They approached the front of the house but didn't go inside. Everything they needed to see could be seen from inside the doorway.

Forensics had rigged a pulley to lift the bodies, aluminum extension ladders descended into a plunging pit, and battery-powered floodlights illuminated the crime scene. She could only imagine what the first responders saw and felt. She looked into the empty pit, moved by the eerie light and its many jagged shadows. She was suddenly filled with so much sadness and dread, her eyes filled with tears and she burped twice, swallowing stomach bile the second time. For a second, she wondered if she was having an out-of-body experience or if she was even there. But it was real, she was there, and dead people had filled the pit.

"Mother of God," Sadie whispered.

Ruiz nodded.

She fought the urge to plug her nose. Brad's eyes watered from the lingering smell, but he wouldn't be the first to hold his nose.

Sadie cleared her throat, wiped her eyes, and said, "Growing up, we lived near chickens. Not too far from here. The summers, smelling all that hot chicken manure—you develop an iron constitution. But this smell is something else."

"What did forensics find regarding the bodies, trace evidence, or anything peculiar about the scene?" Brad asked. "I mean, they weren't murdered here, right? Am I correct in assuming this is solely a dumpsite?"

Ruiz nodded, then talked to them about the cast they made of the tire tracks and photos of several footprints they were running through the SICAR database. "Crime scene techs scoured the house for other, more significant evidence, but not much else was collected."

"Our primary concern is knowing what belongs to the victims and what belongs to the killer. We won't know the difference until we can study the evidence in its entirety and ID the vics; it's a massive undertaking."

"What about the bodies?" Sadie asked.

"Which of the thirty-four?"

"The first bodies," Brad said. "Do we know the times of death?"

Ruiz nodded. "The first ones, yes, we have an idea. All three appeared to have been killed around the same time, which is consistent with the 'family theory' we're officially running with. The next bodies might've expired three weeks ago or more."

"How could you tell?" Sadie asked.

"At around the three-week mark, the skin, hair, and nails start to become loose and the skin begins to split and burst open."

An image formed in her mind, which she quickly wiped away to avoid getting sick. "The first three, then," she managed to say.

"You all right?" Ruiz asked. "Because you look a little green."

"I feel a little green," she said.

Ruiz nodded and said, "The first three were cold to the touch, so they were at least four to six hours dead. The corneas were cloudy on all three, and rigor had already set in and was relaxing around the neck muscles and jaw, which put us at the six- to eight-hour window. Fixed lividity on all three vics confirmed this time marker."

"Blanching?" Brad asked.

"The coroner said no, but she wasn't very forthcoming, not beyond the normal details. That's not always the case with her, considering she's an elected official, but, then again, the last time we caught a case involving nearly three dozen bodies was never."

"I understand," Brad said.

Moving on, Ruiz said, "The bodies were clammy to the touch, two of them had a greenish-red hue to the skin, and full rigor was resolved in all but the adult male. That puts us between eighteen and twenty-four hours, with estimates being closer to twenty-four hours or more."

"Why do you say, 'or more'?" Sadie asked.

"It's cool down here, so the decomp slows, but we also have three different vics in different sizes: the father, mother, and child. Decomp is different in them all depending on how they were killed—by blunt force trauma to the adult male, stab wounds to the neck for the adult female, and a broken neck on the child. The cause of death for the male changes the decomp time due to reduced levels of ATP, presumably caused by a struggle."

"ATP?" Sadie asked.

"Adenosine triphosphate," Brad said. "It's the body's energy source and is stored in the cells. When ATP depletes, the muscles no longer contract, giving us rigor mortis."

Ruiz nodded and said, "That's right."

"What's after rigor mortis when the body is relaxed?" Sadie asked.

"Time and other levels of decomp, such as the loosening of the nails and teeth, and hair for vics who aren't already bald. Depending on the conditions, which are cold and somewhat damp, you can see these changes in about three weeks or more. After that, we bring in the insect dicks and forensic anthropologists."

"Insect dicks," Sadie said with a snort of laughter. "You're talking about forensic entomologists, right?"

Ruiz nodded, unable to keep from smirking. "While the first three vics had maggots inside them, the bodies below were in later stages of decomposition. We found spiders and millipedes and evidence the beetles had already dropped by to eat and run."

Sadie felt her face flush. She gulped hard and nodded as if the conversation were as normal as talking about sports or grabbing a cup of coffee. Brad looked unshaken, but everyone else reacted to the wet, rotten stench that hung heavy in the air.

"So, how can we help, then?" Sadie asked.

"If we have anything too complex or we're short on manpower, maybe you can send it to your lab," Ruiz answered. "Otherwise, for now, we've got many volunteers helping us. I'm not saying this because I'm not a fan of you guys; I'm neither here nor there. I honestly don't know why Chief Miller called you guys. I figured it was to cover his ass if the public turns on us, which they did under the last police chief after Earl Gray went bonkers."

"You're talking about Skip Davenport?" Sadie asked.

Ruiz nodded, then was startled by his ringing phone. He checked the iPhone's screen and said, "Excuse me for a second, Dr. West is calling. She's the county coroner." He stepped outside and took the call.

Meanwhile, she and Brad stared down into the hole. "You gonna puke?" Brad asked.

"Thinking about it, you?"

He nodded.

A moment later, Ruiz saved them from spending another minute there. He said, "Our coroner has prelims on the first three vics."

A moment later, Sadie watched a bald man with shiny, peach-colored skin and the starved, almost gaunt look of a POW make his way up the driveway.

"Coroner just called," the detective said.

"She called me, too," Ruiz said.

"We going?"

"I was just coming to get you," Ruiz said. "Guys, this is Detective Peters."

The detective saw Sadie and Brad, stared at them for a second, then glanced back at Ruiz and asked, "You bringing Mulder and Scully?"

"*X-Files*, that's cute," Brad said. "Not original, but cute."

"The Ken doll speaks," Peters said, which almost made Sadie laugh. Without waiting for a reply, he turned and headed back down the driveway, presumably to their cruiser.

"Don't mind him," Ruiz said. "His dad's a fed, and he hates him."

"My dad's bald and looks like a walking penis, too," Brad joked. "We don't get along either."

Ruiz chuckled and said, "For Feds, you two aren't so bad."

"Give it some time," Sadie said.

thirteen
sadie gray

SADIE AND BRAD arrived at Chapel of the Angels Mortuary on the corner of Race Street and Memorial Lane, where Dr. Eliana West, the Nevada County coroner, was busy conducting the autopsies.

The building wasn't huge by any stretch—just a low-slung, single-story, white building with navy-blue pillars and a decorative roof frame, which wrapped a slightly gabled roof and was at least two feet thick. Parked between the building and a mass of ancient-looking shrubs were a gray hearse and a white panel van; Sadie thought she had seen the van or one like it at the crime scene on television.

The parking lot had nine spots split into two different sections, one facing Memorial Lane and the other parallel to Race Street. They parked in the two spots facing Memorial Lane, and all four got out and prepared to enter the office.

Sadie gazed at the mortuary and the massive wall of evergreen trees behind it. The building looked like it was first built in the '60s or '70s and was thoroughly unimpressive in size. Looks could be deceiving, though. Still, with the sheer number of bodies they pulled from the dumpsite, the county had to be using other mortuaries or some other means of cold storage to preserve the remains. Or were they?

"They couldn't be processing nearly three dozen bodies in *there*, could they?" Sadie asked.

Ruiz said, "Our county coroner unit utilizes three different mortuaries to conduct their autopsies. Chapel of the Angels here in Grass Valley, Hooper & Weaver Mortuary in Nevada City, and Truckee-Tahoe Mortuary in Truckee, where the bones of the oldest victims will await an incoming team of forensic anthropologists."

Detective Peters asked, "Have you ever been present for an autopsy?"

"Several times," Brad offered.

Peters looked at Sadie, who held his gaze unflinchingly but said nothing. He gave a low chuckle and said, "Hope you ate a light breakfast, Special Agent Gray."

"Breakfast is for pansies," Sadie said.

Inside, she and Brad put on protective scrubs that Brad said would prevent them from contaminating the autopsy environment and hopefully protect their suits from any biohazards. Much to her dismay, he handed her nitrile gloves, shoe and hair covers, a face mask, and goggles to protect her eyes.

"Don't be surprised if later that fancy suit you're wearing smells like something died in it," Detective Peters said. "Oh, and if you're wondering about the stench, it's not just the end of your television career; it's the farted-out fumes of the dead, and they're there to stay."

Ruiz and Brad laughed at the comment about her TV career already flaming out, but she didn't think she was that bad for being a nervous wreck.

Inside the autopsy suite, Sadie saw a pretty woman in protective clothing working on the body of a dead man with his face beaten to a pulp. Dr. West looked up when they entered the room, set her tools down, and leveled them with a weary expression. Sadie put the coroner in her late thirties, but she could also be into her forties.

Ruiz made the introductions, then said, "Patterns?"

That was all the coroner needed to hear. "Right now, all I can say is that, of the two adult males I've completed, both died of blunt force trauma to the face and neck."

Sadie smelled the familiar smell, similar to that of the dumpsite, and though she was immediately nauseous and a bit woozy, she planned to fake her way through the moment. If Brad could deal with this, so could she.

"Tell us about the weapon," Peters said.

"It's all in the various prelims, but it looks like a mix of heavy-duty padlocks and combination locks." She made a fist of her right hand and held it up. "Think of them as being gathered together in a loose bundle. There is inconsistency in the spacing and angles, not only on this victim's face but between the two male victims I've seen so far."

"And the women?" Brad asked.

"Only got to one so far, but I'm about to do the second, and, as you can see,"—she said, motioning to a woman on a nearby table with a series of stab wounds to the neck— "this one, like the first woman, has fatal stab wounds. Both died of exsanguination, or severe blood loss."

Sadie stared at the woman's face, and something didn't look right. She took a tentative step forward, bringing her closer to Dr. West but also the dead woman.

"Her eyelids are flat," Sadie noted with an upset stomach.

Dr. West reached out and pulled both eyelids back, revealing empty sockets. Sadie felt her stomach all but jump into her throat. She immediately broke into a light sweat.

"The killer took the eyes of the women," she said.

"So that she couldn't see?" Brad asked.

"Or maybe because she'd seen something and did nothing," Ruiz guessed.

Sadie was about to say the same thing. Instead, she asked, "So, the killer beats the men to death with a bundle of locks, then stabs the women and takes their eyes? Do we have not one but two murderers here?"

"I'm waiting on toxicology, but I don't see any puncture wounds or injection sites—ways to inject the victims with paralytic toxins—so it's possible," Dr. West said.

"What about the kid?" Ruiz asked.

"Complete cervical spine fracture. Whoever killed the child broke her neck in half. It's not an easy thing to do."

Heat stole into Sadie's face, her cheeks beet red, her hands moist inside the gloves. If she fogged her goggles, which was bound to happen, how was she supposed to clear them?

She drew a thin breath, inhaling slowly and hoping not to pull too much of that smell into her lungs. Slowly, she exhaled, trying to settle her body using visualization techniques her father once taught her. But then, as she considered the thickness of the vertebrae, something in her changed. A break like that was no easy feat. There would be incredible violence.

At that moment, involuntarily, she formed a vision of a child, terrified and crying for their mommy and daddy before having her neck snapped in two at the hands of a madman. A cold chill ran through her, causing a hard shiver.

Brad looked at her; she avoided his gaze.

"You've identified the first three bodies," Ruiz said. "Have you IDd the others?"

"My people are searching for next of kin right now, but so far, on the first three, we're not seeing any, so that's slowing the process. IDs are in the preliminary reports if you want to use them for victimology."

"Fingerprints, right?" Sadie asked.

"Fingerprints and dental," Dr. West confirmed. "The farther we go into the pile, the fewer physical markers we'll have for identification. I hope you can use the first three to find the killer or killers because everything will only go slower from here. And with the number of bodies we're looking at? Even with three teams, this could drag out longer than we prefer."

"We just need enough to find, stop, and arrest this psychopath," Ruiz said. "Hopefully, this is enough, but if we need more, or if you can help us out at all with patterns, or you have any idea on motive, let us know."

"Isn't that what you have *them* here for?" she asked, nodding at Brad and Sadie.

"Miller brought in everyone but Santa Claus, hoping we can move quickly and not hump the mutt on this one," Peters said.

"Are you serious, Peters?" Ruiz warned. "Ladies are present."

Peters lowered his head, looked up at Brad, and sheepishly said, "I'm sorry, Special Agent Tulle."

Sadie snorted a laugh before catching herself. Brad nudged her shoulder hard, which she deserved.

"I've asked for bigger miracles than that," Dr. West said, ready to return to her work. "Despite these two clowns, I'm happy to have you here, Special Agents Tulle and Gray. My door is open to you anytime, for any reason."

"Thank you," Sadie and Brad said simultaneously.

"The deputy coroner will have copies of the preliminary reports for you up front," Dr. West said, facing the body. "She's the girl who looks like a mouse and speaks softly. But don't give her grief. She's great."

"Yes, Ma'am," Peters said.

"You, too, Detective Ruiz," she said over her shoulder.

He put his hands up and said, "Why, I'd never, Dr. West."

"And yet you have before," she mumbled.

"Old dogs can change."

"Sure, they can."

Before they left, Dr. West said, "Oh, Detective Ruiz."

The four stopped, and Ruiz took a step toward Dr. West. "Yes?"

"Both men's penises were missing," she said. "Full castration, testicles and all."

The news caused an unnatural stillness in the men, especially Peters. "You waited until we were leaving to tell us this?"

"Serial killers take souvenirs," Brad said.

"Everyone loves a good surprise, right?" Dr. West grinned.

Peters said, "You think our perp has a bag of dicks sitting around his house somewhere, Eliana?"

"My job is to tell you what's not here, and your job is to do the rest, Detective Peters."

They thanked her and left, and out in the parking lot, Detective Peters said, "Have you two seen the murder board yet?"

Ruiz said, "They haven't been to the station."

"Now is as good a time as any," Peters replied. Was he hoping to prolong their hazing or actually help them out?

Sadie got into the car and was about to ask Brad a question when he said, "You realize I'm the case agent on this, and you're new, right?"

"If you'd like me to deny my instincts—"

"This is your first case."

"You've already reminded me I'm not the case agent—"

"Then do me a favor and act like it. For God's sake, you're fresh out of the wrapper. An FNG, dammit."

For the love of God, where did I step out of line? "I feel like I should apologize—" she said.

"Thank you," he said too soon.

"To your ego."

He turned and said, "One week, Sadie. You've been on the job one week."

She sat back and tried not to stew; he was quiet, too. Then she said, "I'm pretty sure I'm going to be amazing."

Brad glared at her; she smiled and blew him a kiss.

"That's cute and all," he muttered under his breath. "I'll be sure to tell the SAC and ASAC Blackwood you aren't taking your job seriously and have no concept of the chain of command."

"So, you're going to tell on me?" she asked.

"I'm the case agent!"

She could not help but take the attack personally. Still, she'd taken the wrong approach, and Brad was right when he said she needed to toughen up and thicken her skin. So, she sat there and tried not to sulk as her body trembled inside. Finally, she managed to let it go, smiling away her discomfort until she found a calm place inside her mind.

Then, she said, "Hey, Brad?"

"What?"

"When you were a kid, how many participation trophies did you get?"

He didn't look at her, but his face deepened two shades of red. The cheap shot wasn't a true victory; it was more of a diet victory —half the fun but none of the calories. The truth was, proving his skin was a little thin felt like a win. And Sadie would take one of those in any way she could.

fourteen
sadie gray

SADIE ENTERED the Grass Valley Police Department's conference room, where they had set up their version of a murder board—several murder boards placed side-by-side because of the large body count. Chief Miller stood with several other detectives, speaking about one of the victims with a slashed throat, when he turned and saw Sadie and Brad.

Miller locked eyes with Sadie, frowned before catching himself, then offered a conciliatory nod. She returned the gesture. Was Miller part of the old guard who hated that her father took justice into his own hands once upon a time?

Brad said, "Chief Miller."

Miller glanced at him. "Special Agent Tulle."

The two walked up to the row of murder boards and saw an organized layout of the victims and notes of what was known about them so far. The photo lineup told a story of their deaths, starting with the most recent bodies, spanning through those in different stages of decay, and ending with the victims whose bodies were reduced to bones inside disintegrating clothing. Sadie scanned the photos, ending on the three bodies Dr. West already examined.

"Did you get copies of the prelims?" Miller asked, referring to the preliminary reports Dr. West provided. Sadie nodded, but Miller wasn't talking to her; he looked at Brad.

"Yeah," Brad said.

Miller nodded, but no one offered much. Sadie almost asked what they were supposed to be doing there.

"Forensic anthropologists are now working the bones in Truckee," Miller said, "but we believe Dr. West's findings will eventually help us find this guy and put his nuts into a freaking vise. Pardon the expression, Ma'am."

Sadie waved him off and said, "I'm not one of those girls who gets offended by every little thing, so don't sweat it."

Ruiz stared at the board with the oldest bodies and said, "There was a literal mountain of bodies in that hole. Weight and decomp are going to be an issue."

Sadie studied bodies four through seven, which might be a week dead or slightly older if she was to guess. All she had were guesses, though. Dr. West was the coroner, so Sadie would rely on the prelims for those details. She and her team would soon make more IDs, allowing the local teams to begin basic victimology and hopefully begin conducting interviews. She knew detectives would be looking for patterns and motivation as well as the scene of the crime. It would be time for Brad to build a possible profile when they had that. Brad, not her. Sadie was there to learn and do what Brad asked since he was the case agent.

She drew a breath and reminded herself to be patient. They needed a starting point, though, and likely had one, but without specific details, it would just be them standing around and scratching their asses.

Brad, Ruiz, and the Chief's phones beeped with text notifications. Ruiz smiled and said, "All right, folks, we have our first address."

"Where are they from?" Sadie asked.

"Reno," Ruiz answered, sounding disappointed.

Sadie almost volunteered to go, but Brad beat her to it. "Special Agent Gray and I will follow up on this lead."

"Great," Miller said. "I'll call Reno PD ahead and get you a contact you can work with there."

"We'll populate as many databases as possible, check for similar cases, and start looking at missing families," Ruiz said.

"Roger that," Sadie said, mimicking Brad.

Ruiz smiled. "How long have you been on the job, Special Agent Gray?"

"Long enough," Sadie said.

"One week," Brad replied, stabbing her in the back with a big, invisible knife. A few others snickered, which bothered her enough that she clenched her jaw.

Brad turned and apologized but with a smirk; Sadie leveled him with the mother of all stink eyes.

"What?" Brad asked. "It's the truth."

She frowned and said, "Now I'm not just a girl—I'm the *new* girl."

"Here's the difference," Detective Ruiz said, coming to the rescue. "You're Sadie freaking Gray, daughter of Earl "Mop Up" Gray—a genuine legend and a vigilante of epic proportion."

"Don't give her props for that," Chief Miller snapped.

"Why not, Chief?" Detective Peters asked.

"Because her father, who is in prison—might I remind you, made this department and our predecessors look like fools. Personally, I've got no issue with him or what he did, but it set us back decades in terms of community support."

"You made yourself look like fools when you ignored those missing girls," Sadie muttered.

"Bullshit," Miller snapped.

"You know it's not, Chief Miller," a female officer said. Sadie turned and saw a woman whose face would never leave her mind.

"Officer May," Sadie said with a growing smile.

"Sergeant May, now," she said. Teresa May's features brightened, highlighting the prominent scar on her face. She met Sadie with a warm hug.

After a second, the two separated, and Sergeant May asked,

"You're a fed now? How did this happen? And look at you—my God, you're stunning!"

"She's not that stunning," Brad said, maybe trying to keep her ego in check because his was wounded.

"Shut your mouth, asshole," Sergeant May barked.

"That's Special Agent—" Brad started to say.

"It's Special Agent Asshole to me," Teresa said, finishing his sentence.

Sadie turned to Brad and said, "When Sergeant May was Officer May, we met under dark and bloody circumstances. I'm only alive because of her."

"Is that how you got the scar?" Brad asked, motioning to her cheek. The entire department was quiet.

"First off, rude," Teresa said. "Second, yes, it is."

Brad looked at Sadie and said, "You did that to her?"

"A sandwich did that to me," Teresa said with a grin. A few of the others laughed under their breaths. Sadie tried not to laugh.

"It's a long story I won't ever tell you, pretty boy," Teresa said. She turned to Sadie, her smile returning. "Anything you need, call me, and it's yours."

Brad returned to the murder boards, the larger group broke up, and Miller spoke with Detective Peters about the current autopsies. The distraction gave her and Teresa a moment of near privacy to speak.

"You remember when I reached out last, right?" Sadie leaned in and asked, keeping her voice down. "My... *mother*?"

Teresa gave her a sad smile and said, "Yeah, I do."

"And?"

"The cold case workload is the size of the Empire State Building, but I have my feelers out."

"Any leads?"

Teresa smiled again and shook her head. "I don't think she's in California anymore. I've expanded the search, but... it's hard to know what to look for. I can say this, though... I think she's still alive. Right now, I'm wondering if she's homeless. That would be my best guess if you were to press me."

Sadie nodded, hugged her again, and said, "Thanks. It was so good to see you."

"Don't be a stranger," she said.

"We're heading to Reno, then we'll be back here," Sadie said before checking in with Brad. "Hopefully, we'll be back here with something worthwhile. My cell number's the same if you need to call."

"Roger that," she smiled.

fifteen
sadie gray

THEY ARRIVED in Reno at Reno PD on East 2nd Street less than two hours later. Brad asked for Detective Swartz and was greeted promptly by a balding man with a large belly, bad skin, and fingernails yellowed from smoking too many cigarettes. He didn't smile but didn't frown either. He brought with him an overwhelming smell of cheap aftershave mixed with cigarette smoke and a hint of body odor. After they shook hands, Sadie wondered if she would smell like him.

"So, you're on that case in Grass Valley, right?" he asked. "The 34 in the floor, I guess it's called."

"Yeah," Sadie said.

"They called you two in because the murders crossed state lines, then?" he asked, looking back and forth between them. "Or are they trying to put prettier faces in front of the media?"

"We're not influencers or entertainers, Detective Swartz," Sadie said before Brad could reply.

He looked sheepish but said, "Sorry, I didn't mean to imply… it's just that we're understaffed and stretched thin on resources while trying to manage impossible caseloads."

"Is that a current thing or ongoing?" Brad asked.

"Why do you ask?" Swartz asked. "You thinking of trading in that suit for a real job in law enforcement?"

"The prettier people get jobs with the Feds," Brad joked back, all in good fun. "Don't feel bad, though; at least you have that belly."

He and Brad laughed like it was no big thing.

"And those crusty fingers," Sadie said with a poorly received smile. The two stopped laughing and stared at her. She raised her eyebrows. "What?"

"Male bonding precludes females from body shaming," Detective Swartz explained.

She stared at him for a moment. "Holy Toledo, you're serious?"

"Of course," Brad said. "Everyone knows that."

Having thoroughly pooped on the male bonding parade, she said, "As fun as this is, those bodies won't identify themselves."

Swartz leaned sideways, covering his mouth, and said to Brad, "What's got her undies in a bundle?"

"I can hear you," Sadie said.

"What did I say, then?" he asked.

"That you have diabetes, and your dying wish is to be helpful."

Brad's face went beet red; he turned sideways and failed to suppress a laugh. Swartz, however, did not hold back—he barked out a laugh.

"That's a good one," he said. "You got the wrong parts for a guy, but I feel you're a guy's gal, so... sorry for coming off as cold."

"No worries," Sadie said, victorious.

He handed Brad a file and said, "Directions and authorization for investigative activity only. We'd appreciate the heads-up if you need warrants or want to make an arrest. I'd go there with you now, but I've also got murders in need of solving."

"Of course," Brad said.

"We're not stepping on your toes, are we?" Sadie asked.

Brad closed his eyes.

"No," Swartz said with amusement.

"Well, we might," she grinned.

He was warming to her. "Are you the case agent?"

"Maybe."

"She's not," Brad said.

Sadie quietly giggled to herself as she turned and headed out to the car. Outside, she waited for Brad to unlock the doors. Before he could open them, she looked at him from across the Impala's roof, and said, "Everyone knows cops hate the Feds and we hate the cops."

"First off, that's not entirely true and you shouldn't utter nonsense like that," Brad said. "And second, no one's given us a reason to hate anyone yet so maybe keep that crap back there to a minimum."

"That guy just put us in a pack-n-play and told us not to crawl out unless we checked with him first."

Brad put on his sunglasses and asked, "Have you ever heard the saying, 'It's better to ask for forgiveness than permission?'"

"Who hasn't?" Sadie asked in return.

"Well, we're asking for neither," he grinned. "We just act polite to keep them off our backs."

She smiled at Brad, thinking she might be quiet from now on.

He opened his door but had yet to get in. Instead, still staring at her, he said, "I don't want to tell you to shut up, Sadie, but you need to shut your mouth around others and let me be the case agent."

"You say that like you're on a power trip. Open my door, please."

"Chain of command," he said.

He got in the car, started it up, and let the A/C run while she stood outside, waiting for him to open her door.

She drew a breath and sighed, finally understanding. Brad unlocked the door. She climbed in, buckled her seatbelt, and said, "Okay, I get it. It's about respect."

Brad didn't celebrate the small victory. Instead, he said, "ASAC Blackwood said you were a fast learner."

"Did he also tell you I have a problem with authority?"

"He didn't have to, Special Agent Gray. We all have that problem, so being the authority is critical to operating efficiently."

"You want me to drive at some point, or can I get a little shuteye?"

"You can get some sleep if you want, but I'll keep the radio on because I don't want to listen to you breathing or snoring."

"That's not nice," she said, feigning offense.

"I don't know you well, and I don't want to feel creeped out by you."

She gave him a sideways glance. "I hear you're good at solving these cases, but you kind of suck at being a partner."

"I was thinking you suck, too."

She watched the scenery go by, mesmerized by the new locale and how different it was from California.

Finally, she said, "Yeah, I guess so."

"You've got twenty minutes to sleep, so maybe be quiet and aim your mouth at the window."

She shook her head, leaned back, and closed her eyes. Brad woke her almost right away, but it turned out that twenty-five minutes had passed.

"We're here," he said. He had parked the bu-car along the sidewalk of a clean, suburban neighborhood. He pointed to the house and asked, "Are you ready?"

She yawned and nodded, unbuckling her seatbelt.

"When we get back," Brad said, "you'll have to tell me why you were calling out my name in your sleep."

She looked at him in shock, but then he winked, and she thought of a few names she could call him. But not now. Now, they were at a possible crime scene.

They walked up the front walkway to a small porch and a closed front door. The face of the wooden door was damaged, though. Brad ran a finger through one of the grooves and said, "What do you think did this?"

"You're asking me?" she said.

"The bundle of locks, I think," he replied.

She nodded. The wood was dented and splintered with several long grooves. Whoever hit it was likely very angry or wanted to intimidate the homeowners.

"This one's a brave one," Brad said. "He's fearless, bold, or too dumb to know better."

"After thirty-four kills," Sadie mused, "he's got a little experience."

"Perhaps he's gotten cocky," Brad said. He seemed to shake off the thought. Then he turned and looked at her. "Gloves."

She pulled them out of her jacket pocket and said, "Got 'em."

"Put them on then," he said as he put on his gloves.

Sadie did as Brad instructed as he unholstered his weapon. Sadie took out her gun and asked, "Is this normal?"

"Someone could be injured inside," Brad said.

He tried the doorknob and found it unlocked. Brad stepped back and looked left and right, checking for witnesses. He had motioned for her to either go forward or get back. *Which was it?* She breathed and entered the house, moving into the hallway the way the instructors at Quantico had trained her. With limited light and stuffy air, it wasn't pleasant inside.

Brad scoffed as he moved in behind her, pushing past her with Sadie covering his six. She cleared the front room and office while Brad disappeared into the main bedroom, another small room, and the kitchen and living room. They rendezvoused in the hallway, where Sadie was staring at blood and bits of broken teeth. A cursory look at the hallway walls revealed several impact points. Blood spotted the walls, along with blood splatter.

"It looks like he damn near decapitated the wife in the master bedroom," Brad said, his face a lighter shade of white.

"This must be our guy, then," Sadie said, feeling sick. More than that, though, she felt like she could maybe see the attack in her mind.

"Yeah," Brad muttered.

She drew a breath and asked about the master bedroom.

Brad swallowed hard, holstered his weapon, and said, "It

looks like a bloodbath on white sheets and tan carpet, with bloody handprint smears along the fabric headboard. In the back room, the child's room, the bed sheets looked torn apart, the pillow on the floor." He shook his head, staring down with Sadie at the broken teeth. "We need to back out of here and call Reno PD."

A few minutes later, from inside the Impala, Brad called Detective Swartz and told him what they found. He promised to have an officer in a black and white Chevy police SUV on the scene to tape it off for detectives.

"How soon?" Brad asked.

"Thirty minutes."

Half an hour later, Sadie and Brad were already knocking on doors. Apparently, no one heard anything. While most neighbors knew the family, they all described it the same way: quiet people who kept to themselves.

Two of the neighbors had cameras mounted in front of their houses. The first woman let them look at the video footage, which was grainy and unclear but clear enough to see a pickup truck parked in the darkness.

"You two want some tea or soda?" she asked as they studied the video.

"No, thank you," both said.

Brad paused it and asked, "How far back does this go?"

"It's motion-activated, so it lasts longer, I guess," she said. She was a thin, nervous-looking woman with arms not much thicker than her bones. Sadie didn't think she had enough body strength to wrestle a cat, let alone deep-six three people. "My husband said a week, maybe?"

Brad pressed the pause button again, unfreezing the footage. A moment later, the three squinted their eyes and moved their faces within inches of the monitor.

"That's an old Dodge pickup, I think," Brad said. Then, they saw three people get out of the truck.

"Oh, my God," Sadie gasped.

The neighbor covered her mouth and said, "I can't watch this."

"Best you don't," Sadie said, shooing her off, even though it was her home.

"What kind of phone do you have?"

"An iPhone," Sadie said.

"Good camera?"

"I have the iPhone 13 Pro, so... yeah."

Brad backed up the video to the moment the three exited the truck. Then he looked at Sadie and said, "Record this."

Sadie took out her cell phone, activated the video feature, and nodded at Brad. Moments later, the murderous trio convened on the porch. Two of the three got into a scuffle, which ended quickly, and then the two leaned in to listen to the big guy. After a short, terse conversation, the big guy started beating the front door with something they couldn't quite see. Then a man carrying a baseball bat opened the front door, and it was on like Donkey Kong. The tall one crashed down on the homeowner like a tidal wave, and the other two flowed inside, with the small one closing the door behind him. Thirty minutes later, the three came outside, each with a body slung over their shoulders.

"This is insane," Brad said.

"You ever see anything like this?" she asked.

"Different things, some just as bad, and others worse. But this is... brazen."

"Did you get what you needed?" the woman asked from the edge of her kitchen.

"We did," Brad stood and said. "Thank you so much for your help."

"Hope it did some good," she said.

"More than you know," Sadie replied with a genuine smile.

The house next door, the second one with a newer, more expensive-looking camera, held more promise.

Sadie knocked; both had their credentials ready. An unattractive woman in a trucker's cap, a sleeveless white T-shirt, and cutoff jeans shorts answered the door, eyeing them suspiciously. Sadie tried to hold her gaze, but the woman's skin was like curdled milk, with varicose veins, minor bruising, and a professional cat tattoo.

Brad greeted her, introduced them both, and asked about her security system when she interrupted him to say, "You the good Feds or the bad ones?"

"We're all good, Ma'am," Brad said.

She broke into a wicked cackle that lasted too long, then crossed her arms to prove a point. With narrowed eyes, she said, "What do you want?"

"There was an abduction on your street the other night, and we would like to see if we could access your security system."

"I didn't see anything," she said.

"We weren't asking to check through your brain, Ma'am," Sadie said. "We asked to look at your surveillance video."

"For what?" the woman asked, looking at Sadie like she was trash.

Brad said, "We have the make and model of the vehicle in question and a blurry image of the suspects, but your system looks more up to date, possibly with a 4K camera."

"My husband just wants to know if I'm banging Lucas."

"Lucas Garcia?" Sadie asked.

Her arms dropped, and she said, "Yeah, that's him."

"Were you?" Sadie asked.

Brad nudged her.

"Was I what?" the woman asked.

"Carrying on with Mr. Garcia?" Sadie asked.

Her face was horrified. "Hell no, I wasn't carrying on with him, but I could tell by the looks he gave that he'd like to be carrying on with me, which is why my husband installed the security system."

"Well, Mr. Garcia is now carrying on in the afterlife," Sadie said, "and we need to see if we can help solve his murder."

"Murder!" she exclaimed.

Brad rolled his eyes and said to Sadie, "I feel like we're on a game show."

The woman's eyes ping-ponged back and forth between them, then she said, "The answer is 4K. To the quality of the camera."

"We'd love to see that surveillance footage," Brad said.

The woman's dry, guarded eyes were now glistening with the start of tears. She wiped them, squared her shoulders, then lifted her chin. "Not without a court order or him asking me nicely." She glanced at Brad, her eyes locked on him, unblinking, her body rigid with some form of manic desperation. Or was that something else?

"Excuse me?" Brad asked.

Those unshed tears never hit her cheeks; she was too busy staring. "I never met a real-life fed in a suit like that, Special Agent..."

"Tulle."

She batted her eyelashes. "Say it nicely, please."

"Could we please take a look at your surveillance video?"

She smiled, satisfied, and said, "With a court order. You think I trust you two clowns after what I see going on?" And with that, she slammed the door in their faces.

Brad shook his head and looked at Sadie, who raised her brows as if to say, "What gives?"

"Top brass isn't making things easy for us with some folks."

"Meaning?" Sadie asked.

Brad shook his head and stalled, wondering how to answer. Finally, he said, "We need to see if we can get local LEOs to lean on her, or we have to get a court order."

"Maybe someone else will have surveillance," Sadie suggested.

They hit a few more houses and only had a little luck, but then they ran into a wrinkly, old woman collecting her mail. She eyed them suspiciously as if they were selling solar or religion—neither of which would catch her interest.

"Afternoon," Brad said. He glanced down the street where a

Reno PD SUV sat in front of the house. The officer finally arrived to put up yellow crime scene tape.

"Who you with?" she groused. She spoke and sounded like she had bad breath to match her bad attitude.

Brad withdrew his credentials. "FBI, Ma'am. There was a break-in in your neighborhood, and we're wondering what you may know about the Garcia family."

She picked the inside of her nose, wiped it down the front of her cotton robe, right alongside a few other smears, and said, "No one likes them."

"Why is that?" Sadie asked, momentarily woozy with revulsion.

"This bring your daughter to work day?" she asked, looking between Sadie and Brad. Brad frowned, probably offended that she considered him old.

"No. It's 'bring your dad to work day today,'" Sadie said. "By the way, I'm Special Agent Sadie Gray. My partner and I are here because terrible things are afoot, and they could spill over onto you and your neighbors if we don't get in front of them."

"What kinds of things?" she asked.

Sadie looked at her robe and squinched her nose. "Worse than all those booger smears you're wearing, I can tell you that."

The woman's eyes flashed with embarrassment or hostility; Sadie wasn't sure which. Either way, the woman glanced at the stains and frowned. She held Sadie's gaze for a long moment, pursed her lips, and then said, "It's a condition."

"So is picking your ass," she said, "but that doesn't mean you need to ruin good clothing."

She wiggled her nose, flicked the underside with the bottom of her thumb, and said, "CPS has been there a few times. The old man makes the girl cry a lot. Yells, says horrible things, smacks the wife around, stalks around the block like his pecker's stuck in a chip clip."

Brad suppressed a grin. "A chip clip?" he asked.

Sadie ignored him and asked, "And you know this, how?"

"Ethel and I are friends," she said. "Ethel lives next door to them, but she's deaf."

"And you're not," Brad said.

"Clearly."

"So, you heard the things he was saying?" Sadie asked.

The woman nodded. "Horrible, vile things. Talking about how he hated them and wished they'd aborted the girl when they had the chance. She's the cutest thing ever. Never says a thing, though, not even to me. And look at me! I'm harmless!"

Brad offered a plausible explanation. "Old people creep out young people sometimes. Not because they're creepy—most aren't—but because kids get scared easily."

"She don't say nothing to no one, not even friends she stands with on the street waiting for the school bus."

"You ever see any bruises on her, or slings or casts—anything like that?" she asked.

The woman seemed to think about it, really digging deep in the organic archives. "Come to think about it, she walks funny sometimes."

Sadie swallowed. "Thank you, Ma'am. Would you mind if we reached out if we had any other questions?"

"That would be fine," she said.

Sadie turned and said, "Why don't you give her a card, *Dad*."

Brad handed her a card but looked unhappy with her. She didn't understand that since they were pushing the ball down the field. Up the street, they saw the RPD officer on the front porch of the house, talking on his cell phone.

Brad waved; he got off the phone and joined them. "You two call this in?" the officer asked.

"That's right," Brad nodded, introducing them both.

"Detective Swartz said this is part of that serial in California," the officer said. "The one with thirty-four dead, right Agent Tulle?"

He asked the question while looking at Sadie, even though he addressed Brad, which was weird. The man's expression was blank, something Sadie found uncomfortable and a bit unnerving. Why was he staring? Did he hate women, or was he quietly taking her in?

Brad nodded and said, "I'm Special Agent Tulle, and she's Special Agent Gray. And yes, we just made the ID."

The guy didn't even look at Brad.

Sadie took a moment to tell the officer about the neighbor who wouldn't give up the security footage without a warrant.

He said, "I'll talk to her. If she doesn't like the Feds, maybe she'll like me. People usually like cops better, anyway. No one likes the Feds."

"We like the Feds," Sadie said.

"Good for you."

They thanked the man and walked off. Sadie said, "Is this kind of unspoken hostility normal?"

Brad unlocked the car doors, and they both got inside. He started the car and turned the blower down. "Everyone seems extra polite on account of you."

"Me?"

"Yeah, you being a girl."

"What, they don't want to offend me? I'm not the kind to lean on HR, or whatever it's called at the bureau."

"It's not that," he said.

"Then what is it?" she asked.

He reached over, flipped down her map visor, and adjusted the mirror to face her. "Look in the mirror and tell me what you see?"

"Someone new, innocent, ready to learn."

He blew a breath out of the corner of his mouth and said, "Don't give me the politically correct answer."

"They see someone they want to have sex with," she said.

"Bingo."

"If I say that's sexist—"

"I'll tell you that you're stupid and not to say such stupid shit."

"But if I say 'thank you'?"

"I'll say it's not me who thinks that," Brad said casually. "Everyone knows I'm into blondes with daddy issues and low self-esteem."

She laughed and said, "Thank you."

"It wasn't me saying it. I'm just telling you what I observe."

They arrived back in Grass Valley after dark. By then, Sadie had texted Ruiz from Brad's phone to tell him what they'd found.

There are three killers? he texted.

Yes.

Holy Toledo!

Ruiz met them at Sadie's Airbnb, and they stood outside the small house in the dark, watching the footage Sadie had recorded earlier. He couldn't believe it. Ruiz said, "Well, I'll let Miller and the others know. Great job you two."

"Detective Swartz said he'd try to get the footage from the other woman, the one with a hard-on for Special Agent Tulle," Sadie said.

Brad laughed, but it was a tired laugh.

"She always like this?" Ruiz asked, grinning.

Brad looked at her through the darkness and said, "She's a bucket of laughs. You ask her if this is normal if you really want to know."

Ruiz turned to her, but Sadie bristled and said, "Don't talk about me like I'm not standing here."

"She's here, Detective Ruiz," Brad whispered, teasing her. "Better watch what you say."

Ignoring them both, she said, "I'll forward you the video, and you can share it with your other dicks."

It was dark outside and getting late, and Sadie was exhausted. Although plagued by first-case jitters, she was enjoying herself.

"What's the latest from Dr. West?" Brad asked.

Ruiz said, "Looks like the knife wounds don't match between three different vics, but the blunt force trauma with the locks appears to be consistent."

"And the kids?" Sadie asked.

"Broken necks, consistent with the Garcia girl," Ruiz said.

"Wow," Brad said.

"Maybe the killer is grabbing knives from the owner's homes," Sadie said. "Not sure why they wouldn't bring their own, but if they're still at the scene... maybe...?"

"Maybe we'll find prints?" Ruiz asked.

She nodded.

"I wouldn't hold your breath," Brad said. "But who knows..."

Sadie yawned, and Detective Ruiz said, "Well, I guess that's my cue. The old lady's been blowing up my phone for the last half-hour anyway."

"Why don't you go home and see her, then?" Sadie asked without thinking.

"Because then I'll have to see her," he said as if it was obvious.

Brad said, "I'm at the hotel up the street, but you have my number. Call me if you need anything."

"Yeah, okay," he said.

Ruiz said goodbye, leaving the two of them together in the darkness. A bare lightbulb outside the front door provided enough light to see each other.

"Are you scared?" Brad asked with a weary grin.

"Yeah, a little," she chuckled.

"That's why you keep the gun beside you with the safety off and one in the chamber."

"Always," she said with a yawn.

sixteen
the driver

THE THREE KILLERS cruised through the rural neighborhood in the dead of night with the windows rolled down, smelling wet grass and fresh manure, and hearing whinnying horses and the sounds of cows saying cow things. Beneath the rural sounds, an orchestra of crickets filled the void, then fell silent to the boisterous sounds of a barking dog far away, barking at whatever—not them. It seemed they were the only people on the road for a while. Then, an old car passed them, a souped-up Subaru that some dumb kid was driving too fast.

The driver pulled up to the front of the property, confirmed the address, and continued for another block or two before parking off the road, deep in a bank of shadows. The psychopath jumped out of the back; Jake had the locks in hand and was raring to go, but she didn't like the feel of it—considering it felt rushed and they were under pressure from various law enforcement agencies. But Jake said the family needed to get in the dirt, so they'd put them there before the next sunrise.

When they were sure there were no security cameras or a guard dog, the three approached the house. Normally, they would plan better, but with the remote location and the discovery of the dumpsite in Grass Valley—if they wanted to hit one last target—

they needed to be quick. In and out. Make the kills, do the body drop, wash the truck, and call it a day, month, or year.

Then it's back to normal life, she thought in her head. Whatever constituted normal those days.

A flash of her life filled her head: work, go home to the morons, start drinking and maybe doing some crack, eat only a little food because food had become too expensive, drink some more and do some more crack, then fall asleep in her bed with the door locked, unless she was horny. Most nights, she slept in the nude and left the door open for whichever of the morons got there first. It was usually Jake, but sometimes it was David.

The three stood in the lightless pocket of the porch before an old wooden door that felt dry to the touch and weak. David was just as anxious as always, Jake had his ear pressed to the door, and she just wanted to get in, get it on, and get the fuck out. They were not killing below the radar anymore. There had been a *press conference.*

When Jake began running the lock bundle up and down the door, she felt a familiar electric charge run through her, a killing chill as ferocious and euphoric as it was steeped in bloodlust. The door opened a moment later to an irate man with tired eyes. He wore a white wife-beater tank top and wrinkled blue boxer shorts, and he carried a steak knife—the one she intended to take and use to stab his wife to death.

Jake struck the man with full force with the locks. The lethal bundle battered his hands and arms until he couldn't hold them up to defend himself. Stumbling backward into the house with his resolve waning, the man dropped the knife on the floor, his arms too damaged to hold up. Jake went to work on his head and face next, the begging and pleading lasting as long as it took to land two big blows. After that, it was the meaty, pulping sounds of Jake administering justice.

Blood drained down the dying man's face, and his head was misshapen from the abuse. Jake let out a mighty roar, doubled his efforts, and finally caved in the man's skull—hitting him even after he was unconscious, or dead.

When the three of them were children, their father hated David the most but treated Jake worse than all of them. So, when the opportunity presented itself at times like this, Jake saw every bad father as if they were his father, and he could finally have his revenge.

David slid past them into the back of the house, where the child was no longer awake or scared. By the time Jake finished with the father, he was wild-eyed, dripping blood, and one supercharged son of a bitch. David carried the limp child out of the bedroom, much to the horror of the mother, who stood there, sobbing and shaking and watching it all.

The driver turned on the lights and saw the woman had wet herself.

"Did she know?" she asked Jake.

He nodded and, "Make sure you get her eyes."

She walked toward the woman, lowering her chin and glaring at the terrified woman, a wicked grin cutting across her face.

"Please," the mother cried.

"That's what your child said before you let your husband do... *what he did*."

The woman looked at her dead husband and the kid, whose neck David had snapped in two. She backpedaled, terror-stricken. The grinning driver purred in the back of her throat, stalked forward after her, then chased her into the bedroom. The woman tried to slam the door, but the driver kicked it open and caught her flatfooted.

"I didn't do nuthin'!" she yelled through the sobbing.

The driver rushed her, then used her husband's steak knife to free her shit-awful soul from that shit-awful body. As the driver carved the woman's eyes from her skull, she felt neither remorse nor sorrow—just pure, unfettered exultation.

Humanity lived in a filthy world with disgusting people and perverts, human trash who did the cruelest things to innocents.

But what these two did to their kid... it was enough to give her pause. The driver's only hope was that their deaths would somehow make the world a better, more tolerable place.

When she finished with the woman, the driver stuffed the eyeballs into her pants pocket, stood, and saw her brother in the doorway, observing.

In his game-show host voice, Jake said, "And in one corner, weighing in at one-hundred and five pounds—dead, blind, and forcibly ejected from this world—lay Susan Costley."

It was all he had.

"Eyes?" David asked.

She touched the bulges in her pocket.

"You know I want 'em," David whispered.

"I always give them to you. It won't be no different this time."

He seemed to settle, and then the three picked up their bodies, hauled them out into the night, and walked them to the truck. They dumped them into the bed, secured them, and then Jake got into the truck and drove them up Highway 80, past Auburn. He took the exit to Colfax, and before long, they arrived at the house with the large barn.

The driver, who now sat in the passenger seat, tried to calm her body, but her heart was racing so hard she wondered if she was about to pass out.

"You already did what needed doing, sister," Jake said. He put a calming hand on her shoulder and nodded.

Jake drove them to the locked barn, pulled alongside it, and parked beneath the upper gable. David hopped on top of the Dodge, leaped onto the barn's roof, opened the hay door, and disappeared inside. A moment later, he pushed the barn door open on the ground floor and stood back, making room for Jake and the truck. When they were inside, David closed the doors. Jake left the headlights on, extinguishing them only when David turned on the dim overhead lights.

"We good?" Jake asked, getting out of the truck.

"Yeah," David said.

The house and barn sat on almost eight private, wooded acres. If someone in the distance spotted the light in the barn, it wouldn't tickle their suspicions, let alone cause them to phone the sheriff.

The three went to work wrapping the bodies in plastic. The Colfax location provided anonymity, which the Grass Valley dumpsite no longer afforded. Using the barn, however, was not as simple as lowering bodies into a hole. That was why there were still so many bodies that needed hiding. It was hard work, though. There, in Colfax, they had to bag the bodies and stake them to the wall studs to hold them in. After that, they would erect a plywood wall and shrink the barn's interior space by six feet in width and twenty inches in depth. The false walls weren't enough to hide the bodies from LEOs if they were hot on their trail and found the place, but hopefully, Jake would have time to drywall, texture, and paint the walls to look like the rest of the barn.

But the smell…

"We should stuff 'em with insulation," the moron said.

"Too expensive," the driver said.

"It's already starting to stink in here," Jake said, glancing at the other false walls.

"Maybe if you go crap in a corner and throw a little straw on it," the driver said, tossing dirt from the barn floor at Jake, "it'll start to smell like a proper barn instead of a morgue."

David went into the corner, pulled down his pants, and squatted. The driver clenched her teeth, exhaled sharply through her nose, then grabbed a tack hammer and threw it at him with everything she had. It tumbled at light speed toward his fuzzy-looking head and struck the side of the barn like a gunshot.

David jumped and stared at her with an awful fright.

"I wasn't serious!" she yelled.

The moron swallowed, yanked up his pants, then narrowed his eyes, clenched his malformed jaw, and charged her. Jake stepped in front of the driver and clocked the moron, looking down on him where he fell, now out cold.

"You kill him?" she asked.

"Just a little tap."

They returned to work, securing a few older, nearby bodies to the new four-by-four posts. By the time David woke, they had just finished nailing the plywood to the studs on either side of the bodies.

"If someone finds this place," Jake told her, "you know they'll find the bodies."

"Some at first, but not all."

She thought about what he was saying, considered what was inside the nearby house, and laughed. "First, they'll find *that*," she said, nodding in the direction of the house. "Then they'll find everyone out here—all of them."

"Who cares?" David asked, rubbing his jaw here Jake hit him. "We ain't doing nothing wrong as far as I'm concerned."

"Me neither," she said.

When they finished at the barn, the three piled into the truck, David lying down in the truck bed despite the blood. He kept saying his jaw felt broke.

The driver drove them home in silence. Jake and David washed their clothes outside at the spigot while the driver took a cold shower and headed to her room. She shut and locked the door, not ready for company. A few minutes later, someone tried the door knob—only a single twist. She opened her eyes, propped herself on her elbows, and watched the door. A moment later, whoever was there went away.

She pulled her new rifle toward her, chambered a round, and slept naked with it like a lover. Twice throughout the night, she woke up rubbing her face along the cold steel, dreaming about how much fun it would be to shoot bad people.

seventeen
sadie gray

SADIE SLEPT FITFULLY MOST of the night. The bed was slightly uncomfortable, the air a bit too cold, and a sudden pounding out front went on for too long. The nuisance finally roused her. She opened her eyes and identified the sounds as someone knocking on her front door. She grabbed her cell phone and blinked as much as possible to see it was just after seven a.m. She sat up in bed, half-stuck in her dream. The part of her brain trying desperately to come to life thought it was too early to be awake. She grabbed her Glock, crawled out of bed, and moved toward the door, somewhat wobbly on her bare feet. Rubbing her eyes and trying to fix her hair, she wasn't sure what was happening. Gun in her hand, she walked to the front door, to more banging, and said, "Hold on, *damn*."

She opened the door to Brad, while standing behind it to hide her body. She wore white boy-cut underwear and a black tank top, no bra. Before saying she needed to get dressed, she watched in horror as Brad strolled into the small Airbnb, holding two cups of coffee.

He turned around, surprised by her bare legs and underwear. Groaning audibly, he said, "Don't answer the door like that, Gray. What the balls?"

She closed the door, crossed her arms over her breasts, and said, "What the balls yourself, *Brad*? I didn't invite you in!"

With closed eyes, he handed her a coffee—a liquid truce—then said, "I won't look if you put some freaking pants on."

Sadie took the coffee, grabbed a handful of Brad's perfect hair, and squeezed it, holding his neck immobile. He fought her the best he could without spilling his coffee.

"I didn't do it on purpose—let go!" he barked.

A moment later, she shoved his head away and said, "One look at my butt when I walk away, and I'll come back and make sure you're wearing this hot coffee."

"I don't want to see your butt, for heaven's sake—just go."

She walked to her room, pulled on a pair of pants, and slipped into a bra and T-shirt. When she was presentable, she fashioned her hair into a ponytail and returned to the living room.

"Why don't you tell me why you're here at the ass crack of dawn without calling," she said, yawning.

"Because it's seven a.m., Gray. We're *not* on vacation, and the early bird gets the worm."

"What does that even mean?" she asked.

"It means I got a text this morning," he grinned, trying to contain his excitement. "The text included an address in Colfax."

"From who, and for what?"

"Not Miller or Ruiz," Brad said, grabbing her attention. Before Sadie could question his response, he gave her the answer. "Detective Swartz sent me a clip of the surveillance video from Reno, the 4K video Reno PD got the woman to release without a court order."

"Holy cow, why didn't you say that?" she sat up and asked.

"Because I was busy wondering why the hell I was looking at your butt," he said in his defense.

She tossed a couch cushion at him, hit his head, and spilled his coffee on his white shirt. "Are you kidding me right now?" he all but yelled.

"I said not to talk about that."

"I didn't look on purpose, for the love of God. You ruined my good shirt."

"We'll get you another."

"In this city?" he asked. "It came from Bloomingdale's."

"You bought that on your salary?" she asked.

"I bought it on credit."

"I was going to say," she commented, "this is California and we barely make enough to live over the poverty level, let alone shop at Bloomingdale's."

"What does California even consider the poverty level these days?" he asked, looking at his stained shirt.

"I think $187,000 or less per year," she joked.

He shook his head but had an amused look in his eye. "Unless you live up here."

"Where people are getting murdered by the dozen," she added. "Did you call the sheriff in either Nevada County or Placer County about the Colfax lead?"

Brad nodded. "I called the Nevada County Sheriff's Office and got a referral to Sheriff Arlo Longmire in Placer County. Longmire is coordinating with the Nevada Count Sheriff's Office; they're creating a joint task force and prepping for a raid."

The statement induced her heart rate; suddenly, she couldn't breathe. "A takedown?"

He nodded, looking like a twelve-year-old boy on Christmas morning. "Longmire is tight with a few judges and getting a search warrant issued. He promised to move quickly on this."

"What about property records, ownership status, outstanding warrants, any priors?" she asked.

Brad nodded again. "The scumbag who lives there goes by the name Brodi Bennett. Bennett owns a 1974 Dodge pickup." He opened his phone, swiped his screen several times, then said, "If he has Mickey Thompson Baja Boss M/T tires, the 35 by 13.50R 20LT F, then we have a tread match at the Grass Valley dump site."

"Tell me about this Brodi guy."

Now Brad grinned—just a bucket of good news so far. He said, "Brodi Bennett is a registered sex offender for crimes committed with minors in San Jose a few years back. While he has a history of involvement with young girls, he also has a history of violence."

"What kind of violence?" she asked, anxious to get ready and go but unable to stop the flurry of questions circling in her mind.

"He practically beat his foster grandma to death when he was sixteen. For that, he served eight months at "the Ranch," a.k.a. the William F. James Ranch for juvenile offenders. After that, he did another year at the Ranch's Aftercare program. He's been quiet so far, but Placer County code enforcement officers and two sheriff's deputies visited his home last year on a suspected cannabis ordinance violation. While he had adhered to most legal growing requirements, he had eight marijuana plants instead of six. The officers let him off with a warning but destroyed the two additional plants. To his credit, he had his papers in order."

Sadie's brain hit a few speed bumps. "So, he's a pot farmer?"

"Maybe, but maybe he's just a pothead who still does bad things. With the truck, the sex offender status, and a prior visit by county code enforcers, Sheriff Longmire said probable cause is in the bag, which is all I care about for now."

"So, what are we waiting on?" she asked. "Just the warrant, right?"

Brad nodded and said, "I want to check the tires, have a look around the house, and maybe turn this scumbag's life upside down if I see anything suspicious."

She nodded and said, "Okay, then. Give me a minute or two to get ready."

eighteen
sadie gray

WHEN SADIE WAS DRESSED and ready for the raid, she and Brad met at the Impala, popped the trunk, and checked their weapons, mags, and boxes of extra rounds. Each put on their slim, custom fit tactical vests, but they also ensured their FBI windbreakers and hats were ready to go, as they were required to wear both at any raid.

Satisfied with their gear, Brad looked at Sadie and said, "Most guys soil their drawers before the first takedown, so make sure you have a diaper change on site."

She mocked laughter and said, "Real funny, *Brad*."

"Just keeping the mood light. For real, though, some guys puke from the nerves. And one guy did pinch off a Hershey's kiss of a turd before a raid once, but we don't talk about it unless we're talking behind his back. Then we talk about him relentlessly." He smiled—that perfect, pretty smile.

"Do you ever feel like you'd be a better agent in the movies than in real life?" Sadie asked.

"No, but with this face and exceptional build, at least I have options."

"Someone is in love with themselves over there."

"Aren't you in love with yourself?" Brad asked as if baffled.

"Not in the least."

He made a sour face and said, "That seems so sad."

She shook her head, "Let's go, butthole."

They set out for Bennett's house in Colfax via state route 174, where they would wait for both Placer County and Nevada County sheriffs and deputies to arrive with the warrant.

Sadie studied Google Maps. "Bennett's place is deep in Colfax, near the Eden Valley community, just off Placer Hills Road, on Hi Pines Ranch Road." She glanced at him and said, "We could have saved a couple of miles going down Dog Bar Road."

"Not sure how you are with winding roads and car sickness, but I figure your nerves are taxed enough with the upcoming raid."

She swallowed hard and nodded, grateful that he thought of that first. "I appreciate that," she admitted.

Sadie fell into a prolonged lapse of silence. The drive to Colfax was beautiful and remote, and though she was leaving Grass Valley behind for now, she felt the nostalgia of being back in the Sierra Nevada foothills. In moments, though, they would raid the house of one of the worst serial killers in American history and certainly the most prolific in decades. With a face so warm it felt hot, and her heart beating thunderously in her chest, she took a deep breath and tried to stabilize herself.

Then Brad's phone rang; he put it on speaker. "Agent Tulle," Brad said.

"Sheriff Longmire, here."

"Go ahead, Sheriff."

"The issuing judge has the warrant now and should sign off in about fifteen minutes. Both teams are ready to roll, but it'll be about an hour or so if you want to cool your heels until then."

"Roger that," Brad nodded. "Call with a rendezvous point and a time when you're ready."

"Will do," he said.

Longmire paused momentarily, then said, "Your partner... she's the one from the press conference, right?"

Brad sneaked a look at her. "Yes, that's her."

"Is she good with a weapon?" he asked as if measuring his words but not doing well. "I trust she won't shoot herself in the foot or catch one of my deputies in the back."

Sadie leaned over and said, "I might shoot you in the foot for asking that, Sheriff Longmire."

Brad tried not to laugh as the sheriff backpedaled. Then he said, "Ask stupid questions, get stupid answers, Sheriff."

"Fair enough," he said. "We'll talk shortly."

They hung up, and Brad looked over at Sadie. "You've got some balls on you."

"They're girl balls, and they're huge."

He squeezed his eyes shut and said, "When I said go with the flow, I didn't mean let it all hang out."

"I take things literally, Bradley, or Bradford. If you want me to be a quiet mouse, say so."

He tried to relax his features. "Be a quiet mouse."

"No," she said.

They didn't speak much after that. When they got to Colfax, Brad spotted the Mi Ranchito Mexican Food restaurant and said, "Too early for lunch?" It was just after eleven a.m.

"First off, it's never too early for Mexican food, and second, is that a good idea?"

He pulled into the parking lot and said, "Yes, it's a great idea. If we take this turd and his two cohorts down, we're going to be too busy and too juiced with adrenaline to eat. We also have forty minutes to kill waiting for Longmire and his homies."

When they ordered burritos, Sadie chose the Regular Burrito while Brad ordered the Super Burrito. Brad asked if they could get a couple of Styrofoam takeout containers with their food. The cashier nodded.

When their meals arrived, Sadie saw Brad's burrito, and her eyes darn near popped out of her head. "You need two colons to hold all of that."

"Fortunately, I have three," he said, taking the first bite.

Sadie stared at him, studying the beans' appearance. "It looks good, but it also looks like the inside of a baby diaper."

"My favorite," he said, speaking with his mouth open and food stuffed inside.

She turned, frowning, and said, "And now I'm not hungry anymore."

"Eat," he said with green and white smears of guacamole and sour cream in the corners of his mouth.

Sadie ate quickly, thinking that the sooner she ate, the more time there would be between a full stomach and an armed takedown. She had finished half her burrito when Brad's phone rang.

He gulped his food down, answered the call, and said, "Agent Tulle." He listened, then nodded twice before speaking. "Okay, we're on our way."

Sadie was already packing her food in the to-go container.

The two headed out to meet the two teams at the rendezvous point a few minutes later, just off Placer Hills Road and Eden Forest Drive.

"Take a right on Manzanita Forest," Sadie said a few minutes later, pointing to an immediate right where she saw several sheriff's cars.

Brad hung the right and pulled up to the five cars, all with men gathered around, donning vests and weapons. Sheriff Longmire met them with the warrant and a brief hello as if his and Sadie's last conversation had never occurred. He refused to look at Sadie, a symptom of a woman catching a guy talking out of turn and that woman taking him to school. She didn't bother gloating because she might have won the battle but lost the war in that interaction.

Brad, however, interacted with Longmire as if nothing was wrong; the man put Brad in the loop. He said, "We'll send in drones first to clear the area and check for possible ambush points or obstructions. Placer County K9 is on loan from Auburn in case this cocksucker tries to run, and the undersheriff authorized air support if needed. He's got a flight crew for the Falcon 30 on deck, which is their quick-response aircraft, complete with GPS, a hi-definition daytime surveillance camera, multi-channel comms for all three agencies, and both night infrared imaging and NVGs for the pilots, who are trained in night flight rescue ops."

"Hot damn," Brad said, excited.

"With so much on loan, Placer County wants to run point on the raid, followed by us, then you and your partner."

Last place, Sadie thought, shaking her head.

"There's a barn adjacent to the main house," one of Placer County's men said. He extended his hand, first to Brad, then to Sadie. "I'm Captain Otis Scott, Field Operations Commander. Which of you two is the case agent?"

Brad nodded, and Captain Scott addressed him.

"If you and your partner want to take point on the barn, it'll need to be cleared. There's only one door headed in but there are second-story dormers, from the look of it."

"The barn," Sadie said before catching herself.

"Yes, Ma'am. You can clear the barn or I can have Sheriff Longmire's team clear it and you can watch my boys' sixes."

She told herself to look on the bright side of things. "I suppose it's best to take the front when your only other option is the rear," Sadie said pointedly.

Captain Scott stared at her with his sunglasses on. Sadie stared at her reflection in the mirrored lenses, unblinking. She looked good. The captain asked Sheriff Longmire, "Did this young lady just say what I thought she said? Or was I imagining that?"

Longmire tried not to laugh when he said, "It would seem the FBI has developed a sense of humor."

Captain Scott nodded once, looked at Brad, and then turned and faced her. "Make sure you stow that shit when we go operational," he said.

"Of course, Captain," Sadie replied with a straight face.

"We'll take the barn," Brad said.

"Yes, you will," Captain Scott said. "We'll kick things off. Just make sure you follow our lead."

"This isn't my first rodeo," Brad said.

"What about her?" Captain Scott asked, nodding at Sadie.

"I've been doing this since before you were even a twitch in your daddy's nut sack, Captain," Sadie said. "Don't you worry about me."

Longmire and Scott laughed, synched their comms channels, then took their teams and trotted up the road. They quietly moved onto the property, and a short time later, Scott radioed that they were in position.

Brad and Sadie were in their positions, too. They were eyes-on with the barn looming before them. They sat in silence, waiting on Captain Scott. Sadie lifted the bill of her FBI cap and swiped a forearm across her forehead. She snugged her hat, wiped her palms on her jeans, and reminded herself to relax.

When the high-altitude drone completed its sweep and made its return to the pilot, Brad leaned her way and whispered, "Weapons ready."

Sadie gripped her Glock 19, touched the extra mags on her vest with her free hand, and tried not to puke. She swallowed hard, feeling bile rising in her throat, and told herself to pull herself together. Still, she felt every acidic bite of the burrito working its way up her throat, and her face was flush.

"Shitting your pants yet?" Brad asked over his shoulder.

"Get the toilet paper ready," she mumbled.

Captain Scott's drone pilot retrieved the drone and signaled that the ops commander and Sheriff Longmire's teams were clear to move in on the house.

All men converged on the house with their weapons at the ready, most carrying rifles, some with pistols. Brad cut across the open yard, heading right for the barn. Sadie moved at his pace, kept her head on a swivel, and tuned her ears to all sounds.

Caption Scott's team reached the house with Longmire covering their sixes. Scott banged on the door and yelled, "Placer County Sheriff's Office, we have a warrant to search the premises! Open the door, or we will open it for you!"

Brad and Sadie arrived at the barn doors, which appeared to open outward based on the frame's construction. Sadie got behind Brad, her weapon at the compressed ready.

Scott's team waited all of ten seconds before the door-breaker smashed the locks on the front door and the team made entry.

Sadie considered the presentation of her weapon, as she had done so many times before in Quantico; this action, however, was live with live ammo and an unsub she had authorization to put down with lethal force should she feel her life was in imminent danger.

Lead with your gun, not your body.

Sweat trickled down her hairline at her temples; she ignored it. And while Brad joked earlier about a potential diaper change, she was much closer to throwing up than crapping in her pants, as her instructors at Hogan's Alley in Quantico had warned her and the other trainees.

The second Scott's team made entry, Sadie reached out and squeezed Brad's shoulder, letting him know she was ready. Brad filled the space with a pregnant pause, then pulled the barn door open and moved inside.

Speed, surprise, violence of action.

Brad crossed the threshold of the center-fed barn door, pushing forward into the space ahead; Sadie flowed in behind him, presented her weapon, then moved to her corner and swept inward to her point of domination.

The two successfully entered a large barn with four stalls, an open loft, and minimal lighting from above. Fortunately, they weren't dodging bullets. Unfortunately, something worse hit them: the rich, rotten smell of decay and decomposition.

"Good God," Brad breathed.

Dust motes hung in the air, and the silence was so thick it threatened to choke them both. Sadie cleared the first stall, her eyes zeroing in on the open loft above and then back to the stalls and any other offensive points before her.

The two cleared the four stalls, and then Sadie made her way up the single ladder into warmer, smellier air. Brad covered her from below because he had no choice; she was first to the ladder and moved up it with purpose.

While Sadie was unsure what to expect from the loft above, clearing it meant securing the barn, so she had to check it. She had climbed halfway up the ladder when she heard the low, constant buzzing sound. She suppressed a groan and kept moving.

The rotting smell crept into her nostrils and flooded her lungs—vapors of the dead. She paused, swallowed hard, and felt her eyeballs sizzling.

Keep moving!

Just before she reached the top of the ladder and the loft's base flooring, Sadie eased her Glock over the edge and led with the weapon, keeping her head and eyes as low to the floor as possible while sweeping right and left for potential threats.

Sunlight from the open dormer window was plentiful, showing her dozens of flies and giving her a nice, warm whiff of the dead.

"What do you have?" Brad asked when he saw her gun arm relax.

"About fifteen dead and decomposing," she called down. She shook her head, and her heart sank—*a second body dump.*

Her comms unit buzzed, startling her so badly that she almost fell off the ladder. *"Subject has been found and identified as deceased. The house is clear."*

Sadie keyed the mic and said, "Barn is clear, too, but we have a body dump."

"How many?" Captain Scott asked.

"From what I can see," Sadie replied, "fifteen deceased, at least."

"There are more down here!" Brad called from below. "They're stuffing them into the damn walls!"

Sadie keyed the mic and relayed the message to Scott.

"We're heading your way now," he replied.

Sadie climbed into the loft and verified that each body was

indeed deceased and not a potential shooter lying in wait. She did this while making as little impact on the scene as possible. The last thing she needed was the coroner barking up a storm about her mishandling of the crime scene.

"All bodies are dead bodies," Sadie called down to Brad, staring at a child with a neck broken in half. Sadness crept into her, gripping her heart and causing so many conflicting emotions that it was hard not to cry. "I'm coming down."

She spotted Brad below, weapon holstered, working hard to pull a fresh sheet of plywood off the wall. The instant he got it loose, Brad backed up fast and gasped.

"The hell?" he grumbled, holding his nose and staring in horror at what he had found.

Sadie hopped off the ladder, turned, and saw the bodies wrapped in heavy plastic sheeting. They were nailed to the false wall like mummies.

"Oh, no," she whispered.

Despite wrapping the bodies tight, the smell was crazy; a few nasty blowflies buzzed out into the open. Sadie wanted to shoot every one of those fat bastards with a force of violence she had never felt before, but that would be stupid.

Control yourself, Sadie.

Captain Scott, Sheriff Longmire, and their respective teams arrived to take over the scene, which Sadie appreciated.

"You two can head to the house," Captain Scott said, holding his nose. "We've got a K9 unit walking the surrounding property now." He turned to his men and said, "No one in here but Sheriff Longmire and me."

Longmire said to the teams, "One of my deputies is calling the Coroner's Unit, and it's our job to preserve the scene for forensics."

Everyone, including Brad and Sadie, knew the drill and didn't need further instruction.

Longmire seemed to think about something, then said, "Captain Scott, I'll leave you the scene while I take the suits to the house."

Sadie didn't appreciate being called a suit, but considering the jabs she had taken from the sheriff earlier, it was par for the course.

In the distance, along the horizon, plumes of smoke boiled into the sky. Wasn't it illegal to burn up there? Or were there controlled burn days? No matter, they crossed the property, heading to the run-down house. They entered through the front door only to be hit with a stench similar to the barn's. Worse, it looked like squatters had recently lived there.

"He's in the kitchen," Longmire said.

They entered the kitchen and saw Brodi Bennett. Someone had stripped him naked, beaten him viciously, and mounted him spread-eagle to the upper and lower kitchen cabinets. Sadie eyed the railroad spikes the killer or killers had driven through his palms and feet.

"My God," Sadie gasped. Brad fell into a respectful silence.

"Yeah," Longmire said under his breath.

Bennett's body looked like shriveled beef jerky. Aside from the abuse he wore like a suit, his mouth had shrunken to reveal a mouth full of broken teeth.

"Did they...?" Sadie asked, looking down at his waist. Brad nodded and covered his mouth.

Whoever tortured Brodi Bennett hated him enough to cut off his frank and beans. Longmire turned and looked right at Sadie. Was he wondering if she was going to puke? The odds were pretty good right then. She spoke to fill the silence and perhaps distract herself from the horror.

"Whoever killed him hated him immensely," Sadie said, noting the obvious. "We need to check on past victims of violence, do a deeper search into his family history."

"Looking for?" Longmire asked.

"Potential rape victims."

Longmire nodded and said, "We're unsealing his records now.

It seems he was an orphan who spent much of his youth in foster care before going to the Ranch."

Sadie said, "We've got a crack team if you want a second set of eyes on it."

Longmire said, "The fact that we didn't have to expense out any more manpower to serve this warrant was good enough for me. I trust you'll be headed back to Grass Valley after this?"

Brad nodded and said, "Agent Gray says there are bodies in the loft. Identifying them will help immensely."

"Of course," Longmire said. "Our coroner surrounded himself with some of the most competent people in the field of forensics, which will help immensely. We should have IDs shortly, barring any physical or political complications. Did you see if the killer mutilated any of the corpses? I'm referring to fingers, teeth, and facial structure."

Sadie shook her head. "None that I could see. And I made sure no one was playing possum and waiting to attack or shoot us when we weren't looking."

Longmire seemed to appreciate her tack.

The comms unit crackled to life, and the K9 unit said, "We've got the pickup in question. Looks like someone set it on fire."

Longmire growled, then spoke into the mic and said, "I'll call Fire and have them send a unit."

"Roger that."

"Great, there went our lead," Brad grumbled.

Sadie was already heading outside for fresh air. She put her hands over her head so as not to bend over and compress her lungs. It was a helpful tactic used to keep her from puking. Aside from inducing vomiting, bending over under that kind of stress could also bring on a wicked headache, something she didn't want or need.

Brad left the house a moment later, looking green in the face. "Well, that sucks ass through a straw."

She glanced up at him, and her eyes said it all.

He spat a couple of times in the dirt and said, "This shit show just got a lot worse."

"You want me to call it in?" she asked, referring to her contacting Blackwood.

"You're not the case agent," he said with a tone.

Sadie watched him go from green to pale as a sheet as he swallowed hard several times to keep the puke down. She watched him try not to puke; it was an admirable effort.

Finally, his color returned and he said, "I'm heading to the car for a minute. We'll wait to talk to the coroner when he arrives. I want to see if there's anything we can do here before returning to Grass Valley."

"What do you hope to find?" she asked.

He raised his hand as if telling her to hold that thought for later, then walked off, holstering his weapon and spitting a few more times.

nineteen
sadie gray

SADIE AND BRAD briefly spoke with the head of the Coroner's Unit, who was on the scene quicker than either had imagined. He met with Captain Scott, Sheriff Longmire, and both Brad and Sadie—the agency leads. While the coroner looked like he dodged a bullet, not having to work the Grass Valley crime scene, he knew he was about to take one with this scene.

The crime scene techs photographed each of them and the rest of the teams' shoe prints, then spoke to Brad and Sadie before releasing them from the scene. They hung around for a bit and spoke with Captain Scott and Sheriff Longmire, but there was nothing more to gain, so Brad called it a wrap.

Longmire stretched his back, blew his nose into a hanky, and turned to Brad. "I'll call you when we get a lead on the first set of bodies. We'll have our people on this, but since it's tied to your investigation, and you have Nevada County and GVPD on it, we'll figure out the best way for interagency cooperation here."

"Thanks," Brad said, shaking the man's hand.

Longmire extended a hand to Sadie, which she smiled and took. "Thanks for your help, Special Agent Gray."

She nodded in acknowledgment.

By the time crime scene techs brought half the bodies down from the loft, several meat wagons had arrived. First responders had used crime scene tape to define the outer perimeter, and a few local reporters and a lone podcaster stood close, hoping for a quick word or a soundbite.

Sadie photographed the small crowd, familiar with two of the faces she saw but not the unattractive blonde podcaster. Before she could say something to Brad, he made a beeline to her; she perked up when she saw him coming.

The blonde smiled at the two of them and said, "I know Special Agent Sadie Gray from the press conference, but who are you, Sir?"

Brad said, "Special Agent Brad Tulle, case agent."

"How many bodies did you find here?" she asked, recording the conversation with her Android phone.

Sadie looked her over, taking in all the details about her, and all the while wondering how a podcaster could call herself a podcaster using an old Android phone for video. The woman had terrible skin, thick but brittle-looking blonde hair, and teeth that needed some attention from a skilled dentist.

"What is your name, Ma'am?" Sadie interrupted to ask.

The woman turned and said, "Riley Sharpe with Sharpe True Crime Podcast."

"Is that your real name?" Sadie asked.

"Is Sadie Gray yours?" the woman shot back.

"How did you hear about this crime scene?" Brad asked.

"I got some of the best private investigators in the area, and we're read-in on everything going on here in Placer County and the surrounding counties. My listeners expect it, and you can only keep listeners and grow your base if you're first on the scene to one of the largest body counts in twenty years or more."

"Well, I hope you're enjoying yourself," Brad said.

Sadie opened her phone and snapped a photo of the woman, who turned away and said, "Hey, you can't do that!"

"Yet, I just did," Sadie said.

The two walked to the car, saying "No comment" to the

reporters or bystanders they passed along the way. A KCRA news van pulled up as they were climbing in the bu-car.

Brad backed out and returned to the highway, ready to be somewhere less chaotic and macabre. On his way through town, he pulled into a gas station and threw his takeout away.

"What about you?" he asked.

"As much as it might turn my stomach, I need to get paid before I start throwing away good food," she said.

He shrugged. "Suit yourself."

They headed back to GVPD and spoke with Captain Miller, apprising him of the details of the raid and their findings.

Brad then asked, "How much progress has Dr. West made?"

"She has preliminaries on several families now," Miller said. He looked a few years older than yesterday, his eyes bloodshot and yellowing. "Peters has been pestering her, though, so her open-door policy is now closed for a moment."

"Okay," Sadie said, dragging out the word.

"Detective Ruiz tried to intervene, to maybe find a way to calm those waters, but she told him her revised policy stands and she'll call if there's anything new or significant."

"Are there IDs on the new vics?" Brad asked, disappointed.

Miller said, "We're running the names through NamUS right now. But we're also setting up a phone bank with volunteers for tomorrow's press conference."

"Another one?" Sadie asked.

Miller nodded. "This case is unique in that our killers are hunting families, but for what reason or to serve what purpose, we don't know. I'm leaning on my guys and gals to develop something that ties the murders together and helps you build a suitable profile. Suits are supposed to be good profilers, so maybe you can take what you have so far and give us something to help speed this up."

Brad said, "I can promise we'll start, but with one or two families and limited information on that one family, we'll need victimology on each person or family unit, something we can use to draw some workable parallels. I'm looking for intersection points, which will hopefully provide triggers and a possible motivation for the killer."

"What do you have so far?" Miller asked. The old man's thinning hair was messy; he had heavy bags under bloodshot eyes, dry skin from too much coffee and dehydration, and cuffs he'd rolled up to his forearms. His dress shirt didn't look pressed. It looked like a day-two or maybe even a day-three shirt. As in, it was day two or three, and he was still wearing it without cleaning or pressing it.

"We know that they hated Brodi Bennett enough to chop off his dick and balls," Sadie said.

That woke up the chief in a hurry. "Really?"

She nodded and continued. "We need to get Bennett on the murder board, and by tomorrow, hopefully, we'll have victimology on one or more of the deceased from Placer County—enough to create a stronger profile on these three. We already know Bennett is a scumbag with a history of violence and sexual abuse, so we're looking for shared criminal history or maybe some shared beef."

"You're telling me the sky is blue," Miller told Sadie.

"Right now, we are, but that's our direction, not a profile," Brad said, defending her.

Miller looked at Sadie and flippantly added, "Why are *you* telling me about a profile anyway? You're brand new. Shouldn't *he* be talking while you listen and learn?"

"What's your problem with her anyway?" Brad asked, finally having her back.

He looked at her, his eyes narrowed with disdain, and said, "You and your family left a stain on this city."

"The kidnapping and subsequent events that took place in this city destroyed my family and left an indelible stain on me, Captain Miller," she fired back. "All because your predecessor and this department failed the girls and families of this town and then refused to take responsibility for it."

"You're talking out of turn," Miller said, squaring his shoulders.

Sadie stepped close to him, ignored Brad's grip on her bicep, and said, "It wasn't your fat ass sitting in that basement around bloodstains and dozens of photographs of murdered children, was it, Miller?" She gave him no time to respond. "No, you were still sitting around in your grandma's undies, jerking off to old *Rockford Files* videos, dreaming of the day when you could sit in that same chair being just as useless as Chief Davenport."

By then, Sadie saw red, her nostrils flaring like a bull's nostrils in mid-charge. She had lost control and was ready to go to blows. Meaning, her temperament sucked.

Fortunately, Miller breathed a sigh and said, "Maybe you're right. Truth be told, this situation has me pretty rattled. It's got the entire community rattled."

"As it should," Brad said, using a calmer voice. "These things snowball, though, which means it's going to get a lot worse before it gets better, and if we can't bring this to a swift and satisfying conclusion, you'll be backpedaling and wondering what you're going to do once your term is up here."

"They're going to hang us all out to dry if we don't find these monsters and bring them to justice," Miller muttered. Then, he perked up. "But that's not happening on my watch."

By now, Sadie's throbbing eyeballs and clenched fists relaxed, but she didn't take her sights off Miller.

"The town is scared now," Brad said, the voice of reason, "but when they hear about the second dumpsite, everyone with a family will shake with terror and start living on high alert. They'll demand answers when they can't take the fear anymore. My partner and I will try to give you those answers. But I can say this: whatever issues you have with Sadie, whatever it is that has a few members of this city tied up, you have to let them go and let us do our jobs."

Miller considered this, then looked at Sadie, who wasn't backing down. Finally, he nodded and said, "I'm sorry Davenport didn't have the stones to level with the people of this town and that there were so many things left unsaid. But this is my city, and you will watch your tone with me moving forward, or I'll speak with ASAC Blackwood myself and ask that he reassign you to another field office."

"Keep my family's names out of your mouth, and I will show you the respect you deserve," Sadie said.

Then, because his ego couldn't take it, Miller turned to Brad and said, "Do us all a favor and tighten her leash."

Sadie's blood pressure dipped with his apology, but now it shot north at light speed. She got in his face and said, "You'd better pray he pulls it tight enough to keep me off you if you don't learn to shut *your* mouth."

"Hey!" Brad barked, loud enough to startle them both. "I've been on serials before, and everyone gets testy, but we don't turn on each other because it's too easy to torpedo this whole case. Now, seriously, knock it off."

Cooler heads finally prevailed, and soon they gathered in front of the murder board. Sadie photographed the names and photos of the recently identified, then sent the image of Brodi Bennett's decayed, mutilated, and posed body to the man in charge of the murder board. He printed the photo and pinned it to the board within five minutes, enough to make a few of the guys hobble off, disgusted.

"Who do we call to see if NamUs produced any results?" Brad asked. "All we need is an address."

Sadie added, "Maybe the database will come up with other missing families."

Brad asked, "Has anyone seen Detective Ruiz?"

Someone said, "He's at the coroner's office. I think Dr. West called him and Peters, although maybe Peters is still persona non grata."

Sadie leaned toward Brad, saying, "Maybe we head there and say we showed up looking for Ruiz. Dr. West might not get bothered at that."

She knew being on good terms with the coroner in any murder investigation was critical to getting up-to-the-minute information. Also, the higher the body count, the testier Dr. West would become. That was human nature, too.

She took a deep breath and blew out a sigh. Were they done there yet? Regardless of her patience, Sadie had been warned that this case could break her and some of the people around her. But Dr. West wouldn't crack. She would probably just get pissed off and start reading people the riot act.

They told Miller they would check in with Ruiz; Miller was on the phone with what could be his wife. He waved them off, most likely grateful to see them go.

When they got into the Impala and headed to the coroner's office, Brad said, "I don't know what that was back there, but if you ever lunge at an LEO again—especially a police chief—I'll send your ass back to the ASAC with the recommendation to run your credentials through the nearest shredder. You got that? Because that was fucking embarrassing!"

She lowered her eyes and head, ashamed that she'd lost control. "Yeah, I got it."

"Tell me it won't happen again."

She couldn't promise that, but she could lie. "I promise it won't happen again."

Maybe.

"I can deal with many things and roll with the punches as much as the next guy, but that was embarrassing."

She sat up and fired him a look. "You already said that. And besides, you heard him."

"Everyone's been treating you like a new girl who doesn't know what you're doing. Back there, you finally acted like it."

Okay, that one shut her up. Not because it was rude but because Brad was right. "I've been playing things too loose, and I'm sorry. It won't happen again."

He struggled to compose himself, then tapped the steering wheel hard a few times and looked at her sideways. While she expected more of a fight from him, his features softened significantly. "Now that's an apology that I believe."

"For what it's worth," she said, "it was maybe one of the first genuine apologies I've ever offered as an adult."

"Please do me a favor," he said. "Before we get to the coroner's office, do something with the rest of that burrito. It's stinking up the car."

Staring at him with a smirk, she took a big bite and chewed loudly with her mouth open, looking right at him with big, unblinking eyes. He frowned, turned away, then pulled in his lips to stifle a laugh. "You know, for a block-headed pain in the butt, you might turn out all right."

Sadie smiled to herself then finished eating the burrito politely and in relative silence. Brad shook his head, unable to get through to her.

"This podcaster, Riley Sharpe, does she look inbred to you?" Brad finally asked.

Sadie coughed out bits of chewed burrito all over the dash, then looked at him and said, "I was chewing, Brad."

He chuckled like he meant to do that and said, "Seriously, though. Something's off about that lady."

"I was thinking the same thing. But you know podcasters these days—anyone can do it, and there's no barrier to entry."

"She claims to be based in Colfax, a town of, what—two thousand people?"

"Two thousand people spread throughout winding roads and endless pine trees."

"So, inbred?" Brad asked.

She shook her head and said, "I'll bet you dollars to donuts that there are several million-dollar homes for sale in Colfax right now."

"Meaning?"

"Funny as you are with your inbreeder jokes, Colfax has some wealthy residents. The same as Grass Valley or any of these other communities."

"So don't discount the lady just because she hasn't seen a bottle of shampoo, conditioner, or even moisturizer in a decade or more?"

"So judgmental," Sadie said, taking another bite of her burrito.

"Why don't you dig up everything you can on her using public records and other open-source databases?"

"And what are you going to do?" she asked.

"Run her name and the names of the identified subjects through NCIC."

"You have access to that here?" Sadie asked.

"My phone's loaded with special software that allows me to safely connect to the NCIC network. I also have secure login credentials. You'll get them one day if you ever become a case agent."

"I will."

"You realize the power I have at my fingertips with this system, right?" Brad asked, as if bragging. He turned to Sadie with his thousand-watt smile.

She feigned awe and said, "Is this where I blush and tell you how powerful you are?"

"This is *that* moment."

"You're stupid," she laughed. "You know that, right?"

Cool and without a care, he said, "Says the FNG."

"What's an FNG?" she finally asked.

"Freaking new guy," he answered with a cruel smirk.

"Only 'freaking' isn't the real word in FNG, is it?" Sadie asked.

He shook his head playfully and said, "Clean up the burrito chunks off the dash before they cement on there, will you?"

She started scraping the bits off the dash, not realizing just how tired she had become. It didn't help that she had wolfed down more than half a burrito in no time flat and that said burrito had become a veritable brick in her stomach, demanding her brain's blood to travel to her belly while making her feel *extra tired*.

She leaned her head back, closed her eyes, and sighed. "I need a hot bath and eight hours of sleep."

"You'll get one but not the other," Brad said. Sadie opened her eyes and glanced at him sideways. He smirked. "Nice visual, by the way."

Without warning, she punched him in the arm, which had him reeling. "Hurt?" she asked. "Because that was my left hand. My *weak* hand."

"Not at all," he lied, using a strained voice. Rubbing his arm where she hit him, and still wincing, he added, "Okay, maybe a little."

twenty
the passenger

EARLIER...

The minute Jake rode his motorcycle to the second dumpsite, he saw a sheriff's deputy pull into Eden Forest Drive, elevating his heart rate. He passed another on Placer Hills Road, which caused that increased heart rate to double. He and his family had finally gotten around to taking care of the rest of the bodies, and now this?

He turned around on Ruf Road, rode back, and took a left on Eden Forest Drive. To the right, along Manzanita Forest Drive, he glimpsed a gathering of deputy's cars and an unmarked black sedan—a Chevy Impala.

He continued on Eden Forest to Ruf Road, hung a left, and then another left. He maintained an even throttle because noise echoed, and he didn't want to alert law enforcement to his presence. But when he reached Placer Hills Drive, he made another left, cruised past Eden Forest, and took a right onto Hi Pines Ranch Road, throttling up a little harder.

When he reached the house, he cruised onto the property, and immediately spotted the rust-colored Dodge that they took for themselves and had belonged to the dead homeowner. It was parked halfway in the barn. But the truck was not his chief concern, the cops were. How had they found them so quickly? Mania rose in him and his first thoughts were that they had to ditch the truck and leave the property *now*. He parked his bike in front of the barn and hurried inside. The ingrate David and their sister were nailing the final sheet of plywood to the makeshift walls.

"We gotta go," Jake said. "Five-0's up the street, getting ready to raid us."

"Are you sure?" his sister asked, her messy blonde hair and old clothing perfect for this kind of crap work.

Jake nodded.

"I'll take you on the bike," he said. "David, drive the Dodge into the trees in back, set it on fire, and meet us the next street over, where it dead ends. We'll get the other car and pick you up after dark."

"They got dogs?" his sister asked.

Jake shrugged, saying, "How the hell should I know?"

"You saw 'em, Jake," she barked. "Not me or the moron."

"I ain't no moron," David said. His hair was extra wild, with crazy eyes to match and a mouth fixed into a scowl.

"If you hear dogs coming for you, call us and change your position," Jake said. David looked scared.

"You smart enough for that, moron?" his sister asked.

"Ain't no moron," he growled.

"Then prove it to us tonight," she said. "Let's go, Jake."

His sister gathered any small tools containing their fingerprints, stuffed them into Jake's bike's saddlebags, and then told the moron to get the rest and put them into the truck bed. Then she said, "Be sure to wipe down the truck before you burn it. They can still take prints, even if it's caught fire."

"How's that?" David asked.

"How do I explain rocket science to someone like you?" she all but yelled, the pressure getting to her. "I saw it on TV, so just do it!"

She hopped on the bike behind Jake, then turned one last time and saw David grabbing a nearby rag. She patted Jake's shoulder and said, "Go."

They raced off in time to avoid being seen by the law. Hopefully, David would get far enough from the house and deep enough into the woods to set the truck on fire and escape.

When they reached Placer Hills Road, she tapped Jake on the shoulder and said, "I want to know about these guys, who they are, and how they found us."

"Don't you listen to your podcast?" Jake asked.

"'Course I do," she said.

"Then you know a couple of them, and *her*."

"That bitch?" she asked.

Jake felt her tension rise enough to ask, "Is it the same Sadie Gray as before?"

His sister was quiet enough for him to think she didn't hear him or was formulating an answer. Finally, she said, "I was thinking 'bout that, but what are the chances she'd be back?"

Jake shrugged. "Not great, but you saw the press conference, right?"

"No."

"I did, and I'm pretty sure she's the one."

She lapsed into silence, the miles passing by without a word. Finally, she leaned in and said, "If she is... if that's *her*..."

"I know," he said after she couldn't finish.

"You *don't* know!" she roared, causing him to flinch.

"I was there, too, so shut yer friggin' pie hole about how I don't know," he said. "I know what you know!"

"Yeah, but you didn't see her in the basement when we was kids—*I did*."

Maybe she was right about Sadie Gray. That meant the killing would continue. "If she's a bad person—" Jake started to say.

"She is!"

"I think it's her, but if it's not *that* Sadie Gray, we should know," Jake said. "First, we need to get the car." On a straightaway, Jake turned to look at her, to see if she was sane; she appeared normal but sounded like a lunatic. "You sure it's smart to go after a fed?"

Jake faced forward but watched her in the side mirror. His younger sister stared straight ahead, the cords in her neck taut, the vein in her forehead as thick as a worm and pulsing. She turned her eyes to the mirror, locked onto his gaze, and said, "We did that kill and stole that car a long time ago. We'll switch the plates after we pick up the moron. But for now, picking up his dumb ass is priority number one. Because if he gets to talking, you know that knucklehead's gonna spill it all."

Jake wanted to go, rip out of there, race home and grab the car and just keep on going. He cherished his safety and anonymity, but he feared his sister was out of control.

When he backed off the throttle, his sister said, "I know you're scared, Jake, but they're onto us now, and that changes everything."

"How so?" he asked.

"We gotta be careful, but maybe we gotta stack the deck in our favor, too."

"If you're thinking what I think—"

"You're darn right I'm thinking that, and you're thinking it, too. After what that thankless turd did to our family…"

"We can't kill her," he said. "She's a fed."

His sister laughed and said, "You wanna bet?"

There was nothing left to say—his sister had officially lost it. While Jake disagreed with her impulsiveness, considering their enemy, part of her was right: if the Feds caught David, he would tell them everything. After all, the kid only had two brain cells and both were fighting for third place.

When they reached the house, Jake and his sister went out to the garage, opened the door, and waved away the dust. Something skittered along the floor. Jake tried to stomp it, but it got away. His sister jerked the old canvas off the somewhat rusted AMC Gremlin, which was painted royal blue with a pair of faded white stripes. The car was old, full of cobwebs, and the paint had faded badly. Jake then watched his sister walk around the car and kick all four tires.

"All good," she said.

Jake climbed into the butt-ugly beater, found the keys, and tried to start it. The inline six started with a wheeze, a cough, and a sputter. But when the engine finally caught, it roared to life, clouds of dust and fumes from the lone exhaust pipe boiling into the back of the garage and stirring up everything that had long ago settled.

A rat, nearly the size of a possum, scurried out in front of his sister: she kicked the thing as hard as she could, sending the disgusting varmint rolling out of the garage.

"Son of a bitch, did you see that?" she exclaimed.

"Let's go," Jake barked.

His sister climbed inside the Gremlin, buckled up, and nodded. Jake backed up, whipped the front end of the Gremlin around, switched gears, and got on it. He buried the accelerator as he shot from the gravel driveway onto an asphalt road. The jolt and squeal of the tires reminded his sister that, as ugly as Gremlins were, they had a fair amount of giddy-up, like a dog-ugly broad who could do sex like a pro.

When they found David, he was breathless and hysterical, hidden in a ravine with weeds and loose soil pulled over him.

"What the heck took you so long?" he asked. "They had a smelling eye dog or something out there."

"Probably looking for cadavers," his sister said. "Besides, if they were hunting for you, they'd need your scent to track you. But if the dog smelled the *actual* you, he'd need a cadaver dog to find him."

"I don't know," David said, ignoring the jab. "All that barking made me think they were tracking me on the smell of my fear, 'cause I was scared."

"I told you we'd come back for you."

"Yeah, but—"

"'Yeah but' ain't a word, fartknocker," she said.

"Leave him alone," Jake said.

She fixed him with a glare and said, "He almost panicked."

"But he didn't."

Narrowing her eyes and clenching her jaw, she pulled her head from side to side, popping her neck, then zeroed in on David. "Momma shoulda aborted you, you know that?" she said.

David looked at her with sad eyes that Jake could see in the darkness; the kid was just scared and feeling abandoned. And she was making it worse. Jake glared at her with hostility, but she returned his gaze with eyes as cold and dead as those she reserved for David.

"You got something to say to me, dummy number one?" she asked.

He punched the side of her face so hard that her head bounced off the window, spider-webbing the old glass. Instead of crying out, she cupped her cheek and then turned her hateful eyes on him.

"Broads oughta know when to shut their mouths," Jake grumbled.

Behind them, David snickered, and it was like a little girl's giggle. She turned her entire body to look at him over the seatback.

"Say one word," Jake snarled at her. "I fucking dare you."

She straightened her body, leaned against the window, and held her face. They drove the rest of the way home silently, which Jake appreciated. He had put in a long day at work, trying to help people twice as dumb as his degenerate family but just as belligerent. Being a decent human at work helped him focus on the day's problems, doing his best to save one kid, one good man or woman, and one struggling family at a time. While he had to listen to their nonsensical ramblings at work without hitting them or bashing in their faces, he could at least hit his sister and tell her to shut the hell up because she needed to, and because he sometimes wanted to kill her the way she always wanted to kill David.

twenty-one
riley sharpe

AS SOON AS Riley played the podcast's opening, she sat back and listened to her work, liking what she heard enough to consider this particular show a point of pride. In the last couple of days, with some advertising money, some good word of mouth, and her growing population of listeners, she had doubled her listenership to nearly two thousand people. Closing her eyes, she listened to her voice and imagined how others would hear her.

Riley's recorded voice said, "The second body dump was no less impressive than the first. The scene of this crime struck me as morbid and eerie, like something out of one of those '80's horror films. It was like when you were young and watching the *Texas Chainsaw Massacre* for the first time. We're talking about a level-10 ick. Anyway, sheriff's deputies, K9 dogs, and even the FBI scoured the scene, moving from the house to the barn and calculating the dead.

"I can't give you an accurate body count as of this hour, but I can tell you that law enforcement has never been so on their heels. Even the FBI is on the scene. In a brief interview with Special Agent Brad Tulle and his partner, the younger, beautiful Sadie Gray, I can say they were out of sorts. Dealing with serial killers, terrorists, rapists, kidnappers, and human traffickers, you'd think these two supposed professionals were more organized, but they looked to me like they'd seen a hundred ghosts at once and didn't know what to do with it.

"When I leaned on an excellent bevy of local law enforcement sources, I learned that the owner of the home—a person of interest—was long dead, laid out spread-eagle, and nailed to the kitchen cabinets. Sources say he was stripped as naked as the day he was born, minus three very important parts."

During the recording, she had paused for effect. Now, hearing this very pregnant pause, Riley sat back in her chair and grinned.

This is such good podcasting.

"From what I'm told, he was missing his banana and bro globes. He's got a man taco now, and that thing is reportedly more rotten than its owner. We're talking about a Broadway Street snatch after a sweltering, abusive weekend. Someone hated him enough to defile him, crucify him, change his gender, and leave him for dead.

"Ladies and germs, we're not dealing with a serial killer here; we're dealing with a sadistic monster who gets off on brutalizing his victims. Never fear, though! The LEOs are hot on his trail and closing in fast. Earlier today, these same LEOs—law enforcement officers for the laymen and laywomen—received an APB on a 1974 Dodge Truck with a crew cab, oversized tires, and rust-colored paint. They found the truck burning a quarter-mile from the second dumpsite. Forensics teams are on the scene now, pulling corpses out of the barn by the dozen and hoping to catch this animal before he bashes in the faces of any more innocent families."

Riley stood and went to the bathroom, checked her teeth, which weren't in great shape, and then fixed her blonde hair, which wasn't great either. For years she promised herself it wouldn't always be like this; now, a better future for her was in reach.

She studied her reflection and said, "You're going to be a different person when you hit ten thousand listeners. And after that, when you reach a hundred thousand listeners, we're getting a blowout, some silicon to fill these saggy titties, and enough glycolic peels to smooth out this asphalt-textured face."

She held her dead eyes unblinking and felt herself aching to come back to life.

"You're gonna be someone that halfway decent men want to take advantage of, and you're gonna let 'em because you deserve it."

She let her head fall back on her shoulders and blew out an exalted sigh, dreaming big dreams of tattooed men ravaging her and making her feel like a desired woman, not something discarded so long ago. If she wanted a chance at life, she knew she had to stop being her real self, something she's been doing for a while now. So far, it was working out well.

When she finished in the mirror, she pulled her underwear aside, hovered over the toilet, and pissed. It was unladylike in every aspect, but if guys could do it, she could do it better. But when she turned to flush, one of her magnetic eyelashes fell off into the urine.

She shook her head and yelled, "Of all days!"

She kneeled, pulled the spider-leg-looking lash out, dried it with toilet paper, and tried to stick it back on her lid. When that didn't work, she licked the strip, dried it, then licked it again and stuck it on. For a moment, it hung there, looking like it would surely drop, but it didn't. Satisfied, she returned to the studio, plopped into her seat, and listened to more of the new podcast, ready to post it as soon as she finished.

"As always, the more we know, the more you'll know, but understand this: we're on the precipice of a new brand of killer, someone or something with a thirst for murder, and they crossed the line when they killed kids. But it's not just the kids. This bloodthirsty maniac killed women, too—a no-no—*and* men. Why the men, though? Why slaughter an entire family? We may never know, but we might also know tomorrow, which is why you need to never miss a show. Be sure to listen to an all-new podcast tomorrow, straight from the crime scene.

"You've been listening to the Riley Sharpe True Crime Podcast with your host, Riley Sharpe. Also, be sure to refer us to a friend, family member, or co-worker if you've got a job. Because if the criminals aren't sleeping, then neither are we. When the story breaks, tune in here and get the dirty, gritty deets from head to toe. I'm Riley Sharpe, signing off for now."

twenty-two
sadie gray

BRAD SENT Sadie a few texts here and there, letting her know what work he was doing with the locals. At that point, they needed to pry something loose, find a thread to pull—*anything*. While she didn't have enough experience to draw up a profile on the killers, shouldn't she at least try? Wasn't that going to be her job one day? To catch the worst of the worst using tools the FBI provided in order to construct a profile she and law enforcement could use?

She had listened to the Riley Sharpe True Crime podcast and suddenly felt a million times smarter than the host. Shaking her head, Sadie could hardly believe some people were trying to do what law enforcement professionals already did a bazillion times better.

"Everyone's got a dream they'll never see," Sadie muttered, "and Riley Sharpe, I hate to say it, but your garbage podcast might've just peaked."

Then again, law enforcement solved many crimes with the help of a fierce and determined public, so who was she to judge?

Rather than focus on things that didn't matter, Sadie studied the information Dr. West provided about the first family, hoping to draw parallels between them and Brodi Bennett. She was anxious to get into the NCIC report on the man, but then her phone rang, drawing her out of her trance.

"Yeah," she said when she saw who was calling.

Brad said, "The Placer County coroner unit sent prelims on the freshest body from the Colfax dumpsite. The good news is that we have an ID."

"On just one victim?" she asked.

"One victim, who is part of a family," he said. "The first family has been on the table since we left. That's one thing. The other is that I'm sending you a copy of the NCIC report I pulled on Brodi Bennett. Oh, and I'll pick you up in half an hour for a late breakfast."

"Breakfast?" she asked. She didn't usually eat breakfast.

"Yes, breakfast." When she didn't respond immediately, he said, "It's part of our per diem pay, Sadie. We're going to breakfast."

"Yeah, okay, sure," she said. "Where are you thinking?"

"Lumberjack's is supposed to be good."

"Who said that?" she asked.

"Your friend, the cold case lady, said to stay away from The Chainsaw sandwich. Actually, she said to avoid it at all costs if it's still on the menu."

"That bad?"

"On the contrary, she said it is deceptively good, but they don't call it The Chainsaw because it goes down smoothly or comes out without incident."

"Sergeant May said this?" Sadie asked.

"Yeah, what's with you two anyway? Aside from some kind of shared past, I guess."

"I asked her to help me find my mother a few years ago, but she was also on the case to find and save me as a kid."

"And did she?" Brad asked.

"Yeah, I lived."

"I didn't mean it like that, ding dong. I meant, was she the one who saved you?"

Sadie thought about it and chuckled to herself, recalling pieces of a story she had largely blocked from her memory. Now, she saw the humor in it.

"What's so funny?" he asked.

"Nothing," she lied, recalling Teresa's most recent recounting of the day Sadie almost died. If she wasn't mistaken, The Chainsaw sandwich played a pivotal role in how the day's events unfolded.

"Truthfully, I don't care," Brad said, "so don't tell me later."

Her jaw dropped. "Okay, butthole, I won't."

"Why are you the way you are, Agent Gray?" he asked.

"Nurture and nature," she answered, surprised by the question. "I'm ready when you are, Special Needs Agent Tulle."

He chuckled and said, "Cute."

"And sexy, but you don't need to say it," she teased. "I can tell by how you look at me that you see it already, and that's enough."

"Have you heard the song, California Dreaming?"

She chuckled and said, "I'll be ready if you'd let me get off the phone and shower."

"So pushy..."

"Just don't make a girl wait."

He paused momentarily, breathing into the phone, but not like a perv, and then he said, "I like you like this."

"Like what?" she grinned.

"Relaxed."

She kind of liked herself like this, too, which wasn't normal. But she was only being lighthearted and fun for now, because the second they were back in the field, she knew she would feel like they were wading through the deepest mires of someone else's version of Hell on Earth.

"I'm relaxed for now," she said.

"But you're bringing a change of diapers for later?"

She grinned to herself. "I think that was a one- or two-time thing."

"It is until it isn't," he said.

"What does that mean?"

"Don't you have to shower or something?"

"Yeah," she said. "Oh, Brad?"

"Uh-huh?"

Sadie immediately pressed the END button on her phone and laughed like a twelve-year-old. She wasn't exactly having fun being back in Grass Valley, working on such a gruesome case, or dealing with all the masculine Joes, but Brad was growing on her, and he wasn't half bad. She felt like maybe she could relax around him and that he might make a great partner.

As she ran a quick shower, she thought about the aspects of the job, how she might like it, how she loved the bump in her earnings from the last job, and how she might actually have a brush with fame if this serial killer case ever hit Netflix or HBO. Then again, everything hinged on them catching the three psychopaths.

Standing in front of the fogged mirror, wrapped in a towel, she reached out and swiped the one-way glass, catching a glimpse of her reflection. "This is how you make something of your life, Sadie Gray." She said that, but then she frowned.

Sadie never took this job to be famous or cling to her fifteen minutes of fame; families were dying en masse, left for dead, and desecrated. Three people were violently assaulting families and breaking children's necks—two generations of people who could make their marks in the world but would no longer impact anyone's future because of filth like these three.

When she looked at it that way, she no longer felt the light-heartedness of earlier. She might have even lost her appetite.

She fought to shake the heavy fog that settled over her, but when she thought of the photos of the thirty-four bodies in the floor and those in the barn in Colfax, she nearly buckled under the weight of sadness and responsibility. These were real people living real lives, with hopes and dreams like everyone else. And they were gone. Just erased.

Tears boiled in her eyes, and she wavered under a rush of dizziness followed by nausea. Before she knew it, she dropped to her knees before the toilet and vomited whatever remained in her system of yesterday's burrito. Her eyes dripped throw-up tears, her nose drained snot, and when finished, she spat about a dozen times to clear her mouth. She had just managed to stand and flush the toilet when the knock on her front door startled her.

Groaning, she quickly fixed her hair and mumbled, "That was quick."

Sadie grabbed her vest and gear and headed to the front door. When she opened it, she didn't see her partner. Instead, she looked down and saw what appeared to be a small, shriveled banana and an oversized walnut sack.

Her brain skipped gears momentarily, but then she gasped, backed up, and froze. Finally, she snapped out of her trance, slammed the front door, and squeezed her eyelids shut.

"Out of sight, out of mind," she whispered frantically. "Out of sight, out of mind."

But out of sight was *not* out of mind, and closing the door on what she suspected were Brodi Bennett's chopped-off genitals did not make the gravity of the situation any better. Instead, she gathered her courage, drew her weapon, and opened the door. With a round chambered and her Glock at the low ready, Sadie searched the trees and nearby brush around the Airbnb for any signs of the person or people who put them there.

A moment later, Brad arrived—jovial Brad with a big appetite and maybe his own dreams of Netflix stardom. However, when he saw her, his looks changed, and he scrambled to get out of the car.

"What's wrong?" he asked, worried.

"Our killers just left me a gift."

He drew his weapon and walked cautiously toward her, scanning the area before reaching the porch. He didn't go onto the wooden stoop. Instead, he glanced down and took a moment to process the sight.

Finally, he met her gaze, horrified. "That's a piss-pipe 'n giblets, right?"

"The beef jerky version of it, yes."

Brad paced for a long second, weapon still drawn, then stopped when he realized he could be trampling over footprints.

"That has to be Brodi Bennett's junk," he said, more to himself than her.

Sadie nodded and said, "Other vics were castrated. Meaning, we already have a 'vics without dicks' problem."

"I'll call it in," he said, shaking his head in disgust. "Don't contaminate the scene any worse than I did now."

"Yeah, okay," she said.

"How'd they know where you're staying?"

"It's a small town," Sadie said, the repercussions of this act striking home.

"You need to change Airbnbs," he said.

"I'm not letting these clowns run me off. It's time to fight back, Brad. Because they're out there, killing families and taunting us, and now they're trying to make it personal."

"This makes it pretty freaking personal, Sadie."

She stilled herself against the fear and anger, then said, "This means justified homicide when I fear for my life." For a moment, she sounded just like her father.

Brad stared at her as if lost and unsure how to take her. Maybe Sadie's father was right when he said there were times when bad people needed to die. Her father, a former contractor for the government, had strong opinions about killers and terrorists, which she never blamed him for. Now that she was dealing with a formidable menace of her own, she wondered if her father was right—that she would see his wisdom and come to believe it.

That begged the question: Given the chance, would she put them down with extreme prejudice? Was that a blessing for the living? Or was this "gift to society" nothing more than cold-blooded murder with a fancy excuse? One thing was sure: she was going to find out, and so were they.

twenty-three
sadie gray

BRAD SAID that Chief Miller was shocked at the reason for his call and the implied threat to Sadie—whatever the threat may be. So far, not even Sadie knew what it meant.

"One of Miller's forensics guys is on his way here, to the Airbnb," Brad said.

"Thanks," she whispered.

Sadie sat on the couch with her gear, feeling like a little girl playing in a grown-up world, not the big, badass, ferocious FBI agent she wanted to portray. The word "coward" came to mind. But "fraudster" seemed to be a better descriptor.

When Miller's forensics nerd arrived, he cordoned off the porch, photographed everything, and studied the dirt in front of the porch and around the house for shoe prints or other trace evidence. After the tech photographed the soles of their shoes to exclude them, he said they were all good and he'd finish up shortly.

Brad and Sadie thanked him and then headed to GVPD to meet with Miller and Detectives Ruiz and Peter's task force. Law enforcement filled the conference room to near capacity. They entered the warm, humid, wide-open space, and it was buzzing with the electric chatter of a motivated group.

Chief Miller saw the two and waved them over to the murder

board, which had doubled in size and data. They now had more names placed next to the grid of victim's photos. Sadie watched Brad absorb the information, wondering what he was thinking and how he processed the information. Did he consider it a puzzle of emotions? Unspoken motivations? A lost childhood with good or bad parents or potential signs of trauma? Or did he see it as she did: the sadness of families gone, wiped off the earth by a pack of monsters?

Miller cleared his throat to get everyone's attention. Then, to Sadie's surprise, the chief briefed the task force about the "meat and potatoes" incident at the Airbnb, which caused one of the other officers to raise his hand.

"What, Garcia?" Miller asked.

Officer Garcia stood and said, "Maybe I'm speaking out of line, but I think Peters should be in charge of the 'frank and beans' incident."

The others laughed under their breaths—even Sadie tried not to laugh—but Miller smacked the murder board with the flat of his hand and said, "That's not funny!"

Everyone fell silent, and Peters shook his head.

Ruiz said, "It was kind of funny, Chief. You see, peters references—"

Miller turned and fired Ruiz a look that could have almost decapitated the man. He fell silent in a flash, his mouth open to speak but unable to find the right words. Ruiz finally closed his mouth, his sentence unfinished.

Miller turned and glared at them all, incensed, his eyeballs slightly less hot than the sun and a degree or two shy of bursting into flames. He finally wiped his slash of a mouth and said, "This guy or girl, or whatever—maybe all three of them—had a deep enough issue with Brodi Bennett to cut off his junk and turn him into a crucified version of DaVinci's Vitruvian Man." He turned to Sadie, the movement so fast you'd need slow-motion cameras to catch it. Sadie nearly flinched, which seemed to please Miller. "And now Bennett's junk ends up on the front porch of *your* Airbnb? Do these three have personal issues with you, too?"

"Yeah, why not Special Agent Tulle?" Peters asked.

Brad said, "I'm at the Best Western Gold Country Inn, which is far more exposed than my partner's Airbnb. Special Agent Gray wasn't supposed to speak at the press conference but got pushed into it, which exposed her to the masses." He glared at Miller. "I wouldn't have done that, but you thought that little dagger in the back would be cute—it wasn't. So, perhaps the killers saw her on TV when they should have seen me."

"Would you have liked to have the dick and balls?" Garcia asked. Everyone burst into laughter, and Miller didn't tell Garcia to be quiet this time.

"Actually, yes," Brad said, catching everyone off guard, including Sadie. "I was going to give it to you to show you what man-sized parts looked like."

"I know what they look like," Garcia said with mild amusement. A bit of heat stole into his cheeks.

Brad said, "I know you're small in stature, and your neck is really thin, but your frank and beans are still supposed to grow after birth, not stay the same size. It might be a bit confusing, something someone should have explained to you—"

Garcia shot out of his chair when everyone started laughing. Brad took a step forward and said, "Keep doing chair squats like that, Garcia, and maybe you'll generate enough testosterone to put some hair on those little baby nuts."

In Miller's defense, when everyone started laughing at Garcia, he never stepped in to stop the commotion; he merely let it continue.

Sadie bristled when Brad and Garcia locked eyes in the mother of all stare-downs. The conference room fell almost to a hush as if the confrontation was about to go physical. Then, Garcia's face broke into a broad smile, and he barked out a laugh.

"You know, for Feds, you're not half bad," Garcia said. He walked up to Brad and knuckle-bumped his fist, the two smiling.

Sadie wondered if that was male bonding or an alpha test. She shook her head, not understanding it at all.

"Maybe you should get a room next to your partner, Special Agent Gray," Miller said, no longer prickling.

Brad said, "The Best Western is undergoing major renovations now and is at full capacity. When given the choice of accommodations, Special Agent Gray chose the Airbnb."

"Is it wise staying there now?" one of the deputies—a woman with a tight bun, sloped shoulders, and an ample bosom—asked. She was sitting next to Garcia.

Sadie straightened her back, squared her shoulders, and lifted her chin. "I'm not going to be run out of my place because of a stack of meat that's supposed to be a threat. Besides, if they found me at my Airbnb, they'll find me elsewhere. This city isn't huge, we're no strangers to the media, and whatever beef they have with me—no pun intended—will draw them out a little quicker."

"What issue could they possibly have with you?" Miller asked.

"Maybe it was the press conference."

"She's not exactly ugly, Chief Miller," another officer said. "It could be that one of them is fixated on her. You know...good-looking *and* a Fed? It could be a love/hate fascination."

Miller gave the statement its due consideration before responding. "Yeah, maybe, but I'm not buying it." He returned his attention to Sadie, fixed her with a stare, and paused to the point of discomfort.

While Sadie remembered much of what she experienced as a child, she had also blocked out the bad parts, which wasn't hard considering she went from living a somewhat normal life to having no family virtually overnight. She swallowed over a massive lump in her throat at the thought of losing her father, mother, and sister in such a short amount of time.

"I have a history here," she said too quietly.

"Yeah, no kidding," Miller said.

Before fourteen-year-old Sadie Gray had a chance to process the fallout from her father's actions and subsequent arrest, she lost her mother and sister and was put into foster care to live with people who saw her more as a paycheck than a human being.

As a child, a survivor, and the product of a broken home, she was put into the system and shuffled from foster home to foster home. At first, several of her host parents deemed her incorrigible, eventually causing her to shut down emotionally. Subsequent families described her as vacant during the days, an empty child. But at night, they couldn't take the screaming, the constant nightmares, or the violent thrashing when they tried to wake her.

When she was seventeen, she was finally able to purge her mind of much of the lingering fear and vicious memories, but she did that by mentally throwing a black blanket over them and pretending they didn't exist. But they did. And though she wanted them gone, they were still there, somewhere in the darkness, lying dormant. Did she want to pull them up, shine a light on them again, look at every angle? No. *Hell no.* But there she was, searching for the memories, trying to pull them into the forefront of her mind, if only to see if they held clues to this disgusting warning and why they targeted her. Unfortunately, her mind was insufferably blank in most places.

"Look at her," someone whispered. "She just disappeared from her body. Like, the lights are on but no one's home."

Another officer laughed, but it was an uncomfortable laugh. Sadie's vapid gaze shifted ever so slightly, her eyes landing on him, unblinking. His eyelids shot open, his nostrils flared, and he shrunk back, unsure of what he was seeing.

Finally, Sadie cleared her throat and said, "Maybe they think they can intimidate me more than my partner, me being a woman." Everyone was staring at her in her silence. "They can't."

"If the media gets wind of this, they'll dig into your past here —they might even say things like 'conflict of interest,' or things like that," one of the officers in the back said.

"That's patently absurd," Brad said.

"The Feds already have such a bad rap," Detective Peters shot back.

"You're riding my last nerve, Ezra," Miller hissed. The room fell silent. Miller blew out a sigh and paced the room. "What's the connection, Special Agent Gray? Paint us a picture of the dead and give us some insight about where we look. That's why you and Agent Tulle are here, right? To craft a profile?"

"I'm the case agent here, Chief Miller," Brad reminded him.

"You didn't get the hot links on your porch, though, did you, Agent Tulle?" Miller challenged. He looked over at Sadie. "We're listening, Agent Gray."

Does he want me to come up with a profile right now? In front of everyone?

Brad mean-mugged her in his own way, hot under the collar but quiet, as if he was angry but just as keen as everyone else to hear what she had to say. The only problem, Sadie knew, was he would use everything she said wrong against her.

She swallowed, stilled her nerves, and said, "These people have an issue with families, which means they likely have a family history that mirrors behaviors they see in their victims. We're looking for three people with a shared history of abuse. Their story will likely fit a pattern of violence, but not like we see here. This pattern suggests repressed anger with sociopathic, maybe even psychopathic tendencies.

"So far, from what we can see, the fathers are savagely beaten to death, which can't feel great, while the women are stabbed viciously in the throat. It would take the women less than two minutes to die—quicker if the injuries persisted. We're possibly looking at a pattern of rape or molestation in their youth, with mothers who saw what their horrible fathers were doing but couldn't or wouldn't stop it. That's why the women have their eyes cut out.

"As for the children, their necks are broken, which means the killers want them dead quickly, maybe even painlessly. Is this a mercy killing? Do the killers think they're saving the children from a future similar to theirs? This measure of killing will likely correspond with Dr. West's findings, who I believe will end up searching for evidence of bad families with innocent, abused children.

"So, in summary, our three unsubs are likely victims of abuse, innocent kids who suffered at the hands of violent parents and grew up to live awful, unproductive lives. They couldn't stop their abuse in real life, so now they're stopping the abuse and its effects for other, similar kids."

"Is this vigilante justice?" Garcia asked.

"To them, maybe," Sadie said.

"Why take the women's eyes?" the woman with the tight bun asked. "Sorry, but what did you say the reason was again?"

Was she even paying attention?

"Because they saw the abuse and didn't do anything about it," Sadie answered, the pieces of the puzzle starting to come together in her mind. "The eyes are punished. It's symbolism."

Detective Ruiz said, "Dr. West said the killer bashes in the men's faces and breaks the kids' necks. Not just in this case, but in most—if not all—of them so far."

Peters said, "The woman's body Dr. West is working on now... the killer bashed her face in, too, using the bundle of locks or whatever's doing all the damage to their faces."

"Men and women?" Sadie asked.

Peters nodded. "Dr. West is certain the blunt force trauma is consistently coming from heavy locks—padlocks and combination locks, likely swung by someone with incredible strength while caught up in a frenzy."

"Some locks are square, others are round," Ruiz said.

"Bike locks and padlocks," Sadie said out loud, thinking about it. She wasn't sure of the connection unless that was just the killer's weapon of choice. She looked at Ruiz and Peters. "How many locks are we talking about?"

"We don't have an exact amount, but evidence suggests multiple locks, like a stack of them, maybe? Or perhaps they're bundled on the end of a rope—tied together like some mass of weighted steel that can do tremendous damage."

"Can anyone see any significance to that?" Miller asked Sadie, then Brad. Sadie shrugged and looked at Brad.

Brad said, "It could be something the unsub used as a kid, or maybe it was something they were beaten with. If there's some significance, we're unaware of it right now without knowing their family history."

Miller looked at Sadie, who indicated her agreement with a nod.

"So, we have three people who kill families that I'm assuming have an abuser, and what...?" Miller asked.

"A wife who sees their husband abusing their children but does nothing to save them," Sadie said again.

"Are *all* the children's necks broken?" the tight-bun lady asked Ruiz.

Detective Ruiz nodded and said, "So far, yes. Dr. West and the deputy coroner have now autopsied five children, and there is no other visible trauma so far. Well, not from the killers. They'll pull medical records shortly, so we'll be able to see if there is a consistent pattern or history of abuse, physical and sexual."

Sadie's mind fell into a rhythm of understanding. "But the kids had old scars, broken bones that didn't heal right, and other, more minor indications of trauma, right?"

Detectives Ruiz and Peters shrugged; Miller watched them both and breathed a heavy sigh. If they were getting somewhere, Sadie didn't feel better. Crafting a profile on these three felt like crawling into a dark hole rather than out of one.

"That could be the thread that connects them all," Sadie said. "They're families enmeshed with abuse. We should find out if it's physical or sexual. It will help clarify their pasts, which might give us clues to the present. That could be what the dick and balls are telling us. Or it could be nothing, just psychos messing with me because I'm a woman."

"Dysfunctional families feels right," Brad announced, as if it made sense.

"Every family is dysfunctional," Ruiz challenged.

"My parents were saints, Detective Ruiz," Brad said flippantly.

One of the other officers muttered, "The Ken doll finally outs himself." Miller shut the man down and Brad ignored the slight.

"What cities are the identified vics from?" Sadie asked.

The murder board had colored tacks pressed into a paper map; Sadie studied them from a distance but would look for patterns there when she could take a closer look.

"Four cities, all a hundred miles apart," Ruiz said.

"Were the families targeted from some sort of database?" Sadie asked, testing a theory that made sense to her. Brad was already nodding.

"Ruiz and I thought the same thing," Peters said.

For Sadie, solving the crime was trying to complete a puzzle where you didn't know how large it was or how many pieces it contained. Hell, she didn't even know where the missing pieces were hiding. They were finding them slowly but surely, and a clear picture was forming.

An idea occurred to Sadie, who suddenly spoke up. "Do you or any of your agencies have access to welfare databases used by CPS or state social services?"

Ruiz's eyes cleared, and he said, "Yeah, SACWIS and its replacement, CCWIS."

"Which is?" Officer Tight-Bun asked.

"Statewide Automated Child Welfare Information System and Comprehensive Child Welfare Information System," Detective Ruiz said.

"Can we gain access to both databases?" Sadie asked.

Miller nodded and said, "Not you or us, but Bart Covey's kid, Rachel, works at CWS—Placer County Child Welfare Services—as either a supervisor or administrator. I'll call her and see if we can fast-track this."

"Will that require warrants?" Sadie asked.

Miller rocked his head from side to side, pondering the question. "Depends on what we ask for," he finally said. "Rachel spent most of her career as a caseworker, investigating cases of child neglect, abuse, and so on. She should be able to cross-reference the data and spot a pattern if there is one. She'll also know people in Reno where we can look at the files from the first family found at the GV dumpsite."

"Great," Sadie said, excited for the first time since she arrived.

Brad, who was uncharacteristically silent, but not looking jealous that Sadie was doing all the talking or asking most of the questions, spoke up. "We'll check in with Captain Scott, get a reference to the coroner's office handling the Colfax dumpsite. If the coroner, Scott, or the Placer County Sheriff's Office can feed us a few names, and your friend's daughter can assist us, we can start pumping names of these families into the child services database and see if they exist and are missing. That might speed up the identification and confirmation processes."

"I'm texting Captain Scott now," Sadie said, typing the question and providing updates.

Things were moving fast now, so fast she almost forgot how scared she was about the morning's threat.

Was Miller right to investigate a possible link between herself and the killers? Sadie was quick to dismiss it at first, but fragments from her past were returning—specifically, fuzzy images of a little girl in a dress carrying a teddy bear.

She sent Captain Scott the text and then took a moment to will her mind clear, which should have been easier considering the traumatic events were only a dozen years old at best. Then again, so much had happened since then, much of it just as bad, scary, and traumatic.

"What?" Brad asked.

"I'm just thinking about my past," Sadie said. "Captain Miller, can you pull the police report on my case from when I was younger?"

"The kidnapping or the killings?" Miller asked.

Brad stared at her, but Sadie ignored him to say, "Aren't they the same thing now?"

Miller thought about it. "I'll see what I can do."

"Weren't there four kids in that family?"

"I didn't work the case," he said, "so I'm unfamiliar with the details."

"You didn't live here then?"

He shook his head and addressed the task force: "Do any of you remember the details of that case? The one with Earl Gray's family?"

"Your dad's name is Earl Gray, like the tea?" an officer asked with amusement.

Sadie glared at him and said, "Yes, it is." The silence that followed was so enormous, you could hear a pin drop in the next room.

Finally, Sadie turned to Miller and said, "Teresa May was here at the time."

"This is Sergeant May's day off," Miller said. "I'll reach out and see what she can tell me. In the meantime, I'll have my assistant access your records."

Sadie's phone pinged, notifying her of a text response, hopefully from Captain Scott. Thankfully, it was. Brad glanced at her phone, then scooted near her to read the text. She turned from him slightly because he was too close.

When Sadie finished reading the message, Brad asked her, "What'd he say?"

"That I should call immediately."

She excused herself and walked into the hallway to make the call. She spoke with Captain Scott for a few minutes. He was gruff and impolite, but straight to the point. She didn't like the man, but she smiled and thanked him anyway. A second later, she received a follow-up text from Captain Scott that made her smile.

When she returned to Miller and the task force, Sadie said, "I have the identities of the most recent victims in Colfax. It would seem that all three were killed twelve to fifteen hours before our raid."

"Fresh kills?" Miller asked, aghast.

Sadie nodded and said, "The killers beat the father's face to a pulp and slit the mother's throat from ear to ear before taking her eyes. The daughter died, too, her neck snapped in half. The coroner said the daughter bore signs of sexual abuse, specifically signs of penetration both vaginally and rectally as recent as a week ago."

"They established the timeline quickly," Garcia said.

"CPS spoke to the father yesterday morning and had scheduled a visit to the house today," Sadie said. "Aside from body temperature, rigor mortis, and lividity, I imagine the visit helped establish a pretty narrow timeline."

"That *was* quick," Miller said, jealous of the speed at which they made the ID and had a story.

"CPS saw the broken back door, blood all over the floor, and signs of a struggle," Sadie said, putting Miller at ease. "The case worker phoned Placer County Sheriff's Department immediately."

Sadie dug deep, tapping into her well of determination. Despite the horror of another dead family, if they could catch these monsters now that they were hot on their trail, perhaps they could stop any future killings.

twenty-four
riley sharpe

WHEN HER RESEARCH ASSISTANT ARRIVED, Riley looked at her anxiously and said, "What have you got?" The young woman was grumpy, a bit messy, and somewhat quiet. In other words, different day, same pile of crap. She stopped and stared at Riley through a pair of scratched glasses. "You okay?"

The girl finally nodded and said, "I wish you knew the lengths I sometimes go to, to make you look good."

The smile that cut across Riley's face was contagious; the young girl smiled in response. She needed her teeth cleaned. Then again, so did Riley.

"What you got," Riley said, "is it enough to get us to ten thousand listeners?"

Her assistant slowly removed her glasses, narrowed her eyes, and started to nod, slowly at first and then faster. Riley could hardly contain herself.

"Well?" she asked. "Tell me already."

"Whoever is killing these families," her assistant grinned, "they're doing it with a lock bundle."

All measure of joy dropped from her face. "A what?"

"A bundle of padlocks and combination locks," the girl replied. "They're bashing them in the head and beating them to death."

"But why?"

The girl shrugged. "Pure and utter hatred would be my guess. Or maybe another reason. I don't know. Isn't that your job? To figure out the motivations, produce the gory details, hook the audience?"

"Of course, but a woman is only as strong as her team, and you—my dear—*are my team*," Riley said warmly.

The girl stared at her for a long, uncomfortable moment, then said, "You look good this morning. What's different?"

Riley batted her eyelashes and said, "They're new."

The girl came in for a closer look, and that was when she saw the bruise on Riley's jawline. "What happened?" she asked.

Riley turned her face, embarrassed, and said, "It's a long story that has to do with a bottle of vodka and a celebration."

"Celebration for what?"

"Five thousand listeners, duh. Aren't you watching our numbers?"

The girl shook her head and said, "No, I'm trying to break this case, just like you."

"Yeah, of course," Riley said in a rush. "Well, can we record this new detail in the case, or is there more?"

"There's more," the girl smiled.

Riley, rubbing her palms together and feeling giddy, said, "Give me all you've got."

"All the kids' necks are broken."

Riley's nostrils flared, and her heart raced. If her face hadn't hurt so much, she would have started jumping around, clapping her hands, and giggling. "Look at you, coming through in a pinch. Do any of the local news stations have this information?"

The girl shook her head. "I don't think so."

"Well, then," she said, "we need to record this podcast and upload it quickly. We need the scoop so the public knows who we are."

The girl took a tentative step toward her, hesitating. "I also have a picture," she all but whispered.

Riley stopped in her tracks. Breathlessly, she said, "Let me see."

The girl handed over her cell phone—an old iPhone. Riley's eyes cleared, and she found herself staring at a photo of a house with a broken door and blood smears all over the floor inside the hallway.

The girl watched Riley stare at the photo as if studying her or looking for signs of... *what*? What was she wanting? Some kind of a reaction? A raise?

"Who gave you this?" Riley asked, handing the phone back.

"Use it as the cover photo for the podcast and see what happens," the girl said. "I'm going to text you the image."

"We might get the entire podcast pulled."

"But we might not."

Riley stared at her for a long moment, then she nodded excitedly and said, "I'm heading into the studio now."

The girl's face lit up, and she said, "Ten thousand listeners."

Riley grinned, nodded, and said, "Ten thousand *motherfreaking* listeners."

twenty-five
sadie gray

SADIE AND BRAD left GVPD and walked to their car in relative silence. The day was bright, the air crisp and clean and smelling like pine trees, and Sadie was in an overall mood of excitement. Was this the wild rush her instructors at Quantico talked about? It had to be.

"Food?" Brad asked.

Sadie said, "Sure, but what should we do now? Because I feel like we should be doing *something*. We've got momentum, Brad. Momentum!"

"I think we have to wait for Chief Miller to get in touch with Rachel at Child Welfare Services," he said, smiling at her unfettered joy.

"Or you could not be a boner-killer and we could go over there after lunch," Sadie suggested with a mischievous grin.

She could see Brad didn't like stepping on people's toes, especially when the chief was reaching out to a friend to expedite things, but lives were on the line.

"We came here to assist them until they assist us," Brad said. "And right now, they're assisting us with what we figured out. We'll let them, no matter how hard we want to push this ball down the field."

Sadie nodded, knowing he was right. She also knew that if she cooled her jets, the pressure would start to ease off the murderers, which would give the three lunatics time to figure out how to continue messing with her at her Airbnb. Or worse, it would give them time to kill more people. She blew out a sigh and crossed her arms over her chest. Maybe she *should* change Airbnbs. Then again, the only thing faster than hunting down the murderers was them knowing where she was and coming after her first. Was that wise, though?

She finally said, "The best chance of us finding these clowns is for me to be bait."

Brad looked at her and laughed. "You're an idiot."

She frowned and tried to smack him, but he ducked too quickly for her. "You think I can't handle them, *Brad*? Especially if I know they're coming?"

Brad kept one eye on the road and the other on her. "Let me spell this out for the slow learners in the car, people who are not me. These three *kill entire families*."

"Families who don't know they're coming," Sadie countered. "I know they're coming."

"Because of the Cajun meat dish on your front porch?"

Sadie nodded.

"As the case agent, I'm saying no. Not just a regular 'no,' a resounding '*hell* no.'"

"Then I'll spend lunch trying to find a room or Airbnb around here better than the one I'm in that's still close to you in this tiny, non-destination location."

He registered her sarcasm but didn't seem to appreciate it. "I'd rather step on the chief's dick and go see Rachel before leaving you to your defenses."

"I'm capable, Brad."

"Says every girl before they're attacked and overwhelmed."

She shook her head and looked out the window, refusing to meet his gaze.

"We're agents who do things by the book, Sadie. I don't have a hero's complex, and I'm not a superhuman or blessed with psychic powers. We have a crime to solve, starting and ending with clues and evidence. That's it."

"I'm not trying to one-up anyone here," she said. "I just want to solve this crime and stop families from being slaughtered and dumped in the middle of nowhere like trash."

"Where do you want to go for lunch?"

"Lumberjacks," she said.

"Do you have Teresa May's number?"

"At home, yes, but not here, and not on my phone," Sadie answered.

"You should have thought of that," Brad said.

He was right. Proper planning needed to be an art form she mastered. *It takes time, Sadie Gray.* She needed to forgive herself for so many things—not being perfect was one of them, but so was being a rookie and looking like a fool.

Brad studied her for a moment before speaking. "What are you thinking?"

She shook off the chaotic, unforgiving thoughts and said, "Let's eat lunch. I'll find a new place to sleep, and then we'll call Chief Miller and see about Rachel Covey at CWS. If Miller doesn't answer, we need her direct number, or Miller needs a court order for us to use their systems. NCIC seems good so far, but we need direct access to their systems, especially if one of the killers has hacked in and is now operating within the system."

"Remind me to ask Rachel, Miller, or whoever we can talk to about tracking inquiries. If one of the killers is part of Child Welfare Services, or someone associated with them has direct access to the database, we need a name or names."

Sadie agreed and kept the ball rolling. "If we get a name and a search inquiry, we could probably help Dr. West ID more of the bodies. Even though there are thirty-four bodies, we can reduce them to maybe a dozen family units—maybe more."

"That's better than making thirty-four IDs the hard way," Brad said. "Captain Scott would probably appreciate whatever info we can gather from there, too; he could pass it along to the coroner for a quicker ID, especially for those bodies that rotted long ago."

She nodded, feeling better already.

"If we get a database user with a name, if we find any kind of reliable connection, I want to take them down before Miller or Scott," Sadie said, determined to polish the FBI's less-than-stellar reputation with a victory. Lord knew it needed it!

"Don't chase the glory; chase the killers," Brad said. "The glory comes from doing your job right. Even then, when you find the monsters and manage to stop and arrest them, that will be all the glory you crave. Trust me, that's a high like no other."

She sat back and thought about it, and it made sense. She was on her first case, but Brad had worked dozens or more, which is why she was beginning to trust him.

Her phone pinged—a YouTube notification. "Oh," she said, looking at it.

"What?"

"New podcast by Riley Sharpe," she said.

Brad frowned and looked away. "That woman's a certifiable nut bag."

"Holy cow!"

Brad jumped. "What?"

Sadie turned her phone and showed him the cover photo for the podcast. She could hardly believe her eyes. Then again, neither could Brad.

"How in God's name did she get a photo of the crime scene?" he asked.

"What if she was there?" Sadie purred. Her skin broke into goosebumps, and she couldn't stop smiling.

"It's more than possible," Brad said under his breath. "But she didn't have access to the house. Unless Captain Scott—"

"He wouldn't," Brad said quickly.

Sadie looked at Brad; he looked right back at her. Then she said, "We need to pull over and NCIC this broad right freaking now."

Brad took the first exit, parked, and accessed the NCIC database from his phone.

"Riley Sharpe," Sadie said.

He entered the data, waited for a response, and scrolled through a few pages until he found what he was looking for. "Riley Sharpe was orphaned as a child," Brad said after studying the report. "The file is thin, but it looks like she spent much of her youth in foster care."

They looked at each other, and then Sadie said, "Call Miller right now and either get Rachel Covey's direct number or make sure she gets our names and calls us. We need a more detailed family history on Riley quickly!"

Brad called Miller, told him about the podcast photo and Riley Sharpe's NCIC profile, and said that Sadie was sending the pic to his phone.

Sadie forwarded the screenshot to Chief Miller.

"Agent Gray will listen to the podcast after we get off the phone with you," Brad continued, speaking quickly. "But, if there was ever an odd coincidence, and I don't believe in those, it's this."

Miller agreed, told them to hold tight, and hung up.

"We need to see if she's been at every crime scene," Sadie said, her skin breaking into goosebumps.

"Miller said to hold tight."

Sadie said, "We don't work for Miller."

Brad nodded at first, shook his head in frustration, and texted Miller, telling him to check the crime scene photos and photos of the media and crowds of bystanders to see how often Riley was there.

"How long is Riley's podcast?" Brad asked.

"Ten minutes with a short intro."

"Play it," he said.

Sadie played the podcast on her cell phone. When Riley claimed that sources inside the coroner's office said several victims died by blunt force trauma, likely from a bundle of padlocks and combination locks, Brad gripped the steering wheel so tight that his knuckles lost color.

Sadie shifted in her seat, a hot charge of fear and excitement blazing through her. "Oh my God," she finally said.

"Shhh," Brad said.

Riley was saying the killer used the locks to kill part of each family, likely the more abusive parent. Then she said, "But we're just taking a few small facts and trying to build a larger story, folks. What do you think? Leave a comment and let us know! Oh, and be sure to subscribe!"

Brad grabbed his phone and dialed Miller's number. He needed to know if Dr. West had a leaker among her staff. Sadie took the time to call Captain Scott to see if Riley Sharpe or anyone else on his team had access to the crime scene.

They both hung up their phones within a minute of each other. Brad turned and said, "Miller claims there's no way Dr. West, her deputy coroner, or their staff leaked a thing. They're too busy to even eat or sleep. And he said Ruiz and Peters are solid, no worries there. We all know it would be catastrophic if this sensitive information were released to the public at the wrong time, like now."

Sadie asked, "What about GVPD's officers? The ones on the scene? I mean, someone had to be motivated to do this."

"Those guys weren't at the Colfax scene."

Sadie closed her eyes to think. Was she looking at the situation too narrowly? Perhaps. But what other possibilities existed if she was wrong?

"Dr. West isn't the leaker, nor is her staff, and not Ruiz or Peters or any of Captain Scott's team," Brad reiterated confidently. "Miller also said that his guys have specific instructions to send him word if the press tries to turn them into sources."

"I'm sure you've worked cases where the media developed sources within an organization without the head of said organization or department knowing," Sadie said.

Brad nodded in agreement but looked like he was still considering the evidence and updates.

Sadie interrupted his thoughts to say, "Captain Scott is checking with the coroner and his guys, but he believes the scene was secure from the moment they were on site until now. And he knows for sure his direct response team refused to allow anyone to enter the scene. It's SOP for those guys."

"Maybe the photo was taken *before* anyone knew about the crime scene," Brad suggested, the gravity of the statement hitting home.

Sadie nodded, agreeing with him. "Should we head to Riley's place first or fuel up at Lumberjacks while we wait for word from Miller or Rachel?"

"Lumberjacks until we can get more information on Riley Sharpe," he answered. "But I can feel this thing gaining momentum, and I want us to be ready to go at a minute's notice."

Although she desperately wanted a peek into Brad's head, Sadie fought the urge to blurt out the question. She lost that fight. She cleared her throat and asked, "Could Riley Sharpe be one of the three killers?"

Brad measured his response. "Yes, we have to consider that Riley might be the woman we saw in the Reno video," he said. But then he paused as if giving it further thought.

Sadie ached to interject but refused to interrupt his thought process again.

"Think about it, Sadie—she's ugly enough to have driven the truck Mary Taggart and Blake Landry saw. And she has the right history and background for the profile we're building."

Sadie looked at him funny. "Are you talking about the real estate lady and her Marine client? Mary and Blake?"

Brad nodded. "Then again, she might be too big, according to the Marine."

"You think it was the smaller one driving the truck?" Sadie asked, thinking back to the Reno surveillance video. "The one with the wild hair?"

"Could be," Brad wondered. "Maybe they're not blood-related."

"They could be, though."

"But, if we consider the CWS angle, maybe they were all part of a single foster family. Is that possible?"

"Not only is it possible, it's likely," she said, liking the idea.

"They could also be siblings who were separated and sent into foster care," Brad said. "Rachel will tell us that, hopefully."

"God, I hate waiting," Sadie said.

"I'm not good at it, either."

Things were shifting in her mind, but they were still distant thoughts, layered in fog, trying to break free and tell her *something*. For a second, she thought she could reach out and grab them, but they proved unreachable, like a mirage that's close but never close enough.

"You got something?" Brad asked as they pulled into the Lumberjacks parking lot.

"I don't know, I think so?" she said, frustrated. "But it's like an itch you can't scratch or the name on the end of your tongue, the one you can't quite remember."

He seemed to understand. "It'll come to you when you stop thinking of it."

He was right. *Again.* "After lunch, if we haven't heard from Miller or Rachel, I say we go to CWS in Placer County and ask for Rachel, see if we can impress upon her the need for her immediate cooperation."

"I don't love it," Brad said thoughtfully, "but it might be the best we have now that we've got a thread worth pulling."

"You know Miller's going to give birth if we go around him to talk to Rachel, right?"

Brad turned to her and said, "That's why I don't love it. But we don't work for Miller, and local LEOs don't like us anyway. We're here to stop these murderers and save families, which means we can't let them slow us down, not even for a moment."

"Make no friends," Sadie said.
"Make no friends."

twenty-six
rachel covey

THE PHONE CALLS RACHEL RECEIVED, first from her father and then from Chief Miller, not only startled and concerned her but also set her teeth on edge. The best way to cooperate, to possibly assist them in taking down the person or people killing these families, was to make sure her office had nothing to do with it. If she could resolve that quickly, she could relax and do whatever she could to help the police, the sheriff's department, and the Feds.

She accessed their central database and started the search history before being called away with an emergency—a symptom of her position. Fires were always starting, and they always needed to be put out. Some days, it annoyed her, but she was compensated nicely for it. While she could generally handle the day-to-day, even the most challenging problems, this wasn't just her father asking a favor; it was Chief Miller and, by proxy, the FBI. So, how was she supposed to prioritize that?

Rachel stopped at her assistant's desk and said, "Nora, I have a priority-one task that needs your immediate attention. It is so critical that I should have finished it fifteen minutes ago before doing anything else."

The perky redhead sat up fast and looked right at her. "That urgent, huh?"

Rachel leaned in and lowered her voice. "This is super hush-hush, too, so no matter what you find, you must come to me first." She wanted to clarify that point because young Nora Weaver had her special needs moments, times in the past when she wasn't as reliable as Rachel would have liked. The girl was getting better, though—more responsible. Then again, she was the only person Rachel could lean on, so she needed her to come through.

"I can *totally* do hush-hush," the twenty-two-year-old said in a rushed whisper. Rachel inadvertently appraised the girl, judging her fairly or unfairly by her looks: big eyes, long fake lashes, too much makeup, thin hair with too many extensions, and a complete wardrobe straight from the Ross, TJ Maxx, or Marshalls' clearance section.

This is who I'm supposed to put my faith in?

"What?" Nora asked.

Rachel shoved aside her doubts about the girl and got down to business. "I need you to do a deep dive on Riley Sharpe." She gave Nora the pertinent details compiled by Chief Miller and his teams, and then she laid a slip of paper on Nora's desk. "This list of names is from two or three families. Run a search history on the asterisked names—the parents—and see if there are any shared patterns, calls, abuse, or other notable problems."

"That's it?" she asked.

"Deep dive, Nora," Rachel said, her expression conveying the importance of this task. "We're doing this for the authorities if you catch my drift."

She leaned in and whispered, "What authorities?"

Matching the volume of Nora's voice, Rachel said, "Grass Valley Police Department, Nevada and Placer County Sheriff's Offices, and the FBI."

"Holy smokes," she breathed.

Rachel nodded and said, "Remember, this comes straight to me."

"You can count on me, boss." Rachel was about to leave when Nora grabbed her by the arm and stopped her. Her eyes were so serious that it sparked her concern. "If this is so important, why are you having *me* do it?"

She shrugged off the girl's hand. "CDSS called to say their servers were hacked, and our data is at risk. They sent us a patch, but IT needs permissions that only I can give them."

"This is Defcon Five, then?"

"More like Defcon One," Rachel said.

"Wait, which is worse again?" Nora asked, clearly perplexed. "Five or one?"

"One."

"Okay, go then. I got this."

Rachel nodded and left, hurrying to meet with her IT department to put out yet another fire caused by yet another problematic person or entity. Shaking her head, she thought, *it never really ends.*

And it didn't.

Forty minutes later, while Rachel was on the phone with a California Department of Social Services (CDSS) rep, Nora rushed into the server room looking concerned. Rachel told the CDSS rep she'd have to call her back to put out a more immediate fire, then hung up the phone.

"You're not going to believe this!" Nora said excitedly.

Discreetly, Rachel grabbed her arm, pulled her out of the small room, and pointed toward her office. "Not here, Nora. My office."

They entered her office, Rachel closed the door, and then Nora turned to her, bursting at the seams to speak.

"We have a major fucking problem," Nora said.

"Language," Rachel said.

"Sorry, but... not sorry? Because... wow. Like, *wow!*"

Rachel put her hands on her hips and fixed the girl with a stare. "Tell me already."

"I looked up the families that are deceased, murdered, or whatever, and they're all in our system, but not all in our county."

"Case workers?" Rachel asked.

"They're all assigned different workers."

"Then, why are you out of breath?" Rachel asked.

Nora didn't need to whisper but leaned forward and whispered anyway, as if telling her the mother of all secrets. "Because a single person accessed each of these cases."

Rachel's pulse doubled as bile rose into her throat. Dealing with the hack at CDSS presented its complexities, but so did two crime scenes and almost sixty dead.

Rachel looked at her breathlessly and asked, "Where?"

"Here," Nora whispered.

"Here?"

Nora nodded and stepped closer, so close that Rachel could smell her hairspray covering up significant body odor. "I also compiled a list of all the other families he looked at for you and the FBI to consider." She paused a moment, looked down, and then away. "But I think I kinda messed up."

"What do you mean you messed up?"

Refusing to meet Rachel's eyes, Nora said, "You were busy, and I know the mission is critical with you. When I heard about CDSS, *the hack*, I knew that would be a top priority, and my task would be secondary, so I went to the person who made the inquiries. I thought I was helping you by, you know—taking the initiative."

Every muscle in Rachel's body seized at once, and she felt the top of her head getting ready to blow off in a near-nuclear explosion. Instead of yelling, she gritted her teeth and tempered her response. "I'm sorry, but you did *what*?"

Nora finally met Rachel's eyes. Her expression was teeming with remorse, and her slouched, sad body gave off an air of need—the need for understanding and forgiveness. Finally, Nora said, "I wanted to know why he accessed them."

Rachel couldn't breathe. "And?"

"Nothing," she said, returning to her young, dumb self. "He

said that *you said* part of his job was to check on abuse cases where the child had not been placed outside foster care but needed to be."

"The severe abuse cases?" Rachel asked, grabbing her phone.

"Yes."

"Give me a name!" Rachel barked.

"Jake Sharpe."

Rachel felt the air leave her lungs in a noisy outburst she couldn't contain. First Riley Sharpe, now Jake? "We need to get the FBI here now to interview him."

"That's kinda where I messed up," Nora said sheepishly, her eyes once again burdened by remorse but also tinged with fear.

"If he had anything to do with murdering these families, you brainless *twit*," Rachel hissed, "then you just tipped him off and let him get away." Rachel's heart lodged in her throat, and her fingers became claws at her side. When she thought of the implications of Nora's actions, all she could do was glare at the young girl, who was all but pissing her pants at that point.

Like a squeaky little mouse trying hard to be *so* small, Nora half-closed her eyes and said, "He's gone."

"What?" she snapped.

"I asked around before I came and got you, and Blake Fiori said he saw him tear out of the parking lot in some butt-ugly blue Gremlin-type car. He said he'd never seen the car before, but Jake got into it and... well, I guess he's gone."

Think, think, THINK!

Finally, Rachel said, "Okay, I'll access outside security footage and see if we can get a vehicle description and a plate number. Find out everything you can about Jake Sharpe. First, see if he's in the system, not as a case worker, but as a child placed in foster care."

"Foster care?"

Rachel wanted to scream in her face, grab her shoulders, and shake the stupid right out of her, but she didn't know if she could shake someone that hard. Calmly, despite the war of emotions being waged inside of her, she said, "If he's targeting families with abusive parents, maybe Jake was in the system and suffered abuse, too."

"Oh, yeah…" Nora nodded.

"Go make this right, Nora," she said.

The girl was smart enough not to utter another word; instead, she left the office quickly, prepared to do whatever she could to remedy the situation. Rachel, however, was terrified she'd only do something to make her and her department look worse.

Rachel didn't want to, but she contacted Chief Miller to tell him what she found and what Nora had done. He wasn't pleased, but he also knew that as much as one leader could lead, not all followers were competent.

"Do you have a home address?" Miller asked through gritted teeth.

Rachel had pulled Jake's address from HR before making the call. She gave it to him immediately and promised to send a follow-up text. He thanked her and hung up. A moment later, Nora returned looking winded.

"He was in the system, along with siblings, all separated at the same time, all with different last names for a while."

"Why were they separated?" Rachel asked.

Nora drew a deep breath and blew it out after three long seconds. "Their father was a frickin' serial killer is why."

Rachel gulped, unlocked her phone, and dialed Chief Miller. While it rang, before the police chief could answer, Nora said, "I have printouts on two of Jake's three siblings, so far." She practically thrust the papers at Rachel. The call to Miller went to voicemail. Rachel hung up and tried again, staring at Riley Sharpe's and David Sharpe's partial profiles.

Miller finally answered, and she quickly told him the rest of the story.

"I need the home address," Miller swallowed.

"I already gave it to you."

He sighed heavily into the phone. "The address *before* the kids were taken away and put into foster care."

"I'll do you one better," Rachel said. And then she told him the kids' father's name.

For a long moment, Miller was silent, and it seemed everyone was holding their breaths, waiting for him to respond.

When the chief finally spoke, he did so with a more relaxed tenor than Rachel would have expected.

"Well, I'll be dipped in dog shit," he replied.

"Excuse me?" Rachel said.

"It means this complicates everything," he said, sounding grave. "But it also explains a lot."

"Was he the—?" Rachel said before Miller interrupted her.

"Yeah, same guy," he said.

"I had a Sadie Gray with the FBI leave a message for me while I was working on a… software issue with CDSS. That's not the—"

"It's the same Sadie Gray," he said, answering her question before she'd even finished asking it.

"How's that possible?"

"I don't know how it is; it just is," Miller said. "I have to go. Great work, Rachel. It looks like you might have cracked the case."

"Really?" she asked, astounded. She thought she and Nora had just botched it.

"Be sure to get me everything you can on that Gremlin Jake was driving ASAP. If he's on the run, and it appears that way, I'll authorize a multi-county APB."

"Will do, Chief," she said. "And I'm sorry about the mix-up here… Chief Miller?"

He had already ended the call, and though she felt happy and proud to have helped the police cap off such a monumental murder spree, she was also acutely aware that one of the worst murderers in US history had been on her payroll and working down the hall from her. Her body shook in an involuntary shiver, one that had her hugging herself to ward off the chill.

"Am I in the clear now?" Nora asked, bringing her back.

"Not with me, you're not," Rachel said.

"Am I fired?"

"No, but you lost my trust, and that just might be worse than me firing you."

"Yes, Ma'am," Nora said, sullen.

twenty-seven
sadie gray

THEY ATE AT LUMBERJACK'S, which was more than enough food with their generous portion sizes; it hit the spot. Sadie had the Ribeye Railslide—a 12oz. cut cooked medium well with the perfect amount of seasoning, and Brad ordered the Chicken Fried Steak—a beef steak with country gravy that looked freaking delicious.

They didn't speak when they ate because they knew there wasn't much time with various agencies working their databases and the killers all but in their crosshairs.

Both were finishing when Sadie's phone rang. She checked the caller ID and smiled. "Teresa," she picked up and said, beaming.

"Hi, Sadie," she said, sounding like she was smiling on the other end of the phone. "Or should I call you Special Agent Gray now?"

"For you, Sadie," she grinned.

"Chief Miller said you needed my help jogging your memory?"

"Yeah, I've somehow managed to put much of my past out of my head. Specifically, around the time of... the kidnappings."

"Your kidnapping."

"That's what I meant to say," she said, feeling an awful pull at her insides.

"People who suffered what you and your sister did at the hands of that monster... I understand how blocking it out might help you cope better."

"It was that and a miserable childhood *after* that," she said, eyeing Brad, who was listening but pretending he wasn't. "You know, with the various... foster families."

"It was just you, right?" she asked.

Sadie nodded and said, "Yeah, just me." An image of her little sister came to mind, but she shoved it away to spare herself the pain. "Before that, when Natalie and I were taken—I don't remember much about the kids there, in the basement, but I keep seeing a little girl in a green dress holding a dirty teddy bear. I think she had blonde hair, but I'm not sure."

"Oh, yeah—the girl," Teresa said. "There were four of them. And when, well... when everything went down the way it did, after that, the surviving kids went to different foster homes. The caseworker and supervisor thought the kids would normalize if they sent them to separate homes. They did at first, but not in the long run."

"The long run?" she asked. "You kept an eye on them?"

"I watched them for a few years, checking in and whatnot, and though the girl—Riley—didn't seem to have issues, Jake and David were problem children."

She swallowed at the mention of Riley's name, gripping the table as a sudden bout of dizziness ran roughshod through her head. She closed her eyes and said, "David is the small one, right?"

"Yeah, he was also sort of, like... I don't know—just wrong. God, I hate to say it, but David was a defective child. Something that should not have been born."

"And the fourth kid?"

"You forgot?" Teresa asked.

Suddenly, it came to her, and like a light switch flipping on, Sadie remembered everything. "Oh, my God, Teresa."

"What?"

"It's *them* doing this."

She suffered a long, debilitating silence. Even Brad, who tried to keep up despite hearing only one side of the conversation, said nothing.

Teresa finally asked, "Are you sure, Sadie, because—"

"What are their last names now because they aren't using their given names?" Sadie asked, breathless.

Brad stood and mouthed, "Going to wash my hands." She acknowledged him with a nod.

The second he turned his back, she watched him walk off, thinking he'd been a good teacher but hadn't needed to teach her much. She was naturally curious, liked mysteries, and excelled at finding and interpreting patterns. In other words, she was going to make this job her bitch. But figuring things out also meant understanding the horrors of the situation, the motivations of deviants and killers, and the sick minds of people better off locked away with the key tossed into a bottomless pit.

When Teresa told her Jake's and David's last names, the ones they had used for a while, and that they all had taken Riley's foster parents' last names because of what happened, Sadie refused to breathe, knowing what she would hear next.

"You're so quiet," Teresa said. "This is bad, right? I mean, what's happening, these three?"

"Yeah."

"Riley was always a… wait, Riley Sharpe," Teresa said. "Like the podcast."

"Not 'like the podcast,' Teresa—*the* podcast." Suddenly, everything that slowed her processing of this information sped up at once, her mind charging forward at a dizzying pace. "Teresa, I gotta go. You're a lifesaver—thank you!"

She ended the call, walked up to the front counter, and said to a nearby server, "I need to make a quick local call if I can."

"Sure," she said. "Just dial 9 to get an outside line."

Sadie thanked her, opened her cell phone to check her notes, and then called. The woman answered the phone a moment later.

"Riley Sharpe True Crime Podcast, Riley speaking."

Stilling herself against the pit in her stomach and the sweat that had broken across her forehead, Sadie said, "Hi Riley, this is Special Agent Gray with the FBI. First and foremost, as a listener, I want to say that I enjoy your podcast and your reporting."

"Oh, wow, thank you!" she said, gauging the woman's reaction to Sadie's name. Surely she remembered...

Her heart thumped so hard that she was afraid it would leave her gasping for breath and give away the ruse. Instead, Sadie calmed herself and said, "I have a bit of free time and wanted to stop by and see if you could help us with the investigation."

"Oh, I'd be happy to," she said.

"You know when the media plants stories to draw out the unsub?"

"Unsub?" Riley asked.

"Unidentified subject," Sadie said.

"Oh, yeah, unsub," she replied. "I've heard of that."

"Well, your listener base is starting to multiply, and I wanted to talk to you about that if you have time."

"I just uploaded the podcast earlier, so I have time now," Riley said. "If you're coming down, maybe you could also answer a few questions for me—on the record."

"If I can," Sadie offered, "I definitely will. My partner and I are about fifteen minutes away. Would it be okay to head over?"

"Oh, that would be great!"

"What did you say your first name was, Agent Gray?"

"Sadie," she said. "Sadie Gray."

The woman paused, then said, "From the press conference, right? The cute brunette?"

Sadie smiled—Riley Sharpe knew *exactly* who she was. Still, her heart was all but boxing the insides of her ribcage, the beating so fast and ferocious she felt she might pass out. "The first part, yes, the second... I think my looks are average, as a matter of opinion."

"Well, I can assure you, my opinion is good," Riley said with a singsong voice.

Sadie thanked her and hung up the phone; Brad had seen her on the phone and expensed the meal.

"Well?" he asked.

"We're meeting Riley Sharpe in fifteen."

He glared at her, disappointed, then said, "I'm the case agent, Sadie."

"Yeah, well, while you were off taking a dump or washing your hands or whatever, I was doing official FBI business. Oh, and by the way, I know our killers."

"Are we talking to Riley Sharpe or arresting her?"

"The latter," Sadie grinned. But then she put that smile away. "Unless you feel otherwise because you're in charge."

He nodded and said, "You're telling me everything on the way there."

Oh, she could scream! "Okay," she said excitedly, "but you'll have to drive."

He frowned. "I've *been* driving, Sadie."

With that, she told Brad most everything, omitting some of the more private details of her past. And then, when Brad lapsed into a moment of silence, Sadie pulled out her Glock 17, chambered a round, and said, "If you put a bullet in your past, will it die inside your head too?"

"Are you shitting me right now?" Brad asked, overly concerned.

"I wouldn't shit you, Brad—you're my favorite turd."

twenty-eight
sadie gray

BRAD DROVE TO COLFAX JUDICIOUSLY, making excellent time on the straightaways, passing slower traffic in the tighter spots, and once even on the shoulder to get around someone doing five miles per hour under the posted speed limit (*rude!*).

When they finally arrived in Colfax, Brad dialed down the *Speed Racer* driving and managed to catch his breath. He pulled into a parking space across from the local market next to the podcast studio, which looked like an abandoned building with a makeshift sign that read: Riley Sharpe True Crime Podcast.

Sadie worked to find her inner calm and to be at her most focused and least scared place. They were onto Riley Sharpe —*that murderous fiend*—so she could not induce her heart rate, let alone bump it, but that was only possible if she managed to control her breathing. Breath work was everything.

They parked in a diagonal parking space in front of Railhead Saloon, a few doors down from Main Street Tobacco & Gifts, the Pastime Club, and the Colfax Market—on the corner of N. Main and Grass Valley Street. They got out of the car, checked their surroundings, and were startled at the loud sounds of some kid on a street-legal motorcycle on Grass Valley Street goosing the throttle. Both turned and watched the bike tear off.

"Riley?" Brad asked.

Sadie still felt heat in her face and lower back and slight heart palpitations at the idea of confronting Riley. When she caught sight of the rider, it looked like a girl in stature, but she was wearing a helmet, and Sadie only glimpsed her for a moment.

"Doesn't look like her," she said. "Too small."

The Riley Sharpe she had encountered was a woman with broad shoulders and narrow hips, the body type often associated with football players. If Sadie had to guess, the girl on the motorcycle could be a kid, maybe eighteen or younger.

Sadie turned her attention to the brick façade's wood-framed glass door, approached it carefully with Brad, and knocked. Riley Sharpe appeared moments later, answered the door with a smile, and invited them inside. The woman quickly fetched them cups of water from a five-gallon Alhambra water jug, then smiled generously and took a deep breath. Was she trying to be a good hostess, or pretending not to be a mass-murdering serial killer?

Brad and Sadie thanked her for the water, but neither drank from the cups. Brad took the lead, asking Riley several questions regarding her podcast, how she approached covering a crime, and whether she had really developed contacts among the locals or merely said that to establish social proof among her listeners. She politely answered all of Brad's questions, letting him know Placer County Sheriff's Office was just around the corner, and she saw deputies from time to time in Grandma C's Kitchen, The Basement, and the Colfax Market. The Basement, Sadie recalled, was the pizza shop a few doors down. Riley rattled this off with stars in her eyes, seemingly excited that they were there.

Sadie's instructors at Quantico often told her that people were either enamored with you or hated you by association and didn't want you there—seldom was there an in-between.

Sadie waited for Brad to glance over and let her know it was her turn to ask any follow-up questions. When he wasn't giving her the opportunity, and his questions didn't seem that important, she interrupted with the question that needed to be asked and answered.

"How did you get such a great shot of the inside of the Colfax crime scene?" she asked.

Riley shifted in her seat, smiled at Brad, turned back to Sadie, and answered, "My part-time research assistant and investigator is amazing. The girl has her finger on the local pulse, but it also helps that she's from the area."

"Whereabouts?" Sadie asked. She ignored Brad as he shifted from one foot to the other, a little heat stealing into his cheeks.

"Auburn, last I heard," Riley replied. "Although I think she lives in Meadow Vista now. I'd have to check, but is that something you need to know?"

"Maybe," Sadie said.

Auburn was about seventeen miles west of Colfax and considered a California Historic Landmark, rich with its Gold Rush history and the county seat of Placer County. On the other hand, Meadow Vista was only about ten miles west, a little over halfway between Colfax and Auburn.

"What is your researcher's name?" Brad asked.

"She's named Riley, too."

That surprised Sadie, but she kept her emotions neutral as if it were nothing more than two agents talking to a woman about her job. If anything jumped her heart rate, though, it was this revelation.

"Riley, what?" Sadie asked, trying to maintain her calm.

"Why do you want to know about her?" Riley asked, her soft and friendly demeanor changing for the first time since they arrived.

Brad leaned toward her and said, "Do you realize that the photo you took of the crime scene was from *inside* the crime scene, Ms. Sharpe?"

The question was Brad's cue to Sadie that they were taking Riley in no matter what she said. The judge would issue a search warrant based on the photo, allowing them to take her cell phone, computer, and car, and maybe even get a search warrant for her home if they found evidence of her involvement in the crimes.

"My researcher took that photo," Riley said rather sheepishly.

"You don't seem sure of it," Sadie pressed.

Riley swallowed hard and realized for the first time that she might be in trouble. "Why are you here?"

Brad's phone alerted him to a text, which he glanced at, read, and then considered. Sadie eyed him with discomfort in her heart; she wondered what he was reading that was so important, and then she saw the look in Brad's eyes and knew what was next.

He stood and said, "We would like to invite you to the Grass Valley Police Department to answer some more formal questions."

"Regarding?" Riley asked, gripping the edges of her seat.

"What do you think, Ms. Sharpe?" Sadie said pointedly.

"I'd appreciate it if you'd just tell me so I don't have to guess," she said, her face flush.

There was a breathlessness in her voice that spoke volumes. *Do we have her right now? Is this the catch?*

"Do you remember me?" Sadie looked at her and asked.

"From the press conference, yes."

"Don't bullshit me, Riley."

Sadie looked the woman in the face, trying to see the girl she had met almost a decade and a half ago in a basement.

"I'm telling you the truth," she lied.

"Would you like to come with us voluntarily, or should we take you?" Brad asked.

Sadie was growing frustrated because she wanted Riley to admit that she knew Sadie from when she and her sister had been kidnapped and held prisoner. But freaking Brad just kept vying for control, which he was entitled to as a case officer despite it being annoying. Couldn't he see how personal the case had become?

"Did you leave the Cajun cock and balls on my porch?" Sadie

asked, speaking faster and with enough intensity to match her rising anger.

"What?" she asked. "No!"

"Are you coming with us or not, Ms. Sharpe?" Brad asked.

"Not!" she turned and snapped. Standing tall in defiance, she leveled them with cold, hateful looks. "I know my rights enough to know this ain't right."

"You don't have the right to kill people," Sadie hissed.

Riley's jaw flopped open, displaying all kinds of janky teeth, broken molars, and old metal fillings.

Brad removed his set of cuffs and went for her wrists, saying, "Riley Sharpe, you are under arrest for trespassing on private property, and if we find that you did so after the house was designated a crime scene, not only will you face trespassing charges, you will be charged with obstructing peace officers from performing their duties. And that's if we don't arrest you for the murders of dozens of people, which is the most likely scenario."

"I didn't kill nobody!" she barked, the trailer park side of her coming out. "You got the wrong friggin' person!"

"Everyone says that but seldom are they right," Brad said as he locked her wrists behind her back. After that, they perp-walked her to the bu-car.

"Don't you gotta read me my rights?" Riley asked. "These cuffs are too tight!"

"No, we don't have to read you your rights," Brad answered truthfully. "Not yet, at least. And the cuffs are tight for your safety."

"I don't feel safe!" she said, that deer-in-the-headlights look on her dog-ugly face.

They put Riley in the back of the Impala, Brad pushing her head down so she didn't smack it on the car, then said, "My partner will buckle you in. Any aggression you take toward her is illegal and considered resisting arrest and possibly assault of a peace officer, and we will prosecute you to the fullest extent of the law."

"I ain't aggressin' on no one!" she cried.

People on the street were now watching them through windows and from their store fronts or just slowing as they drove by on N. Main Street, slack-jawed and rubbernecking. Sadie climbed into the back seat with Riley, buckled her in, and Brad started the car and pulled onto the street.

Sadie made sure she had easy access to her weapon in case Riley got belligerent. "I know you know me, Riley," she finally said. "No reason to be coy."

Riley flared her eyes and nostrils, her teeth barred like a rabid animal. "You two are sick, and this is an abuse of power."

"Killing entire families is an abuse of power," Brad said from the front seat.

"I didn't do squat, and I don't know you or this broad, but I can say with one-thousand-percent certainty you got the wrong woman."

Sadie pinned the woman down with her eyes, but she also looked her over, taking careful note of her skin, the size of her pores, and the texture of her skin around her neck. Riley glared back at her, but Sadie was not intimidated. Instead, she studied Riley's face even deeper, eyeing her laugh lines and the start of crow's feet around her eyes.

"How old are you, Riley?"

"Twenty-eight."

Brad barked out a laugh, but Sadie found no humor in the statement. If she was the age Sadie thought she was, then maybe Riley was right about being the wrong woman.

"Twenty-eight, my ass," Sadie growled.

"I am," she said without conviction.

Sadie narrowed her eyes but refused to blink. You didn't have to be a genius to know when you had someone on their heels; Brad and Sadie had Riley in a vulnerable position where telling the truth might get her in trouble, or it might get her life in prison with no chance for parole.

"You're a hard thirty-five," Sadie finally said, "and that's me being generous."

"I haven't aged well," she muttered, looking away.

"You're thirty-five and haven't aged well, *not* twenty-eight."

"I want my lawyer," she said.

"You'll get one, dummy," Sadie hissed. "Because you need one badly, someone smarter than you to sort out the lies."

"Sadie," Brad warned. "Let her lawyer up. That's what guilty people do."

"It's also what innocent people do against corrupt FBI agents, and there's no shortage of you un-American assholes."

"While you might be right, although I doubt you're *that* right," Sadie said, "I can say that whether or not some bought-and-paid-for clowns at the top of my food chain are corrupt doesn't change the fact that you and your brothers killed families."

"Brothers?" she asked.

"Jake and David," Sadie said.

"I ain't got no brothers!" she snapped.

Sadie wanted to spit fire on this woman but was getting tired of the charade. Finally, she turned and said, "With lies like those—and I'm talking about real whoppers—the best defense attorney on planet Earth won't be able to save you, you miserable twat."

Despite speaking with conviction, Sadie was afraid. For that very reason, she continued to press the issue. The truth she thought Riley would confess was not what she wanted, but there was a thread here, and Sadie had to pull it.

"How old are you really, Riley?" Sadie asked. "Be honest, and it will help, but lie again, and we will make your life very difficult."

"I already said I wanted a lawyer, which means you can't talk to me no more."

Brad chimed in with, "Nothing you say can or will be held against you in a court of law right now because we haven't read you your rights—yet."

"You're as dumb as the day is long," Sadie told her. "Can't you see I'm trying to help you? All you have to do is tell me the truth about your age. Answer that, and I'll shut up."

"Promise?"

Sadie nodded.

"Forty-three, and I look old because I'm a recovering meth addict."

"From where?" Sadie asked.

"You said you'd stop asking questions."

Riley was not their killer. Sadie tried to mask her disappointment, but it wasn't easy. "I know you're not our suspect now, but I want to know why you lied."

She didn't answer.

Sadie glanced at Brad's eyes as they shifted in the rearview mirror to watch her and their suspect, or former suspect. Riley was still conflicted over something, and Sadie needed to know why.

"Where are you from, Riley?" Sadie asked again.

"San Jose," she muttered.

That was where Sadie went out on a limb. "What's your real name because it's not Riley Sharpe?"

Riley swallowed hard, her eyes bobbing back and forth as if holding onto something big, a secret she was reluctant to divulge. She finally turned away, which was so annoying that Sadie lashed out. Without thinking, knowing that time was of the essence, she grabbed the podcaster by the shorthairs and jerked her face around.

"What's your real name?" she barked.

"Agent Gray!" Brad turned and warned.

"Get yer hands off of me!" Riley growled.

"Tell me your real name!" Sadie screamed in her face.

"June Grendel, all right? June Grendel!"

Sadie let go of her hair, shoved her head away, and moved back to her side of the back seat.

"You ain't real Feds," June growled. "You're the Fartsucking

Bureau of Intimidation, and this is a *clear* abuse of power. If you don't think I'm gonna report you now, you're as dumb as you say I am."

Sadie knew she'd crossed the line but wasn't sweating it, yet. "It's an abuse of power if I open the door and throw you out of the car going sixty with the cuffs still on you. Right now, you lied to federal agents in an attempt to obstruct justice, on top of the trespassing charges. We can charge you with both, and make them stick."

"I didn't obstruct nuthin!" she cried.

"Yes, you did," Brad said.

"Why did you choose that name, of all names?" Sadie asked.

June went from outraged to embarrassed and then straight to shame. "My assistant, the smaller blonde, that's her name. She gave it to me to use."

The girl on the motorcycle—the one who raced away. *Oh, God. Did June say something to her, warn her? Did the real Riley Sharpe know we were coming?*

"Turn the car around, Brad."

He was already slowing down.

"I need the real Riley's actual address," Sadie said, "not a guess or general location. You have one chance to save your bony ass, and that's through relentless cooperation."

"It's back at the office," June mumbled.

Brad met Sadie's eyes in the rearview mirror; she almost smiled but held back when she saw the heat in his gaze.

"Now, June Grendel, why did you change your name?" Sadie asked, undeterred. "What are you trying to hide that was so important that you lied to federal agents?"

"My past," she admitted, a defeated look on her face.

"We're not mind readers," Sadie said.

She cleared her throat, adjusted in her seat because the cuffs were tight, and said, "I have a long history of drug abuse, narcotics distribution, and domestic violence."

"Domestic violence?"

June nodded. "I broke my husband's balls," she said. She met Sadie's eyes and said, "Both of them. Literally."

Sadie suppressed a laugh. "How'd you manage that?"

"Well, after I caught him having sex with our daughter, I waited for the right time to drug him, and when he didn't even know his name because I got him that wasted, I knocked his ass out with a mean right hook. I busted a finger, but it was worth it."

"And then?" Sadie pressed.

"He was lying on the Pergo flooring, which made it easy to yank down his pants. The second I got his filthy drawers circled around his ankles I was staring at the offending member. I pulled out his saggy balls, grabbed 'em in a bundle, then laid them on the floor and lowered my knee onto each one.

Brad grunted from the front seat, but Sadie listened, rapt.

"It took a few times to get the job done, and I fell over once, which hurt my injured finger like a mother-effer. But then I cracked both those eggs, and it felt *good*. What didn't feel so good was finding myself in jail 'til my lawyer got me out. I took a plea deal for a limited sentence but lost custody of our kid, who still won't talk to me. My husband is now in prison and hopefully getting his salad tossed by guys twice his size."

"No one should wish for anyone to be raped," Brad said.

"Says the pretty boy with no kids," June said. She nodded in Sadie's direction. "She gets it. She doesn't have kids, but she doesn't have to, and *still* she gets it." Looking at Sadie with the eyes of a beaten dog, she added, "God in heaven, trust me when I tell you I hate men."

"Yeah, well, men hate you too, you feckless degenerate," Brad said from the front seat.

June didn't seem offended by Brad's hostility, but she surprised them both by saying, "Yeah, I guess you're right. If I give you Riley's address, you'll let me go, right?"

Sadie nodded. "We won't press charges."

"For real?"

"For real," Brad confirmed. "But we will be referring you to the Placer County Sheriff's Office, considering you have a photo of a crime scene that only a deputy, crime scene tech, or the murderer could take."

"Riley gave that to me—my research assistant, the *real* Riley Sharpe."

"What did you give her in return for using her name?"

"Anonymity and a job," she answered. "If I flood the internet with the 'Riley Sharpe' name from my podcasts and become a big name online, the real Riley will get twenty percent of the business, and pretty soon, her name will be buried under dozens of search pages, and no one will ever know either of us, not the real us. I figured that was her motivation, and I got no problem with that. In fact, I'm good with that."

"What did she say *she* was hiding from?" Brad asked as they pulled in front of the office.

"She said her daddy was a murderer. Killed himself a bunch a girls, fifteen or twenty years ago. Youngins. Barely even got their periods. Anyway, he got found out, and got his ticket punched by some psychopath, apparently."

Brad glanced at Sadie again but said nothing.

"Address," Brad said.

"Soon's you get me outta these cuffs, cocksucker. Then, I'll give it to you."

Sadie stared at her, aghast. The woman turned and looked at her after the outburst, her eyes once again brimming with rage.

Sadie's gaze burned with the same intensity but for different reasons. "You might be innocent, but for the record, you're ugly, disgusting, and unbelievably offensive."

"Which is my right!" June barked so loud that spit flew from her filthy mouth.

Sadie zeroed in on the woman's temple and knew if she drilled her with a straight right, she could knock her out and make the noise stop. Before she could get the chance, though, Brad opened the back door and hauled her out into the street. She complained about the rough treatment, but June Grendel was a piece of work.

So, Brad spun her around, removed the cuffs, and both pushed her away from him and stepped back.

Irate and likely embarrassed, June turned and faced Brad, then postured up like she planned to hit him.

Sadie was suddenly standing beside her. "You touch him, I touch you, but about fifty times harder, June. You can't threaten a federal agent without suffering some serious blowback, so I would advise you to turn around, head inside, and get us that address."

June shoved past Sadie and charged inside the office like a tornado blowing through an open building. A few minutes later, she walked outside, thrust a piece of paper at Sadie, then spat on her shoe.

Without thinking, Sadie kicked the woman in the gut, transferring the glob of spit on her shoe to the front of the woman's shirt, while hurting her in the process. June bent over, gasping for breath, and raised a defensive hand.

Brad grabbed Sadie's arm, but she turned and said, "Don't touch me, Agent Tulle." She turned to June, looking her dead in the eyes. "Spitting on a federal agent is the same as assault, you moron."

June backed up, still gasping for breath, still holding her hand up to ward off Sadie.

"Let's go," Sadie told Brad.

Brad got into the car; Sadie climbed into the passenger seat next to him. They took off at a less than leisurely pace, and when they cleared the scene, Brad pounded the dash with a fist hard enough to startle her. Sadie moved away from him when he spun his head and glared at her. "Are you kidding me right now?" he roared.

"What? She spat on me."

"That happens, Sadie! Even when we're wearing our best suits and don't deserve it. Some people like us, and most hate us when we're on the job. You can't just kick the crap out of people because they insult you or spit on you. It's saliva, Sadie. Saliva!"

She avoided his eyes but lifted her chin, refusing to let him make her feel small. "I did the right thing."

"Really? Assaulting a citizen? Because if someone caught that on camera, they might have missed her spit but caught your kick. You know, you could not only face suspension, but you might also end up before the OPR begging to keep your job!"

"For *that*?" she asked.

"You should know better," he said, lethally silent.

"I do now."

"The Office of Professional Responsibility does not mess around, Sadie," Brad said. "You don't want to find yourself in their crosshairs."

She lowered her head and felt foolish and reckless.

"I looked into your father," Brad admitted after a moment of stern breathing.

She turned to him, no longer feeling small. Emboldened by her family history, she told herself she was big, tall, and ferocious, like her father. "Yeah, he's a violent felon."

Brad didn't flinch. "Seems that if you don't watch yourself, you're going to be the apple that didn't fall too far from the tree." She bit her lip and refused to take the bait. But Brad was right—she was out of line.

With whatever humility she could muster, Sadie said, "I'm sorry. You're the case agent, and I haven't been very respectful of that. I acted impulsively rather than professionally, and it won't happen again."

As hard as that was to say, the apology seemed to diffuse him; if anyone asked, she'd claim that making the apology cost her a bit of her dignity and some of her soul. June Grendel deserved a kick to her face, not her gut, but dirtbags will always be dirtbags, and she had to carry herself by a much higher standard if she was going to honor her FBI credentials.

"It's all right," Brad said, calming down. "I mean, it isn't, but it is. I can vouch for you if anything comes up with Blackwood or the OPR."

"Do you think it will?" she asked.

He shook his head and said, "If we save the day, no, but if we save the day wrong, then definitely yes."

"How do you save the day wrong?"

"You get the killer but botch everything up to that point," he answered. "Quit asking questions right now and just be the navigator."

She nodded wordlessly, humbled and humiliated, and opened Google Maps on her phone. A moment later, she entered Riley Sharpe's address into the app and called out directions.

He followed her without comment.

The sun dipped into the horizon, just behind the soaring tree line. A few minutes later, she said, "Slow down; it's just ahead."

The moment they rounded the bend, a figure on a motorcycle shot out into the road and crashed in front of them. Brad was a great driver but not good enough to avoid hitting the rider. No one could have dodged something like that.

He braked hard and cranked the wheel as best as possible to avoid running over the rider; the back wheels broke loose. Brad steered the Impala into a controlled slide, but it wasn't enough. The tires bumped over the body twice and the car came to a smoking stop sideways in the road. Fortunately, they were now facing the street where Brad had intended to turn, the same street from where the motorcycle had emerged.

What they saw standing in the road, caused them both to gasp.

Sadie had hung on for the ride so far, but was so shaken that when gunfire broke out, she hadn't even drawn her weapon. A rip of bullets suddenly punched through the windshield, the noise so loud and shocking she could hardly think to breathe.

twenty-nine
riley sharpe

EARLIER...

The moment she heard June talking on the phone with that rotten Sadie Gray, she knew the Feds were on to her and her dumbass brothers. Scrambling for a quick escape with a plausible explanation, she told June that she started her period and was having the worst cramps.

"The podcast is already loaded and getting views," June said. "You did great, so go ahead and go."

She hopped on one of the motorcycles she had stolen from Brodi's place and high-tailed it out of there just in time. Before long, Sadie and her pretty male partner would find out that Riley Sharpe, the podcaster, was actually June Grendel, the recovering meth addict, and it would be over.

It was time to move from operational to damage control.

Riley stayed on the throttle throughout town, leaning right and left on the tighter turns and corners to maintain her speed before goosing it on the straightaways. She rode to Placer Hills Road, avoiding the mayhem of Highway 80, while heading west to Meadow Vista, to the abandoned house where she and her brothers were squatting.

She passed through Meadow Vista and hung a right on Combie Road, still making good time as she passed Wooley Creek Lane on the right and Volley Road on the left. She ripped past a few clean-looking houses set back on beautiful properties among the trees, as well as some run-down houses likely inhabited by inbreeders and Section Eight failures. And then she saw the familiar house, a prize-winning dump with rusted-out car parts, abandoned tools, and all measures of miscellaneous trash among the weeds in the front yard. Before the bend in the road, just past the nasty house and a utility pole in front, Riley slowed for the unmarked easement road ahead. Three small green plates, mounted on a warped four-by-four post in the grassy shoulder along Combie Road, marked three residences—hers being one of them. She braked hard, leaned into the turn, and shot up the asphalt road with no time to spare.

Riley parked the bike next to the faded blue Gremlin and David's bike, which was similar to hers. She killed the engine, pushed out the kickstand, and hung her clamshell helmet on the handlebar grip. She hated the house but knew she would have to leave it. It was her fault. She was showboating with June when she gave her the crime scene photo. But didn't the best killers eventually boast to the cops and public? It was a staple of pride, a way of saying she was smart, law enforcement and the Feds were dumb, and she could kill whomever she wanted, whenever she wanted, and no one could do a damn thing about it. Now that she'd overplayed her hand, she realized she and the two dummies were not that good, so it was time to do what needed doing, what had *always* needed doing.

The second she walked in the front door, she found Jake pacing the room like he was fit to burst. "What the hell are you doing home?" she asked.

"They're closing in on us, Riley."

"Yeah, no kidding."

They had an old TV hooked up to an even older VCR playing tapes they found in the house: *Matlock* and *Perry Mason*. Right now, Perry Mason was in court arguing a case while David sat on the couch without pants or a shirt—just a pair of dirty tighty-whities—chewing on his toenails like a dirtbag. His feet and toenails were gross; he was gross.

"Can't you open a window or something?" Riley asked. "It's hot as balls in here and smells like ass."

"David is cold," Jake said.

Riley read the stress in Jake's features and knew something happened. "Put on some fucking clothes, you jackass!" she finally screamed at David.

"You're cold because you're out here looking like trailer park trash in your damn underpants," Jake added.

David turned and spat a chewed-off shred of toenail at her, hitting her in the cheek. Riley gasped, looked at Jake, and flared her nostrils. Her eyes, expression, and demeanor told Jake it was *that time.*

A gleam of reflective dying light caught her attention—the bundle of locks.

"Those clean?" she asked in an attempt to calm down.

Jake was standing on the edge of a proverbial cliff, though. "Don't take that tone with me, sister," he snarled. "I've got all my clothes on."

"This whole room smells like body odor and unwashed butts, *David.*"

David, eyes still glued to the TV, lifted an arm, smelled his pits, and snickered.

"Is it time, then?" Jake finally asked. The weight of his question hung heavy in his eyes and pulled at his weathered features.

"Yeah," she mumbled.

She walked into the back, opened her closet, and pushed her clothes and shoes aside. After removing a cedar wood panel revealing a false wall, she grabbed her LWRC International AR-15 and shoved a ten-round mag into the mag well. She palmed it into place, seating the mag, and yanked the charging handle to chamber a round. Finally, she flipped the safety selector to "live fire."

She took a moment to gather her courage, but then she realized how much she hated them both and knew it was time to cut bait on David. He would buckle under pressure and squeal on them anyway; she couldn't have that.

The second she entered the living room, David saw the weapon, jumped out of the chair, and bolted for the door. Jake overhanded the bundle of locks at him, hitting him in the back, but the little turd was wicked fast, had a high pain tolerance, and knew the score.

Riley rushed out the door as David kick-started his motorcycle, goosed it, and rocketed out of there. She ran out onto the asphalt easement road, where David was making a run for Combie Road. If he got there, he was as good as gone, and they were as good as caught. That was unacceptable.

Riley lined up a shot, fired a three-round burst, and sunk one of the three bullets into his back, not ten yards from Combie Road. He crashed, landing hard on his leg. The bike lay on him, not exactly pinning him down but making it hard to get up. Breathing heavily, consumed with hostility and an ocean of rage, Riley stalked past a house on the left and one on the right, her weapon at her side.

An old woman in the ramshackle house on the right must have heard the gunshots; she stepped onto her porch in a housedress and diabetic swell socks. Riley paused and turned to look at her. The older woman was pushing four hundred pounds, with swollen tree trunks for legs, ham hocks for arms, and a neck as thick as Riley's waist. In other words, she was an easy target. Riley lined up a quick shot and fired once, the bullet punching through her throat.

Six rounds left.

By then, David had crawled to his feet and climbed onto the bike; he was now trying to start it. From a distance, Riley saw his left leg streaked red with road rash and that he was bleeding from the gunshot wound that struck his back.

"Stop, David!"

"NO!" he screamed over his shoulder.

The engine caught, and David dropped the bike into first gear and took off. Riley had already lined up the shot. Just before David could turn right onto Combie Road, she pulled the trigger and put a bullet through the back of his head. Gore exited his face, and he collapsed onto the road, the bike sliding across the asphalt and landing in a nearby ditch.

Riley lowered the rifle, conflicted but mostly happy at finally putting him down. Before she could turn to head back home, she heard the sounds of locked brakes and tires skidding across the asphalt surface. Half a second later, she watched a dark sedan run over David's body. The car came to a stop, but David's body was a lump in the road.

A lifted truck coming from the opposite direction and moving way too fast hit its brakes to avoid the sedan and David. But the driver who hit David saw he was about to get t-boned and gunned it. He drove over part of David with the rear tires and headed straight to her, the front wheels all but smoking. The sedan escaped impact just in time, but the lifted truck locked its brakes and skidded over David's body, dragging him down Combie and out of sight.

Riley stood paralyzed, her mouth agape, but then she saw the two agents in the sedan heading right for her. She opened fire, pulling the trigger as fast as she could without sacrificing her aim. She stitched a quick line of fire across their windshield, ran the mag dry, then dropped the rifle and sprinted toward her bike. Riley wished she could deep-six the two agents, with her and Jake going two-on-two with those pricks, but there was no way she was going to have a shootout with one gun, twenty-five bullets, and Jake's shotgun.

The best course of action was to flee.

Riley fired up the bike and glanced at Jake, who appeared at the window. He was staring at her, but there was no way to communicate what was happening and what was about to happen. Hopefully, he would read the panic in her eyes and run.

But by the time she dropped the bike into first gear, the sedan had given chase. Riley shot out of there like a bat out of Hell, ripping around the side of the house while working through second and third gears. She snuck one last look over her shoulder and saw Sadie leap from the sedan and run back down the road. What for, though? David's bike?

Riley cut through heavy trees and brush, following a narrow trail fast enough to create distance between her and the Feds but not so fast that she risked crashing her bike. A deep and painful churning roiled in her stomach at the idea of leaving everything behind, including her clothes, toiletries, makeup, and what remained of her stupid family. But what other choice did she have?

She pulled to a stop, shut off the engine, and listened. Moments later, she heard the other motorcycle and knew Sadie had grabbed David's bike and taken chase. Then, in the distance, she heard a volley of gunfire and knew Jake had stayed in the house and was now in a firefight with the pretty boy and maybe the local LEOs if they'd already been alerted. She started her bike and took a different path, deciding to head back to her birth home in Grass Valley, where everything terrible first began.

thirty
sadie gray

EARLIER...

Sadie should have ducked or moved sideways behind the sedan's A-pillar when gunfire broke out, but had she done that, her face would have an extra hole. As it was, one of the half-dozen bullets that punched through the windshield zipped past her ear and drilled the headrest, blowing stuffing out the side. She whipped her head around and saw that Brad had moved slightly, which saved his life. The nearest bullet to him blew through his headrest, missing his face by fractions of an inch. Instead of backing out of there and getting to safety, he gassed the engine and raced toward the shooter, who had abandoned her rifle and run toward the house.

"When I stop, jump out and grab your vest and weapons from the trunk," Brad said, strangely calm.

"No time," she said, gripping the door handle for when he stopped.

She saw the girl hop on the motorcycle, and then she saw a butt-ugly Gremlin parked in front of a disgusting, falling-apart house. Beyond that, framed in a large picture window, stood a large man with a face void of expression. Instead of going after him, commandeering the shitbox on wheels, or waiting with Brad for backup, Sadie leaped from the car and sprinted back down the road toward the dead kid's bike.

Several people had stopped their cars in the middle of the road where a large pickup had veered off into a ditch after running over the body she and Brad ran over first. Sadie glanced at David's skinny, pale corpse, where he lay bloody in the street, dead. A long, red, meaty trail preceded him, and half his face was gone. She paused momentarily to take it in. He lay there, half-skinned with broken bones showing, and his tighty-whitey underwear properly soiled and soaking up whatever blood it could. She couldn't deal with that now.

Instead, she crossed the road and headed for the Apollo motorbike with the number 36 printed on the side. The bike in the grassy ditch looked street-legal, with abundant black- and red-colored plastic. She hadn't been on a bike like that since before the kidnapping. She went and stood it up, straddled it, and tried to start it. It roared to life immediately. In the distance, down Combie Road, Sadie saw flashing lights and a pair of sirens from two incoming Placer County Sheriff's cruisers.

Good, the cavalry is here.

She dropped the bike into gear, planted her foot in the dirt and weeds, and goosed the throttle. She then dumped the clutch while cranking the handlebars inward. The back tire spun up a rooster tail of dirt and weeds as she whipped the back end around. She let off the throttle now that she had a straight shot to the house, looked both ways for traffic, then let off the clutch and launched across the two-lane road.

Brad had taken a defensive position behind the sedan with his rifle out and his vest on over his shirt. The man in the window—presumably Jake—had just broken out the glass with the barrel of his rifle and started shooting. Brad hadn't had time for his FBI windbreaker and ball cap. Did it matter, though? He was taking fire.

Sadie roared past Brad, heading for the trail alongside the

house, but something massive—a shotgun slug perhaps—blasted through the front of the bike, blowing apart the plastic front fender. She all but hugged the motorcycle as she raced behind the house, and to safety—*for now.*

The established trail was only inches wide, like a well-traveled bike path cutting through the weeds and brush. Sadie stuck to it, moving as fast as possible, knowing Riley had a substantial lead. Sadie had to make up for lost time, but there was no sense in wrecking the bike or getting injured. The last thing she needed was to abandon her partner in a shootout and end up hitting a freaking tree.

She raced up the winding trail for more than a mile, keeping her eyes peeled for an ambush or any other signs of Riley Sharpe. When she reached a narrow backwoods road and saw no sign of the killer, she blew out a disappointed breath, unsure of which direction to go.

Make a freaking decision!

She eased the throttle open and crossed a narrow one-lane road before cutting through an expansive space into a grove of mature trees. Once she cleared the trees, she rode into the open, over a small hill, and picked up speed until nearly t-boning a wooden fence. She backed off the throttle and worked the brake, leaning hard to the right. She barely avoided crashing, but time was against her. She goosed the throttle again, racing alongside the fenced property of a dilapidated single-story home. A snarling, barking pit bull charged her, running toward her like something out of Satan's lair. She negotiated the fence line long enough to hit another one-lane, tree-lined road.

"Son of a bitch!" she growled.

The trail abruptly ended at a single-lane country road. Sadie paused to consider her options, then chose to follow her instincts and go right. But her instincts failed her, and she ended up on Combie Road.

Shaking her head, itching to let out the mother of all screams, Sadie killed the engine and let the stillness of the day flood her ears. She strained to hear, listening for a motorbike. All she heard were the soothing sounds of nature.

Across the two-lane road, which was painted with clean white and yellow lines, stood a bank of locking metal mailboxes. Behind that was a wall of trees. With no one around, no one in sight, and not even the sound of an engine to follow, she was fresh out of luck.

She breathed a long, frustrated sigh, took a right, and returned empty-handed to the bend in the road, where sheriff's deputies had arrived and cordoned off the road. She slowed for the makeshift barricade, slowed to a stop, and flashed her credentials.

"The shootout?" she asked.

"You missed it," the deputy said, deadpan.

"What about my partner, FBI Special Agent Brad Tulle?"

Now the deputy looked at her. "You two were first on the scene, right?"

Sadie nodded. "Is he okay? Wait... did he make it?"

The man glanced up the road, then back to her, and shook his head.

He's dead?

A car moving too quickly approached the scene and braked hard; it was an old but clean-looking Ford Mustang. The deputy would have to check the driver and their license and then escort them through the gruesome accident scene. He didn't attempt to clear the way for her but was still in the way.

"Move!" Sadie barked.

Startled but compliant, the deputy stepped aside, glaring at her but also understanding. She ripped the throttle and shot past him, heading up the easement toward the house. Placer County Sheriffs cars crowded the driveway near her and Brad's sedan, which was pumped full of holes and looked shot to shit.

Her heart sank, and she felt sick at the idea that Brad might be dead. She reached the house, dropped the bike, and strolled toward the open front door.

Sadie grabbed her credentials but slowed her pace when

Captain Scott walked out the front door, his round face pale. She passed the bu-car, glanced back, and reeled in horror at the damage. Shotgun slugs had Swiss-cheesed the side of the Impala, spider-webbed the ballistic glass, and flattened a tire.

With a sense of dread so deep it supercharged her sadness and remorse, she knew then that she should have covered Brad. If Jake or someone else killed him, if he was truly gone… how could she live with herself? The blame for his death would land squarely on her shoulders, just as it should.

The second Captain Scott saw her, he said, "There you are."

"Brad…"

He shook his head. "Boy, you sure screwed the pooch on this one." He took the mirrored Aviator glasses from his pocket, slid them on, and said, "You never leave your partner, especially during a shootout. You don't need to be a real cop to know that. But you're not a real cop, are you? You're just a brand-new suit with credentials."

"Is he alive?" she heard herself ask, her eyes glistening.

"Even a broad like you should have common sense enough to know that, but you didn't know, did you?"

She swallowed hard and took the reprimand, but she didn't care because the blood had drained from her face, her knees felt weak, and she fought the urge to drop down and puke. She hated that Captain Scott was probably getting off on this.

"You're too pretty for law enforcement, Ms. Gray," he continued, walking so close that she smelled his aftershave and sour breath. "Maybe you should stick to beauty pageants or go be an Instagram influencer or something like that. Just"—he looked down at her and paused for effect— "leave this kind of work to the professionals."

She snapped out of the moment, registered the insult, and said, "With all due respect, Captain, you can eat my ass with a spoon, and then you can shove your opinions right up that shovel butt of yours."

His jaw went slack, and his mouth fell open; he stared at her, unable to find the words. Sadie breezed past him, pushed through the front door, and stopped when she saw all that blood and the body.

He lay there, deader than Disco, with someone from forensics kneeling over him, snapping photos. It looked like a shotgun blast had destroyed most of his face, the hanging flaps of skin an unholy sight. *Oh, dear, sweet Jesus.*

"Shotgun, right?" she asked, swallowing bile.

The deputy looked up and nodded. "Yeah, to the face."

"Any other injuries?"

Returning to the body, he said, "The first shot blew off a chunk of his shoulder—that happened just before the fatal injury."

thirty-one
brad tulle

MOMENTS EARLIER...

Brad watched Sadie hop out of the car and sprint down the asphalt easement as if running for her life. *The hell?* He shook his head and couldn't figure out why dumb girls did such dumb things, and running away from a firefight was the dumbest thing he'd ever experienced in all his years with the Bureau.

"You're on your own, Brad," he mumbled as he kept himself low and popped the trunk. He donned his tactical vest, but then someone broke the large glass window and started shooting. He ducked a few close shots, the shotgun slugs doing damage to the car.

Down the road, when he heard a small engine turn over, Brad squinted and caught sight of Sadie—she had mounted the dead kid's bike. She looked both ways and shot across Combie, then roared up the easement road, flying toward him and the kill zone. Brad spun around and lifted his head in time to see the shooter adjust the barrel of his shotgun and open fire on Sadie.

Brad squeezed off three quick rounds from his Sig Sauer P226 handgun, missing the first two shots but winging the shooter with the third. The man he suspected of being Jake Sharpe ducked inside the house; Sadie kept going, unharmed.

He sighed—*thank God.*

Brad turned his attention back to the house. He had to survive this lunatic and make a clean arrest, but that probably wasn't in the cards. Brad quickly holstered his pistol and pulled the Rock River Arms AR-15 from the trunk. He popped the mag, quickly checked its notched-out indicator window, and verified it was full. He jerked the charging handle to seat a round and took a defensive position behind the bu-car.

The second Jake appeared at the window, Brad let his AR rip. The 5.56mm bullets penetrated the house, obliterating cheap wood paneling and aged drywall and creating a noisy, violent show of force.

Jake repositioned himself in front of what looked like the smaller kitchen window, but when Brad saw the shotgun barrel appear, he moved behind the Impala's rear wheel, making himself as small a target as possible.

Gunfire resumed, followed by noise and destruction, stopping only when Jake ran his shotgun's tube dry. The side of the Impala suffered nominal damage from the slugs, which was a testament to the bu-car's ballistic glass and panels.

Instead of continuing the assault, Jake broke into a furious tirade of obscenities Brad heard from his position. Was he mad that he missed Brad? Or was he finally hurting from that 9mm slug he caught earlier?

Brad shifted position to the other side of the Impala, ducking behind the front wheel, which was closest to Jake and the house. He waited for a beat and was about to stand and return fire when Jake fired three more slugs. One slug hit the passenger window, spider-webbing the ballistic glass but not punching through. That would only happen once, Brad told himself. A second shot to the same place would break the glass, not that it would matter at that point.

Jake's cursing changed tempo, the words becoming filthier

and more laced with wrath. Brad sneaked a peek and caught sight of the idiot standing in the window, trying to clear a feeder jam. Seizing the opportunity, he stood and opened fire. He rushed the first shot, slapping the trigger, but his second and third shots nicked parts of Jake's face, blowing through flesh as evidenced by a light pink mist.

The levels of screaming and cursing rose to all new levels. Brad changed position again, hurrying back to the open trunk. Staying low, he changed out the AR for his Remington 870 tactical shotgun, which was not bu-car-ready, a lapse in judgment.

He grabbed a box of 2 3/4" nickel-coated shotshells with flite control and ducked behind the rear wheel, again using it for cover. He thumbed six shells into the mag tube and fed in a final one as his plus-one. He flinched at the sound of an errant round, making himself small now that Jake had cleared the jam. He barely finished the thought when another shotgun blast shattered the silence. The slug thumped the Impala's door, indicating that the ballistic sheeting was holding for now.

He tuned back in to the sounds of movement and agitated screaming inside the house. So far, Jake had not come outside or retreated deeper into the house, a good sign if Brad could find a way to make entry.

With double-aught buck now in the tube, he grabbed a Velcro-based five-round side saddle, slapped it on the gun, thumbed off the safety, and got ready to work. While he was not currently, nor had he ever been, part of the FBI's SWAT unit, Brad grew up firing shotguns and was comfortable enough to have spent years working on short stocking techniques, a.k.a. close-quarters battle, or CQB, for shotguns. Now was his chance to put his training into action.

He took a deep, stabilizing breath and crept around the front of the Impala. He sneaked another quick peek, saw a clear line of approach, and raced for the front door, staying low. Fortunately, Jake didn't see that he'd advanced on the house and opened fire.

Brad tried the knob and found it locked. He stood back,

angled the gun just right, and fired a load of buck into the locking mechanism. Without hesitation, he kicked in the door but hung back. From inside, Brad heard the scampering of feet running from him as if toward the back of the house. He brought his shotgun to the high ready but rotated the gun ninety degrees and balanced the flat of the stock on his shoulder, significantly shortening the weapon's length. He could now index the gun to where he would need his rounds to go while making himself less of a target.

Go, go, go!

Brad entered the house and switched to the low-ready firing position due to the tight space ahead. That would give him a much shorter arc if he needed to lift the barrel into the high-ready position.

He used the short front hallway as a point of cover, believing that the large room opened into a dining room, kitchen, and living room—or a great room concept. The second he entered the open space, he reminded himself to lead with minimal barrel length.

He knocked a knuckle on the wall between him and any potential shooters; it was too flimsy to provide adequate protection. In other words, he had poor cover at best. Knowing the risks, he worked the angle quickly, aware of his footwork, and moved fluidly into a position where he could check the dining room, kitchen, and living room for targets and better points of cover.

A shotgun blast startled him, as did the sound of wood paneling and drywall coming apart behind him. Jake was still shooting slugs rather than buck or birdshot, which comforted Brad. A more experienced shooter knew seven, eight, or nine smaller projectiles upped the odds of survival far more than using one massive slug when it came to defending the home.

"You can't come in here, you sorry son of a bitch!" Jake screamed, his voice hoarse, as if something was severely wrong with his mouth.

"Why not?" Brad asked, ducking and backing up.

The deafening sound of shotgun fire and the slug blasting through the partition where he stood moments ago startled him. Worse, bits of drywall and splintered wood had peppered his cheeks, some piercing his skin. He ignored the pain, trusting that any injuries were minimal.

Jake answered, yelling, "You can't come in without a warrant because we didn't do nothin' wrong!" His voice was raspy and forced, and he sounded like he had significant damage to his jaw from where Brad thought he had hit or grazed him earlier.

"I don't need a warrant when there are shots fired, you moron!" Brad said, ducking.

Rather than firing another slug, Jake took a breath to speak; Brad capitalized on the opportunity, moving into the open, where he fired from the short-stocking position, using the push-pull method to stabilize the weapon and manage recoil. His aim was off, though, for he'd induced his heart rate early on and had just bumped it another notch.

Now in the open and vulnerable, Brad pushed the weapon forward, ran the action, and transitioned into a shoulder-mount position. He saw Jake's shotgun barrel appear, giving away his position. Brad fired another round. All three rounds of buck chewed holes in the walls in front of Jake, but Brad wasn't sure which shots, if any, found their mark.

Trapped in the open, he was in a sit-and-wait situation with nothing for cover but crappy furniture any shotgun slug could punch through in nothing flat. He flattened himself against the closest wall to minimize himself as a target but aimed the shotgun toward the hallway, where Jake lay in wait.

"Who are you anyway?" Jake snarled, sounding worse by the minute.

"Special Agent Brad Tulle with the FBI."

The second Brad spoke, Jake rushed into the living room, vested-up with ammo spilling out of his sweatpants pockets and his shotgun at the high ready.

Brad fired two rounds of buck on the way to three before Jake could get off a single shot. The first load blasted Jake's vest; the second took a massive chunk out of his shoulder; and the third shot, which Brad took because Jake chose slugs rather than double-aught buck or bird shot, was a gorgeous shot to the target's face.

The spread was tight, and all pellets did significant damage. Brad racked a fresh load only to find he'd run the mag tube dry. He thumbed a shell from the five-shot side saddle into the ejection port and hit the activator; he shoved two more into the mag tube for a total of three, then closed the action and prepared for anything. He didn't think he'd need another shot, let alone three, but safe was better than dead.

He had reduced the downed man's face to a raw ball of meatloaf, but still, Brad proceeded with caution. He kicked the fallen shotgun out of reach, bent and checked Jake's wrist for a pulse—which he didn't find—then stood, satisfied with the kill enough to clear the rest of the house and vacate the scene.

When Brad stepped outside, local Sheriff's deputy cars were flying up the road. He closed the trunk lid, placed his shotgun and handgun on the lid, then stepped away from his slug-blasted sedan to wait for the cavalry.

Captain Scott was first on the scene from the Placer County Sheriff's Office; he wasn't halfway out of the bu-car when he started pressing Brad for details. Brad let him know the sole target was down and the house was clear.

Brad talked the man through the action, but they had yet to walk the scene, which he verbally turned over to Captain Scott, who said one of his guys would call forensics shortly. Then, to one of his deputies, Captain Scott said, "Clear the house and wait for me inside."

"It's clear," Brad said.

Captain Scott nodded but chose not to repeat the message to his deputies as the pair—one with his pistol drawn and another carrying a camera bag and gun—approached the house.

"Where's your partner?" Captain Scott turned and asked.

Brad was wondering the same thing; he gave the only answer he had. "She took off after Riley, the sister. That was right after the girl shot her brother in the back of the head, then opened fire on us." He pointed down the road to Combie. "Her brother is the run-over kid you passed down there."

"She killed her brother?" Captain Scott asked.

"Smoked his ass right in front of us."

"She shot at you first, then?"

Brad shook his head. "First, she killed her brother, then she saw us coming and stitched a line of fire across our windshield. By the grace of God, the shots missed us. But I assume she ran the mag dry, which was why she abandoned her rifle before running for a dirt bike she used to escape. Sadie grabbed the dead kid's bike down on Combie and took chase."

Scott seemed surprised. "Leaving you here alone?"

Brad squared his shoulders. "We're capable agents, Captain Scott. We spend a lot of time at the range and run drills in shoot houses alongside our SWAT teams. All that is to say that I'm comfortable with this kind of action."

Captain Scott nodded thoughtfully before meeting Brad's eyes. "Still, she shouldn't have left, okay?"

Brad was already tired of the seasoned LEO dad chat. It was the kind of "we hate Feds enough to question your tactics" B.S. that he didn't need. So, it was time to nip that nonsense in the bud.

"You worry about your team, and I'll worry about mine," Brad replied using a calm voice; he followed with a disarming grin. Captain Scott said nothing. "At any rate, I appreciate you and your men coming."

Captain Scott nodded and said, "How many are dead besides the lady shot in the throat, lying on her porch, the one you killed inside, and the meatloaf surprise down on Combie?"

"That's it," Brad said. "The kid in the road, his brother, Jake

—the guy on the living room floor—and the lady you're telling me about. So, three total."

"Might as well show me now," Captain Scott said. He shouted to another one of his deputies. "Tell the coroner to bring three body bags!"

"Yes, Sir."

The two entered the house with Brad leading. He felt that Captain Scott was still bothered about something. The gruff old guy finally said, "You know, I always try to like you guys, but y'all come off like a bunch of high-brow know-it-alls with your ivy-league talk and your fancy clothes, if I'm being honest."

"It's a little too late in the game for flattery," Brad scoffed.

"I'm not saying it rubs me the wrong way, even though at times it does," he said. "Considering how you approached this, though, I'm just saying y'all are a confident bunch."

Brad suppressed a grin. "We work extra hard to make sure our shit never stinks."

The older man broke into a low chuckle. But then, he stopped and surveyed the scene, taking in the damaged walls where slugs and buckshot had blown holes in them or torn apart the drywall and studs. He turned his attention to the dead shooter's body lying on the floor. For a second, Brad wondered how shocked he was by seeing that much blood.

Captain Scott cleared his throat and asked, "It was just you in here with a shotgun?" Brad nodded. The old man blew out a breath. "Damn, son… nice work."

Brad appreciated the compliment despite the toll it might have taken on the captain's ego to give it. He asked, "How hard was it to say that, Captain?"

With glossy eyes and a hillbilly smirk, the salty dog said, "Harder than you know."

Under his breath, Brad muttered, "That's what she said."

The sarcastic yet unexpected comment caused them both to break into laughter, which Brad appreciated, as the Feds were often met with hostility by local LEOs. It also felt good to break the ice, even if it happened at the tail end of the hunt.

Outside, Brad heard a motorbike racing up the road. "I'm pretty sure that's my partner," he announced.

Before heading out to meet her, Captain Scott excused himself and said, "I'll tell her you're in here."

"Thanks, Captain."

Brad took the limited time he'd have to try to decompress. His heart was still working overtime, considering the gun battle he'd survived. And then, suddenly, he realized how close he had come to dying and felt his emotions threaten to surge.

Sadie walked inside minutes later, terrified. She saw Brad, and her expression changed completely. The look of relief was so profound that Brad expected Sadie to stroll across the crime scene and hug him. Instead, she took a tentative step into the living room and focused on the body lying on the floor.

She asked the deputy with the camera, "Shotgun, right?"

He looked up and said, "Yeah, to the face."

"Other injuries?"

The deputy was focused on photographing the body but offered a response anyway. "The first shot blew off a chunk of his shoulder—that happened just before the fatal injury."

They both looked at Brad, who shrugged. "I've been working on Shotgun CQB for a while now. These are tight quarters, which made it the perfect scenario."

Deadpan, without an ounce of emotion or range to her voice, Sadie said, "The live action must have been so exciting for you."

He moved in her direction but paused, grinned, and said, "You know, it was. Now, why don't you tell me about Riley Sharpe."

After a moment's pause and a doleful look, she said, "She got away."

Sadie suddenly became easy to read. Was this because she wanted him to know she felt terrible about returning empty-handed? Brad did his best to mask his disappointment but knew he likely failed.

"How did you manage to lose her?" he asked, tempering his tone.

"She had enough of a head start," Sadie replied as if the answer was obvious.

Captain Scott popped into the house again and said, "Everyone clear out; forensics is on the way. Oh, and Ms. Gray, we've got an APB on Riley Sharpe."

"It's Agent Gray," Sadie said.

"That is yet to be determined," Captain Scott grumbled.

Brad watched Sadie's expression change, and it was clear she wasn't about to let the comment slide. She looked right at the old man and said, "You want to see my credentials, you fat-headed ball washer?"

Brad suppressed the urge to laugh. Instead, he solemnly nodded in agreement and said, "She's got them, Captain, so you might try a more respectful approach next time."

"Nevertheless..." Captain Scott replied with rosy cheeks and a flush of red circling his neck like a scarf.

Sadie wasn't one to let something like this go, as Brad was learning. She said, "While you're out front, Captain Scott, perhaps you could have someone change our bu-car's flat. I'm sure you have a spare in one of your many untouched vehicles, an obvious benefit of showing up late to the party."

Captain Scott stared at her and said, "Everyone's a comedian these days."

"Welcome to the clown show, *Otis*," Sadie replied with a wink.

The brash but somewhat humorous response left Captain Scott searching for a reply he'd never find.

Old school, meet the new school, Brad thought.

"You just remember what I told you about a career on Instagram," he said in a playful but forced tone.

"Save your fantasies for your boyfriend, Otis—I'm happy with my career path."

Nearby deputies laughed, but Captain Scott took his licks and refused to get butt-hurt about it. "Okay, I admit I might have misjudged you, and you should probably get your due."

"I'm sure you're right," Sadie said, pleased.

Captain Scott narrowed his eyes at first, then relaxed his face and acknowledged her with a nod. After that, it was back to the business of finding and arresting Riley Sharpe.

thirty-two
sadie gray

SADIE AND BRAD remained at the scene for as long as Captain Scott and the coroner needed them. Afterward, Captain Scott had one of his deputies change out the bu-car's front tire, calling it the consolation prize for being last on the scene.

Meanwhile, Riley Sharpe was out there somewhere, which was unnerving to Sadie. APBs were out for her in Sacramento, Placer, El Dorado, and even Amador counties. If they came up with nothing in the next day or two, local authorities would expand the APB to Sutter and even Yolo counties.

Unfortunately, no one heard anything from Riley, which could make their job difficult. If she had gone to ground, the next move would have been to alert every media outlet available and use them to disseminate her name, face, and physical description. Social media could also be helpful, but Sadie didn't know how to navigate those channels—where would she even begin? She assumed Brad or the locals could spearhead that if they thought it was worthwhile. Many criminals have been caught that way, including serial killers, so hopefully, *something* would work. Until they got a hit, though, it was all about the "hurry up and wait."

"Dinner?" Brad finally asked.

Sadie missed her bed and Droolius Caesar but didn't confess this to Brad for fear of ridicule. He would probably tell her to quit being a girl, and he'd be right. Either way, it was nearly nine o'clock when they left the scene, so she was hungry, tired, and more than ready for a hot bath and a bottle of wine—in that order.

"Yeah, I could do dinner," Sadie said, "but maybe fast food. Not a sit-down meal."

"That's how every LEO gets that swollen belly and a big, gelatinous butt," Brad said flippantly.

"I've been dreaming of having a body like that for days," she said.

"So... Taco Bell?" he asked.

"Yeah, I guess."

From the Taco Bell drive-thru at the Colfax Mall, Sadie ordered a six-pack of tacos with hot sauce, while Brad ordered two super burritos with fire sauce. They collected their bags of food and headed back to Grass Valley.

"About your Airbnb," Brad said when they reached the outskirts of Grass Valley. "I think you should sleep with me tonight."

"What would the other kids say?" Sadie joked, her heart not into the back-and-forth banter—not after wolfing down half her tacos and unable to abandon the other three. She took a bite of taco number four.

"I'm not asking for sex," Brad said.

"I know that, dumb-dumb," she said, talking with her mouth full.

With a tired grin, he said, "Although sex after an intense situation is a perfectly acceptable response. It might even be healthy, according to experts." She stopped chewing and looked at him. He grinned at her. "I think we should follow the science, Ms. Gray."

She quickly finished chewing, gulped down the whole load, then looked right at him and said, "I think so, too." Her tone was soft and seductive. "I'll call a hooker for you. I'm sure you two will bond."

He cleared his throat and said, "Sex worker, Sadie. *Sex worker.* Man, you can be offensive sometimes."

She slugged him in the shoulder, putting a little extra stink on it for effect. "I told you I'm a virgin."

"I am, too," he said, rubbing his shoulder.

"Yeah, right," she laughed.

"Same to you, butthole," he said, still frowning. "And quit hitting me. Your stupid little knuckles are sharp enough to hurt."

They drove silently the rest of the way, except for the calls from ASAC Blackwood and Chief Miller.

When they entered Grass Valley's city limits, Brad said, "What do you want to do? If you want, I can switch with you—take the Airbnb for the night."

"I'm fine."

"This is not smart."

"Everyone in law enforcement is now looking for this inbred mouth-breather," she said flippantly and with a twinge of hostility. "Someone else will find her first—I promise."

"You're the FNG, so your promises don't carry much water," Brad said impatiently. "It also means I trust my instincts over yours. But you're stubborn, which is fine."

She hated being called the FNG, so she refused him a reply. But, much to her chagrin, Brad wasn't finished.

"I want to check your place out first," he said. "That's non-negotiable."

"I'm a trained agent, Brad. I think I'll be just fine."

He shook his head and said, "You're unbelievable, *Sadie*."

She grinned. "Believe it, *Brad*."

Bested, he said, "So... I'm going to sleep in the car tonight to keep watch over you whether or not you like it or agree with it."

"That seems extreme," she yawned.

Brad pulled up in front of the Airbnb, and it felt like he had conceded. He turned to her and said, "You sure you're okay?"

She yawned a second time as the adrenaline, long days, and scope of the case took its toll with her. "For real, man—I'm not some damsel in distress, so stop being 'Captain Save a Ho;' it's only making me think that you think I'm weak, which I'm not."

He turned and slugged her *hard,* then smiled that sexy, Hollywood smile and said, "I know you're not weak, tough guy."

She cupped her aching shoulder, her mouth falling open. With wide, shocked eyes, she stared at Brad, who winked at her—the same as she did to him. Still, it felt as if he hit her with a sledgehammer, which he had to know by her response. Instead of apologizing, he raised his eyebrows like he was cute and funny and it was all good in the hood. Well, it wasn't.

"Are you kidding me?"

"Turnabout's fair play, butthole," he said with amusement. "Now get out of the car—I've got to take a leak before I babysit your grumpy, belligerent ass."

"Go home, douchebag," she said, still floored that he had socked her. The minute she opened the door, he leaned over and pushed her out. She nearly fell onto the ground but managed to get her balance enough to stand and slam the door like a bad date. He waved, and she flipped him off before he could drive away. When she lost sight of his taillights, she turned and headed for the porch and front door, still rubbing her shoulder. The second she stepped inside, she reached for the light, and that's when she sensed movement from behind.

The intruder punched her in the side of the face so hard that Sadie staggered sideways and nearly collapsed into the cheap TV stand. She barely registered the fact that she'd been clocked when the intruder drilled her again, this time with a vicious barrage of punches to her ribs and the side of her face and head. She covered her face as best as possible, but her timing was off, and her brains were officially scrambled.

Dazed and trying to get off the X—the center point of her attack—her mind whispered desperate messages her body couldn't obey. She took more than a few blistering shots while she covered up—several to her arms and hands and once to her ear, which hurt like crazy. No matter how hard she tried to back up and get away, her attacker pressed forward and kept hitting.

Flashes of her training at Quantico and her Everlast heavy bag appeared. Even in Quantico, a formidable adversary could off-balance you, put you back on your heels, and get in your head with pain, violence, and an unending attack. And the Everlast bag? Well, that fucker never hit back; not like she was being hit now.

Before she knew it, Sadie had been beaten across the room and pinned against the wall, where she took what felt like the brunt of the attack. The speed and savagery by which the attack persisted began to wane, her attacker gassing some.

Sadie focused all her energy and attention on landing one shot, which she needed to time and place just right. But the second she opened her guard to throw the punch, her attacker blasted her in the mouth, cutting her efforts short. That was when she saw her: Riley Sharpe.

Sadie composed herself enough to fire a cheap shot with some spunk on it; the punch landed perfectly on Riley's somewhat saggy right boob. She winced, stepped back, and frowned. Sadie followed up with a glancing blow to her chin; Riley ate the shot but shook it off. She launched herself at Sadie, their bodies clashing. With wobbly legs and pain radiating everywhere, Sadie was driven into the wall. She guarded herself, but Riley crashed through her defenses. With nowhere to go, panic set in.

Riley unleashed a ragged war cry so raw and animalistic it chilled Sadie's blood. Then she grabbed Sadie by the hair and began smashing the side of her face into the window. Each blow sapped more and more energy from Sadie until doubt and terror threatened to undo her.

Sadie blindly palmed Riley's face, found her eyeball, and shoved her thumb into it. The girl yelped. Yeah, it was time to fight dirty. Riley, however, backed up and kicked Sadie's floating rib, which knocked the wind out of her and hurt like hell.

Sadie felt the blood dripping from her nose and mouth, and there was a slight ringing in her right ear where Riley hit her.

She pushed off the wall, still in the fight. But Riley was too strong, her drive to survive unmatched—she charged Sadie again, pushing her back to the windowed wall despite eating a few of Sadie's shots. While she made contact, her punches were desperate and didn't land right. The effect was demoralizing, to say the least.

Riley grabbed her head again, flew into another terrifying frenzy, and resumed bashing it into the window, stopping only when several glass panels shattered. Sadie tried to push off the wall again to create some space, but Riley punched her in the stomach. Terrified of what was next, she covered her midsection, eyes bulging and gasping for breath.

This time, Riley stepped back and drilled her with a nasty kick. Covering up hadn't helped much—the force of pain cut through her hands and arms, the energy of it radiating like sickness through her insides. Sadie folded forward, groaning, not realizing she could get rocked so hard and thoroughly by a girl of Riley's size.

thirty-three
brad tulle

BRAD DROVE up the road to take a leak, buy some beef jerky, and maybe grab a couple of energy drinks despite the two cooling burritos calling out his name. He might even buy a few beers since he was technically off-duty.

He had nearly reached the main road when a reflective flash of light and color in the trees caught his eye. He braked hard, put the Impala into reverse, and backed up to where he saw a red and black motorbike stashed in the woods against a tree.

He hustled out of the Impala, flashed his Maglite on the motorcycle, and froze. "Oh, no," he whispered.

He jumped into the car, put it into gear, and smashed the accelerator. He spun the wheel, whipped the back end around, and corrected his steering as he shot down the narrow road. He liked to give Sadie grief because she was good and could take it, but if something happened to her—if he was too late...

He hit a straightaway, pulled his weapon, and jammed it under his thigh where he could get to it quickly. Slowing, he barreled first into a curve and then into Sadie's driveway, where he locked the brakes and skidded to a stop almost against the porch railing. With no time to grab his vest, the AR, or the Remington from the trunk, he chambered a round in his Sig and exited the car.

Moving quickly with the weapon at the low ready, he approached the house, saw the inside lights and broken glass panels, and immediately kicked in the front door. When he saw what he saw, he damn near had a heart attack before raising his weapon and screaming, "NO!"

thirty-four
sadie gray

SADIE TURNED, spat blood all over the floor, and pushed the hair out of her face. "I remember you, you sorry little turd," she muttered when Riley paused to catch her breath. She felt blood splattered all over her face and several open wounds.

"You don't get to speak after what you did!" Riley growled.

Sadie stood despite everything hurting. "I didn't do anything, and you know it, but maybe you broke your head then, and you grew into a bigger dummy. Is that the case, Riley? Are you just a big, dumb moron now?"

Riley erupted in a guttural growl, then leaned toward Sadie, ready to let out the mother of all screams or mount another attack. But, by then, Sadie had recovered enough to catch the little bitch in the nose with a straight right. There wasn't much stink on the shot, but she had body mechanics on her side, so it did some damage.

Riley reeled and cupped her nose immediately. Blood poured through her fingers, startling her but encouraging Sadie.

With the thin advantage Sadie finally created for herself, she closed the distance between them and went to work on Riley, punching and kicking her like she was the heavy bag, beating her with vicious fists while keeping her on her heels.

Riley's timing was off just enough to leave her guard open,

and Sadie capitalized on a second wind. Each shot was Sadie trying to break bones, flatten her organs, punch the ever-living crap out of her. She could hardly stand, but she refused to quit.

Riley finally stumbled into the edge of the coffee table and fell over. She managed to roll over and get to a knee but was not fast enough or prepared enough to stop what came next.

Sadie launched forward and drove her knee into the side of Riley's jaw with all the force she could muster. The shot was clean, the impact producing a hollow ringing. Riley crumbled before her, her eyes rolling up into her head.

Sadie stood tall and sucked in a deep breath, the edges of her vision crowded with darkness, her head spinning. It wasn't over, though—not yet. When she caught her breath, she pulled her weapon, knelt before Riley, and shoved the barrel into her mouth.

Within moments, the killer's eyes fluttered, and she took a breath. Riley was suddenly aware of the gun in her mouth and the fact that Sadie had put it there.

"See, you've put me in an untenable position," Sadie explained, feeling hostile and unstable, almost like she was having an out-of-body experience. To put an exclamation point on the moment, she turned and spat a huge glob of blood on the floor. "You know my father and what he did to your family, so you have to wonder, how much of her crazy daddy does little Sadie Gray have running through her veins? Well, *you little bitch*, I can tell you: I have plenty. That means it won't take much convincing for me to squeeze off a few rounds."

"Go ahead," Riley mumbled, her teeth knocking against the Glock's barrel.

"Although I appreciate your tenacity, I can shoot you where it won't kill you, but you'll be sucking down dinner with a straw for the rest of your worthless life, wondering why nothing but your eyes and nose work."

"You won't," Riley mumbled.

"This thing you're blow-jobbing, Riley—it's not a lollipop." When Riley tried to swallow, Sadie shoved the gun in deeper, forcing a gag reflex. Using a lethally calm voice, she asked, "Why did you and your stupid brothers do it? Why did you kill all those families?"

Riley stopped choking and freaking out enough to flick her eyes up at Sadie. The hatred burning in those enraged spheres could have started a brush fire.

Sadie slowly removed the weapon. "Speak the truth only. If you lie to me, I'll kill you."

"We didn't do it," Riley said, swallowing hard before falling into a coughing fit.

Sadie waited until she was finished, then flicked her wrist, striking Riley's eyebrow with the barrel of her gun. A small gash opened, and the wound began to weep red. The instant Riley registered the pain and gasped, Sadie knocked her again in the same place, opening the wound even wider.

"I said the truth!" Sadie roared.

"We was saving kids from the abusive parents," Riley managed to say. "If you were worth a crap at your job, which you probably aren't, you'll know them kids got the worst of it."

"Jake found the families, right?" Sadie asked. Riley glanced away, a confirmation. "And David? What did that good-for-nothing bucket of dick meat do?"

"He killed the kids," Riley confessed. "Me 'n Jake couldn't do it, but something was wrong with David's head, which is why we volunteered him."

A darkness more than night passed through her eyes as she considered her past. But then her gaze cleared, and she looked up at Sadie. "You remember when I told you I watched my daddy kill my mother with a hammer? It was back in the basement when we was kids."

Sadie recalled that particular detail of her kidnapping before Riley mentioned it, but then she had a clearer memory of the little girl in the green dress, holding a filthy teddy bear, and suddenly she felt ill.

"I remember," she said softly.

"The way we was raised, we was just putting our talents to good use for those in need of salvation," Riley said as if proud of her actions.

"Slaughtering entire families was your version of salvation?"

"Still is, asshole," Riley said. "No kid wants cuts or broken bones. They also don't like getting raped over and over again, which I can say from personal experience."

"So, you took it upon yourselves to fix that problem with... *murder?*"

"Mercy killings ain't the same as murder," Riley said, her tenor rising. "It's not like what your dad did to my family."

"Your family sucks now worse than it did then," Sadie said, exhausted.

"Then arrest me and get it over with," Riley mumbled. "Jake ain't saying nuthin', which means you got your suspicions and fuck-all for evidence."

"When my partner blew your brother's face off with a shotgun, we found the bundle of locks on the floor near the front door. We got plenty of evidence. Meaning, I know you and your brothers did all that killing."

The statement and mention of the locks broke something in her. Defeated, she said, "Fine, arrest me."

Instead of trying to cuff her, which would leave Sadie vulnerable to attack, she jammed the gun into Riley's mouth again, chipping a few teeth in the process. Riley gasped, and her eyes and nostrils flared when Sadie leaned on the weapon and said, "What makes you think our system of justice will be the best way for you to answer for your crimes? I think me doing to you what you did to David will save taxpayers a bunch of money and time testifying in court. We can chalk it up to a mercy killing. Because that's not the same as murder, right?"

"Already told you to do it," Riley struggled to say while choking on bits of broken teeth and blood.

Outside, Sadie heard a car approaching and knew it was now or never. Frantic, she glanced around the room to see if she could stage the kill for forensics. But would the team and later, OPR, see through the façade? Brad kicked the front door open before she could end this sick broad the right way and yelled, "NO!"

Sadie lost her chance to pull the trigger; time ran out, and thank God, because after the killing spree Riley and her brothers went on, she ached to reunite them in Hell. When the anger and hysteria in her mind began to fade, common sense set in, and she backed off. She was law enforcement, not a vigilante killer.

"Sadie, holster your weapon," Brad warned, his tone evening out as he lowered his weapon and raised a hand to signal calm.

Was Brad doing enough to make her change her mind? Yeah, probably. But then, the things Riley said moments earlier surfaced, coming wholly and sharply into focus. The families she and her brothers killed were abusers, and they were there to save the kids from further abuse, by killing them. Ending everyone's lives solved the problem in Riley's eyes, but she and her brothers never gave the kids a chance at life.

"What happened to you in foster care?" Sadie finally asked, pulling the Glock's barrel from her mouth.

Riley turned and spat out bits of broken teeth and blood, then glared at Sadie. "What do you think happened? Did you listen to anything I told you? Because, *I already told you.*"

"Feel free to repeat it," Sadie said.

Riley's face broke into a cold, sadistic grin. "I left the hint on your porch, you brainless halfwit," she growled, coughing up more blood. "Can I wipe my head and face where you cut me, or are you gonna hit me again?"

Sadie nodded, holstering her weapon now that Brad was there for cover. Riley wiped the blood out of her eye and off of her cheek, then ran her hand across her pants.

"The skank hit me for no reason," Riley turned and told Brad.

"Looking at her face, I'd say you had it coming."

"Back to the frank and beans," Sadie said.

Riley rubbed her sore jaw and said, "Brodi Bennett was my foster brother, my *older* foster brother. As a little girl, he loved showing me how to be a young woman capable of pleasing an older boy. He showed me over and over again until I wished I didn't have girl parts. And my foster parents? Well, they was too busy collecting state checks to worry about a loser like me getting preyed upon by an even bigger loser like Brodi. When I finally told my foster mother *in detail* what happened, she told her husband—my filthy fucking foster father—and he joined Brodi in teaching me the lessons of older boys and men."

She and Brad were silent, too sickened and stunned by the revelation to respond immediately. Brad broke the silence when he said, "We have enough to book her for murder in the first while not worrying about any of the charges sliding."

"I'd rather she shoot me," Riley said.

"And that's why we're cuffing you and taking you to jail," Sadie said, now resolved to let the justice system do its job. "Unless you want to resist arrest. How'd you like that?"

"I'd like that," Riley surprised her by saying.

She grabbed hold of the butt of Sadie's gun, where she kept it holstered, moving faster than expected. But Sadie rolled her shoulders and fired a left-handed punch into her cheekbone. The shot rocked her so hard that Riley grabbed her face with both hands and howled. Sadie withdrew the pistol, spun it around so she could hold it by the barrel, and pistol-whipped her forehead, opening another mean gash.

"Stop resisting," Brad said without volume or emotion. Sadie looked at Brad, who appeared lackluster. He nodded before saying it again. "I said, stop resisting."

Sadie drilled Riley again, deepening the same bloody wound. When Riley finally fell back on her butt and broke into tears, Brad felt safe enough to proceed. He grabbed her strongest hand, cuffed it, and said, "If you continue to resist, Agent Gray will have to continue to assist me in securing you. It's for our safety, of course."

Riley willingly gave him the other arm. Brad cuffed both wrists, hauled her to her feet (she grunted in pain, tears leaking down her face), then turned her body and marched her out to the Impala.

Just as they had done with June Grendel—the fake Riley Sharpe—they put the actual Riley into the back seat with Sadie, who had her weapon easily accessible, just not to Riley.

"That was a cute trick, you and your brothers taking different last names for a while," Sadie said. Riley refused to speak or acknowledge her. "I would've recognized your piece of shit father's last name and arrested all three of you far sooner than now had you not done that."

A firestorm of heat and anger gathered again in her eyes, but she didn't turn and face Sadie. Low in her throat, her voice scratchy and raw and teeming with animosity, Riley said, "You killed my brothers, and you'll have your way with me in court, but I saved lots of families from living bad lives, and you can't never take that from me." Riley's eyes were so dark and empty that they appeared black in the low light. "I wish my daddy woulda raped and killed you and your dumb sister when he had the chance."

"I wish he would've killed himself before he did what he did and given you three a chance at decent lives."

"Four," she spat. "There were four of us!"

"Now there's just you—the one. And man, the courts are going to crucify you. Worse, the entire world hates you, fears you, and will beg for your death."

Riley performed a theatrical head bow, smiling and showing a mouth full of broken front teeth. Then she said, "You wanna bet on how long I can stretch my fifteen minutes of fame?"

From the front seat, Brad said, "You can stretch it out as far as it will go, and it won't make a bit of difference to me, Agent Gray, or anyone else."

Sadie added, "Think about that while you're crapping in a hole and dreaming of all the ways you could kill yourself. And while you're doing that until they back-door parole your bony ass, we'll sleep comfortably in fluffy beds, eat gourmet food, and take down more vermin like you."

"So, you say," Riley mumbled, exhausted and turning away.

Sadie told herself to be quiet, but there was still more to say. "I hope you know that once we hand you over to Chief Miller, we won't give you a single thought. We'll be onto bigger and better things than you and your dead, degenerate kin."

"You already cut open my face, broke my teeth, and got me to confess—what else do you want?"

"I would rather have killed you," Sadie admitted. "This is me trying to square that circle, but I'm having a hard time."

"Well, good luck with that," Riley whispered, her hair falling over her face.

When they arrived at GVPD, they handed Riley over to Miller and Detective Ruiz, who took her into custody, but not before June Grendel could snap a few pictures from the dark edge of the parking lot.

Sadie turned to the woman, who held a camera, and let her snap a photo of her battered face. Before she went inside to join Brad, Chief Miller, and whoever else was there from the task force, she told June, "I hope the photo helps."

June stared at her for a long moment, then nodded. "That should get me over ten thousand listeners, thank you very much."

"How'd you know we'd be here?" Sadie asked.

"Canceled APB."

Sadie grinned but didn't look away from the woman. "Good luck with your podcast, June. I hope you do something worthwhile with your life."

She nodded her thanks but didn't say a word. Brad popped his head out the door, saw them talking, then waved halfheartedly to June. She blew him a kiss, which made him laugh.

Speaking to Sadie, he said, "Time to get you to a hospital—your face is still bleeding. I need to get checked out, too."

He still had some splintered wood embedded in his face. Either way, she nodded and didn't put up a fight, which seemed to surprise Brad.

Neither spoke until a proficient male nurse cleaned up Sadie and sanitized the minor injuries on Brad's face. When the hospital cleared them to leave, it felt like the end of an unbearably long day.

In the bu-car, Brad called ASAC Blackwood and told him what had happened. Blackwood listened carefully and then asked to speak to Sadie. He handed her the phone.

Sadie's face was swelling now and hurt like a mother, and one of her eyes had almost closed and would need more ice, but she had no problem talking.

"Yes, Sir?" Sadie asked.

"I don't want to blow a bunch of sunshine and unicorn dust up your ass, Agent Gray, so I'll keep it simple: I could not be happier with your success, and we both know you don't owe it all to Brad."

The two laughed at Brad's expense, but then Blackwood said, "I know you're listening, Brad. I teamed you two up, not just so you could show her the ropes but so she would come to listen to you, trust you, and hopefully learn from you on this case and the cases ahead. I'm sure you've earned her respect, and she yours."

"I have," Sadie said, looking at Brad when she said this.

"I have, too, Sir," Brad told Blackwood.

When they said goodbye and hung up, Sadie said, "You said I earned your respect—did you mean that?"

Brad shook his head and said, "No, I'm just pacifying the ASAC; he seemed pleased with us. You?"

"Yeah, I don't respect you either," she said, staring straight ahead through her good eye. "I miss my dog."

"Your dog loves your boyfriend more, I'm sure."

"He's not my boyfriend."

Brad considered this statement for a while, then said, "You won't be anyone's girlfriend for a while, not with your face looking like that."

She chuckled, then lay back against the seat and said, "I can pack up the Airbnb in about five minutes."

"It'll take me the same to pack," he said. "We'll go to the

Airbnb first, then my place. After that, we'll hit the road, and you can sleep all the way home. I promise not to touch you... *much*."

"You know, you're all right, Brad Tulle," she said, closing her good eye.

He smiled and said, "You, too, Sadie Gray."

thirty-five
sadie gray

WHEN BRAD DROPPED her off at her midtown loft, Sadie thanked him for the ride and walked inside, feeling like a resuscitated corpse. She breezed past Yo's place, and even though she knew Droolius Caesar was inside, she went straight home, undressed, and crawled into bed, where she slept hard for a while.

Around four a.m., she woke screaming, the nightmares as vivid as they were unending. She sat up for about an hour, crying from both eyes, but only able to see out of one. Finally, she crawled out of bed, put an ice pack on her eye, and sat at her kitchen table, weeping in her black tank top and a pair of boy-cut underwear. A soft knock on the loft's door startled her.

"Who is it?" she asked. She kept her gun on her nightstand, a round chambered. Should she get it?

"Hey, lady?" a voice said.

She sniffed hard and smiled. "Yo."

"You all right?" he asked through the door.

Sadie wasn't sure she wanted him to see her, but she also didn't care after everything she had survived and figured he wouldn't either, especially if the super was right and he wasn't the dating kind of guy.

She opened the door, and he just stared at her.

"My God, it *was* you." She stood there, wearing next to nothing, and Yo couldn't take his eyes off her face.

"What's your real name?" she asked. "I know it's not Yo, so I'm not calling you that anymore because I sound dumb saying it."

"Cassius Hayes," he said.

"No wonder you opted for 'Yo,'" she said with a half-smile.

"I'm assuming you're Special Agent Sadie Gray with the FBI?" he asked.

"In the flesh. You coming in or what?"

He stepped inside and said, "As long as Caesar stays asleep, yeah. Maybe you could tell me what happened to your beautiful face."

"I'll tell you everything I can, but if you hit on me, just know I'm vulnerable enough to maybe sleep with you, but if that happens, I'll probably hate you in the morning."

"You'd sleep with me?" he asked.

Even though it hurt, she offered a warm smile and said, "I haven't had a Cassius yet."

He rolled the door shut and said, "You go first so I can stare at your butt."

She turned, led him to the kitchen table, and said, "Tea?"

"Please."

"Why are you up this early?"

"I paint best at this time of night," he said.

She glanced at his hands and shirt. "But, you're clean."

"I ended my night early when I heard you come home. I tried to sleep, but then I heard you crying and didn't feel great ignoring you."

"That's sweet of you."

She made tea, sat down with their cups, and told him about the case, the bodies, and the three deranged killers. He listened to it all, not saying a word, and when Sadie was finished, Cassius said, "It's going to take everything in me not to take advantage of you right now, Sadie Gray."

"And why is that?" she asked.

"I sort of have a thing for women like you."

"Yeah?" she mused. She sipped her tea as she thought about the statement. "I guess if I had a dick, I'd probably want me, too."

He finished his tea, stood, and politely said, "And that's why I'm going to go. If things happen between us, I want you to want me in the morning."

She nodded, saddened if she was honest with herself, and said, "Here I was, all ready to hate you tomorrow."

"Sorry to disappoint," he smiled. "Come get Droolius whenever you're ready. We're getting along well, though, so there's no rush."

She was happy to hear that, and even though she needed him to leave, a small part of her loathed the idea of returning to her bed alone. Sadly, she would settle for emergency sex just to have someone by her side and not be alone in the dark. But alas, Cassius left, and Sadie ended up sleeping alone. Thankfully, when she managed to nod off, she slept soundlessly for the next four hours.

thirty-six
sadie gray

SADIE WOKE up to a raging headache, a deep ache in her ribs, and a face that felt like Mike Tyson worked out on it the night before. If an elephant had parked its big gray butt on her head, it would have felt far better than this.

She pushed herself out of bed and sat there, trying to psyche herself for the day. Finally, she stood, shuffled to the bathroom, and looked in the mirror. *God, what a mess.* She turned to the left and right, hating every angle, knowing it was the face she'd have to live with for the next few days. Fortunately, most of the swelling had gone down enough for her to pass for normal... from a distance.

Sadie sat on the toilet, tried not to cry, and started the shower. There was no reason for a hot shower; she wanted the water ice cold. After the cold shower, which felt amazing, she fixed her hair and applied her makeup the best that she could, not that it helped the train wreck of a face staring back at her in the mirror.

She thought about picking up Droolius Caesar but couldn't make the mental leap yet, so she went to work, arriving on time. When she got into the office, she lowered her head and eyes and tried to walk to her desk without drawing attention to herself.

But then someone said, "There she is!" And suddenly, people began to stand and clap. Sadie stopped in her tracks, cautiously looked up, and saw so many smiling faces looking right at her. The smile that broke over her battered face was unexpected and genuine, and she couldn't lie—the applause felt good. But the face she was happiest to see was Brad's face. He stood, too, a bright smile on his blood-speckled face, clapping with the rest of them.

When the applause died down, Brad raised his voice enough to say, "You got your first big win and helped give the FBI one, too, which means it's time to get our butts chewed to the bone for everything we did wrong."

Brad said it loudly enough for everyone to hear, but Sadie got the idea that this was standard operating procedure. She frowned as best as possible, and then ASAC Blackwood stepped out of his office, spotted them, and said, "Gray, Tulle—my office."

The "oohs," "aahs," and "busteds" rose from those who had applauded her only moments earlier. While a lesser person would have been embarrassed, Sadie believed the hazing was all in good fun.

When she entered Blackwood's office with Brad, Blackwood saw her face and said, "Criminals would never have taken you seriously with that once-perfect face anyway. Sit down, please."

"Yes, Sir," she said.

Blackwood tried to brush off her injuries at first, but then he couldn't take his eyes off of her. "For the love of God, Sadie."

She merely nodded.

He drew a breath and got down to business. "Now that you have a few good scars, let's pray you don't get more. I can safely say we all enjoy the way you looked before, even if you're not so bad now."

Sadie took the compliment at face value, no pun intended.

Brad nodded. "I said she was too pretty for the job, and she solved that problem for us. Now she's one of the guys."

"Mission accomplished," Sadie muttered with a half-cocked grin.

Blackwood beamed. "I knew you were the right woman for

the job, and I knew you and Agent Tulle would figure out any differences and solve this case."

"I hate to admit it," Sadie said, "but it was a good call, through and through."

Blackwood asked, "Aside from the murders, were you able to resolve other, more private matters?"

She nodded, grateful that he asked. "I still have a little more work to do emotionally, but being back there shook a few things loose, put me in touch with an old friend at GVPD, and made me think I *am* right for this job."

Blackwood leaned forward on his desk, tented his fingers, and didn't bother to blink when looking at her. "Even though you're not on the East Coast?"

Sadie nodded, knowing she was where she was supposed to be. "Most serial killers are here in California anyway, right?"

"Yes, but we do more than track down killers," Blackwood said.

"Of course," Sadie replied.

"You ready for your next case?" Blackwood asked. "Or do you need time and counseling? Because you can have a bit of both, but not too much."

"I'm good, Sir."

Blackwood raised his brows, thought about it, and nodded. "Okay, then. I'll put you two back in rotation."

"What about my face, Sir?" Sadie asked.

"This isn't a sorority, Princess," Blackwood said with mild amusement. "The only person who cares about your good looks right now is you. Don't sweat it, though. Brad will help you write your reports."

"Reports?" she asked.

Brad started ticking off his fingers, saying, "We've got investigative reports, evidence reports, after-action and arrest reports, a case summary, and our closing report."

Blackwood said, "You done yet, Agent Tulle?"

"Yes, Sir."

Blackwood looked directly at Sadie, focusing solely on her. "You met some good old boys on this case, Agent Gray—that's good. You'll meet more like them, many of them hardened detectives or agents with decades of experience handling some of the worst crimes you can imagine. We're talking felony assaults, gang-related task forces, domestic disputes, terrorism, and every other thing you can think of that sucks. They're good at what they do, enough that some might not like Agent Tulle and certainly not you."

Brad cleared his throat and said, "Did you say 'hardened detectives,' Sir?"

Sadie snorted to herself and smashed her lips together, finally covering her mouth as she fought not to burst out laughing.

Blackwood stared at Brad; Brad stared back, barely containing his laughter. Then, both men broke into fits of laughter, Blackwood laughing despite Sadie or her face.

"If you get it, you get it," Brad said to Sadie.

She shook her head and said, "Such an overgrown child."

Blackwood cut the laughter short and said, "Dick jokes aside, our job is important and we need you at the top of your game, Agent Gray. You displayed courage under fire, according to Agent Tulle, as well as good judgment. That's why I'm keeping you together for now. Do you have any objections?"

Sadie looked at him and said, "Of course not."

"Good," he replied. Apparently, Blackwood had nothing more to say, so he glanced down at the paperwork on his desk, frowned, and waved them off, saying, "Get me those reports."

"Yes, Sir," Brad and Sadie said simultaneously.

Brad stood, opened the door for Sadie, and went to his desk. He pulled a pack of chewing gum from his top drawer, popped a piece into his mouth, and offered her a stick. Sadie shook her head and thanked him, but he said, "Trust me, you need it."

"Like the great Captain Scott said," Sadie replied as she took a stick, "everyone's a comedian."

Brad laughed and stuffed the gum back into his drawer. "We can't do our reports until we have one very important thing."

"What's that?" she asked.

"Coffee."

Now, he was speaking her language.

"I also got the motor pool to assign you your car," he said with a grin. "You're welcome."

"Really?" she asked. "My own bu-car?"

"It'll be ready after work," he said as they left the building. "Until then, I'm driving, since I'm the case agent and you're still the FNG."

"That won't always be the case," Sadie said, opening the next door for Brad, who stopped flat and looked at her.

"You think I can't open my door?" he asked.

"Suit yourself," Sadie said. She walked through the open door and let it close in Brad's face, then she flipped him the bird. She heard him behind her, laughing to himself.

Yeah, she liked this job; she was going to crush it, and she was pretty happy that ASAC Blackwood had partnered her with Agent Brad Tulle.

The man was a peach.

END OF BOOK 1
Sadie Gray returns in The Sight Unseen! But first...

If you haven't already read Sadie Gray's thrilling origin story, be sure to grab your FREE copy now as it has become an unexpected fan favorite and a "must-read companion" to the Sadie Gray series! Before Sadie Gray was with the FBI, she was a young girl drawn into a nightmare by a monster no one suspected, one wreaking havoc on a small town already mired by scandal. This pulse-pounding, edge-of-your-seat thriller packs a big punch and will leave you breathless, surprised, and laughing out loud when you least expect it. Scroll ahead for a quick summary and a link to The Blinding Light: A Sadie Gray Origin Story, *which is currently FREE! If you are reading this in paperback format, use the link below to download a FREE PDF version of Sadie's origin story or read online by simply following the online prompts. You can also purchase a paperback copy on Amazon. This free book is only available using the link at the end of The Blinding Light book description (scroll down to FREE BOOK: Sadie Gray's Origin Story). Also, before you leave, keep scrolling and be sure to check out the next book in the Sadie Gray series, titled* The Sight Unseen.

your voice matters

If you enjoyed this and other Sadie Gray stories, please refer this series to a friend, or on your social media accounts, and consider leaving a kind review on Amazon letting me know what you liked most about this particular story—your feedback allows me to craft future stories to your and other readers' liking. But please, NO SPOILERS. That said, your reviews mean more than you might imagine to me and potential readers. Not only do they make my day (yes, I read them all!), but they help a young series in a very competitive genre get its legs, allowing me to write more Sadie Gray stories!

QUICK NOTE: The way Amazon's review system works is five stars is good, four stars is all right, and three stars or less are just degrees of *no bueno*. That said, I hope you enjoyed your Sadie Gray experience and will continue on to the next book!

*Be sure to look for a new Sadie Gray story at the beginning of each month, and thank you in advance for your reviews, readership, great word of mouth, and kindness—you truly are the best!

**If you happen to see any errors (typos, etc...), they sometimes show

up uninvited and can get overlooked (sad face!), feel free to email me at SadieGrayBooks.com/contact. Thank you!

sadie's free origin story: the blinding light

Two missing girls. No suspects. A police department mired in scandal.

Earl and Gabriella Gray's lives are shattered when their daughters, Sadie and Natalie, are kidnapped in broad daylight in the quiet town of Grass Valley, California.

As a frantic manhunt begins, led by Officer Teresa May, the investigation stumbles over shocking secrets buried deep within the town's history, secrets that may have played a role in the girls' disappearance.

With no faith left in the system and time running out, Earl and Officer May take matters into their own hands, determined to bring Sadie and Natalie home and enact justice, even if it means sacrificing everything they have left.

While *The Blinding Light* is the origin story of FBI legend Sadie Gray, this is also the story of a young officer trying to make a name for herself, a protective father at odds with his violent past, a mother struggling to cope with life, and two small sisters forced to face the ultimate evil. Will they all survive? And, if so, will anything ever be the same? Find out this and more now by tapping or clicking the following link:

Head to SadieGrayBooks.com *and follow the links to read this book for FREE! A paperback version is also available for sale on Amazon.com*

the sight unseen: a look ahead...

A painting she couldn't live without. A life she will fight to keep.

After a brutal case in Grass Valley, California, Special Agent Sadie Gray and her enigmatic partner, Agent Brad Tulle, are barely catching their breath before being thrown into a new and perplexing mission—a missing persons case that the FBI's San Francisco field office wouldn't, or couldn't, handle.

The local sheriff has reason to believe it's more than a disappearance; he suspects Leona Kolsch has been kidnapped. But there's a twist—the last sighting wasn't even in California. *It was over 700 miles away... in Utah.*

As Sadie and Brad dig in, they find themselves entangled in a tangled web of questions: Was Leona on the run from someone close? Is a kidnapper targeting the rich and powerful? Or is there something far darker—a predator lurking in the shadowy corners of the internet?

One thing is clear: nothing is what it seems.

What begins with a priceless painting and a woman's insatiable desire to possess it turns into a race against time, as Sadie and Brad uncover a case far bigger and more sinister than they imagined. With lives on the line, including their own, they'll have to untangle the truth before time runs out...

Head to Amazon.com to grab your copy now!

also by r.b. schow

THE SADIE GRAY SERIES (*w/ Bailey James*):

THE 34 IN THE FLOOR
THE SIGHT UNSEEN
THE BROKEN GIRL (*January 5, 2025*)
THE MURDER SOCIETY (*Coming Soon!*)

THE COMPLETE ATLAS HARGROVE SERIES:

THE TEARS OF ODESSA
THE BEASTS OF JUAREZ
THE BETRAYAL OF PRAGUE
THE DEVIL IN COLOGNE
THE BUTCHER OF CARACAS
THE MARTYR OF NOGALES
THE CAPE TOWN MASSACRE

about the authors

Million-copy selling USA Today best-selling author R.B. Schow is the mastermind behind the pulse-pounding *Atlas Hargrove* thriller series. A second-degree black belt and adrenaline junkie, Ryan thrives on crafting fierce, flawed characters who battle impossible odds. His stories are rich in character development but also packed with plenty of chaos, where the lines between right and wrong blur, delivering gripping, high-octane adventures at every turn. He and his wife live in California.

Bailey James, her husband, and their two little ones live in the Sierra Nevada foothills in Northern California. Surrounded by many small towns rich in history and intrigue, Bailey immerses herself in true crime culture, drawing inspiration from more than a few local, unsolved mysteries. Her writing journey began in editing and has evolved into crafting fiction, with a focus on capable yet realistic heroes and heroines, formidable villains, and the unique charm of small-town life.

Leveraging decades of fascination with true crime, Bailey joins forces with bestselling author R.B. Schow to create high-stakes stories that captivate even the most discerning mystery enthusiasts.

About The Authors

For more information about the authors or to chat with them about the current books, upcoming releases, or cover reveals, be sure to join the private Facebook page, called *The Edge of Your Seat Book Nook!*

Made in United States
Troutdale, OR
02/08/2025